"A charming fantasy . . . a cute, smartly told pastiche of Tolkien and Terry Brooks."

"Odom has created a likable, believable character who will continue his adventures as a newly promoted Second Level Librarian in charge of great books. Fans of the movie version of Tolkien's *Fellowship of the Ring* will be looking for books to satisfy their interest in weefolks. Readers will enjoy the wealth of creatures in this tale of magic, mystery, and self-discovery, and will stand up and cheer for this little guy who reaches for his best shot and saves the day."

THE ROVER SERIES FROM TOR BOOKS

seaspray:
the quest
for the
trilogy

mel odom

TOR®
fantasy

A Tom Doherty Associates Book
New York

This is a work of fiction. All the characters and events portrayed in this novel are either fictitious or are used fictitiously.

SEASPRAY: THE QUEST FOR THE TRILOGY

Copyright © 2007 by Mel Odom

Seaspray was originally published by Tor Books in 2007, in Mel Odom's *The Quest for the Trilogy*.

A Tor Book
Published by Tom Doherty Associates, LLC
175 Fifth Avenue
New York, NY 10010

www.tor-forge.com

Tor® is a registered trademark of Tom Doherty Associates, LLC.

ISBN-13: 978-0-7653-5426-6
ISBN-10: 0-7653-5426-8

First Edition: November 2008

Printed in the United States of America

0 9 8 7 6 5 4 3 2 1

To my son, Chandler.
Daddy created this world with you in mind. Enjoy it.

seaspray:

the quest
for the
trilogy

foreword

Ordal the Minstrel

The rain followed *Moonsdreamer* into Calmpoint, further evidence that the storm wasn't a natural occurrence. The ship was at sea for six days before making port, all of them filled with anxiety.

No one knew why or how Craugh had disappeared. The wizard's blood—at least Juhg assumed it was the wizard's—still stained the cabin where he'd been lodged for the voyage. All of his effects were gone as well.

"This is a dangerous place, scribbler," Raisho declared as they stood on deck. In the rain cloak he wore, with his ebony skin dappled and inked with blue tattoos marking him as a sailing man, he looked every inch the warrior. Lantern light gleamed on the red fire opal headband. "I've been here before."

"So have I," Juhg replied. "Long before you were born." He smiled at his friend. Raisho, because of the disparity of their sizes, tended to sometimes treat Juhg as a child. Juhg didn't mind because there was a difference between being protective and being patronizing.

Raisho dropped a hand to the worn hilt of his cutlass. "True, scribbler, I keep forgettin' ye've been around a lot longer than me."

The coastline looked gentle. A solid harbor fronted the Gentlewind Sea to the south. To the west, the Forest of Hawks offered a barrier against any fierce weather that might wander in from the Gentlewind Sea. Although the local shipwrights lobbied every year to start logging the Forest of Hawks, the elven warders there denied them.

Shantytown occupied the area right behind the docks, but there were much nicer houses to the east behind the Customs House and Harbor Watch headquarters. To the far east stood the three tall buildings that housed the three shipwrights' guilds. The middle sector of the town was a mix of shops that provided services or sold goods either made in Calmpoint or imported from other places.

Juhg stood at the railing and remembered past times he'd been there. It had always been with Grandmagister Lamplighter.

Now Craugh was missing and Juhg felt he was putting Raisho at risk in the search for things that might have been better off forgotten.

Except the past will always return to haunt you, Juhg thought. Then he thought of the bloodstains on Craugh's cabin floor. *Or maybe it will kill you*. The possibility was sobering.

"Do ye think mayhap it might be best to put this behind ye for a time?"

Juhg clambered into the longboat over *Moonsdreamer*'s side and looked back at Raisho. For six days his friend had been trying to talk him out of what he was going to attempt.

"No," Juhg said.

"Whoever these people are that are tryin' to keep whatever happened at the Battle of Fell's Keep from becomin' public knowledge, they're serious about it."

"I know," Juhg said. He could recall the bog beasts with distinct clarity.

"An' they got Craugh," Raisho pointed out. "Right under our noses."

"It might not be the same people." Juhg sat in the longboat's stern. He disliked looking up at Raisho because the incessant rain kept hitting him in the face. "Craugh had—" He stopped, realizing the slip he'd unconsciously made. "Craugh *has* a lot of enemies. What happened aboard *Moonsdreamer* may be about another matter entirely."

Raisho gave a disgusted snort. "What are the odds of that?"

"I don't know. But I have to do this."

"Go seekin' Minstrel Ordal?"

"Yes."

Raisho waved an arm toward the city. "Calmpoint is a big place. That's a lot of lookin'."

"I won't find him here in Calmpoint," Juhg explained. "He'll be in Deldal's Mills."

Frowning, Raisho said, "I've 'eard of it."

"It's a lumber town farther up the Steadfast River," Juhg explained. "Lumberjacks float logs down river to Deldal's Mills rather than all the way to Calmpoint. They've had to go farther and farther upriver to claim them these days and don't want to risk the long ride when they can get just as much from Deldal's Mills."

"'Ow far away is this town?"

"A day. The Steadfast River is usually lazy, not too hard to paddle upstream. With this rain, that may change."

"Ordal the Minstrel will be there at that town?"

"Yes. Ordal, in one form or another, has been there for generations."

"Is 'e an elf?"

"No." Juhg smiled. Everyone always thought that. Dwarves weren't known for their singing voices even in a dwarven tavern, and elven minstrels were rare.

"A 'uman then?"

"Yes."

Placing his hands on the railing, Raisho shook his head. "Ye know I'm far too curious for me own good."

Juhg said nothing, but he smiled.

"An' I like even less settin' ye loose on yer own, scribbler, without someone to look over ye."

"Beggin' the cap'n's pardon," one of the young sailors in the longboat said, "but I resent that. Ye asked us yerself to care for the Librarian, an' we're gonna do that."

"No disrespect intended, Tellan, but I own up to a pertective nature when it comes to this particular scribbler."

"We can see him safe to this Deldal's Mills," Tellan said. He was tall and youthful, his hair the color of straw and eyes blue as the sky at twilight. Dressed in a cloak, he looked large and ready. A sword hilt stuck out above his left shoulder. The other men in the longboat were similarly equipped.

"Mayhap ye can an' mayhap ye can't," Raisho said. "But ye ain't gonna do it alone." He pointed at one of the men. "Outta the boat, Trotner. Ye're stayin' here."

Looking relieved, the older sailor climbed back out of the longboat.

"Raisho," Juhg said, "you shouldn't come."

"Because it's dangerous?" Raisho shook his head. "If it's dangerous, I shouldn't be lettin' ye go, now should I?"

"Not because it's dangerous," Juhg said. "Because you're captain of this ship. You've got obligations and duties here. This is my task to see through."

"Oh no ye don't, scribbler. There'll be no war of wits this time. 'Cause I win. Craugh done vanished offa me ship an' I don't know the reason—yet. I'll not 'ave ye disappearin', too."

"You've got a family," Juhg said, knowing it was his last point of attack.

"I told ye all them years ago, an' I'll tell ye again now, scribbler. Ye're me family. Just as much as me wife an' kids. Just as much as me ma an' da ye 'elped me find when we went looking fer *The Book of Time*." Raisho caught a kit that one of the other sailors tossed him, then dropped it into the longboat and followed it. "Until we find out what 'appened to Craugh, I ain't leavin' ye outta me sight. An' that's that."

Some of the tension Juhg felt melted away at Raisho's words. It felt good not to be alone in the world, and facing unknown adversaries and odds. He respected his good friend's wishes and didn't protest any further.

"Thank you," Juhg said.

Raisho picked up an oar and settled it into its lock. "What ye're a-doin', scribbler, I know it's fer the good of a lot of people." He grinned. "Just make sure ye give me proper credit when ye write up the story of this 'ere journey."

Juhg took up an oar, too, then waited for Raisho to call off the count. Together, then, the longboat crew rowed for the public dock.

Juhg paid for horses at the livery after negotiating a fair price for them. The seller threw the tack in for free because Juhg had paid in gold rather than offering something in trade.

"Ye know payin' in gold could cause some problems," Raisho said as they guided their new mounts out into the rain. "Word gets around town quick when ye're an outsider payin' in gold."

"I know," Juhg said. "If I didn't feel pressed for time we would have walked to Deldal's Mills."

At the mercantile, Juhg purchased a few supplies for a cold camp to enhance what they'd brought from the ship. Raisho made it a habit to keep some supplies on hand for times when they had to go ashore because of bad weather, to repair the ship, or to avoid pirates, but Juhg wanted to ease the trip if he could.

Once he had everything squared away to his satisfaction, Juhg pulled up his cloak and went back out into the rain.

Raisho and the other sailors divvied the supplies among them, placing them in bedrolls and saddlebags. Then they headed out.

They rode along the river, on the hard-packed trail that lined both sides of the Steadfast. Under Crossing Bridge, called that because it was the only bridge in Calmpoint that crossed the river, Juhg made certain they were on the Deldal's Mills commercial side rather than textiles.

The river's running high farther north, Juhg thought. *The storm front covers more than just the Gentlewind Sea.* He wondered if he should think any more about that, or worry any more. Although, frankly, with Craugh inexplicably missing from *Moonsdreamer* while at sea, Juhg didn't know how he could worry any more. *Grandmagister Lamplighter, I do wish you were here right now. You've had far more experience with this kind of roving than I have.*

The wet saddle leather creaked. The horses' hooves thudded against the muddy ground. Gradually, Calmpoint fell behind them as they rode deeper inland. Instead of the forest that had once grown there after the land tried to heal, only scrub brush and farms could be seen.

To the right, within a cornfield that stood tall and green, a garish scarecrow kept watch. As he passed the straw man, Juhg got the uncomfortable feeling that it was staring after him with its charcoal-blackened eyes and stitched mouth.

It's your imagination, he chided himself. He turned his attention northward again, focusing on the narrative he'd translated about Grandmagister Lamplighter's adventures in the Cinder Clouds Islands. How had the Grandmagister fared in Wharf Rat's Warren while seeking the thieves' guild known as the Razor's Kiss?

Juhg knew his mentor had survived, but what must Grandmagister Lamplighter have seen there? And why had the Grandmagister never seen fit to tell Juhg about it? Of course, just from reading books in the Vault of All

Known Knowledge, Juhg knew that there were a great many things Grandmagister Lamplighter hadn't told him.

He sat the horse as best he could, though it was not a favorite mode of travel for him.

"Ye doin' okay, scribbler?" Raisho asked beside Juhg.

"I'm fine," Juhg replied.

"Ye appear to be doin' some deep thinkin' there."

Juhg hesitated a moment. "I am."

"We'll get Craugh back," Raisho said. "Ye got nothin' to worry about. The stories I 'eard about 'im, he can tree a bear with a switch."

"Perhaps," Juhg said, "but it wasn't a bear who took Craugh from a ship at sea." *It was something far worse.*

"'E's 'ard to kill, scribbler. Ye just got to remember that."

"It would help if I knew who was after us."

"Ye said yerself that it wasn't Master Oskarr who betrayed the Unity at the Battle of Fell's Keep there in the Painted Canyon during the Cataclysm. According to the information Grandmagister Lamplighter uncovered, why, it was Master Oskarr was one of them betrayed."

"Then why didn't Grandmagister Lamplighter let people know when he found out?"

"Could be like Craugh pointed out to 'im all those years ago. 'E just didn't have proof."

"He had the rubbings he took from Master Oskarr's forge table."

"Ye're talkin' about a thousand years of 'ard feelin's. They don't just go away like sugar in tea."

Juhg sighed. "I know. But I have to wonder why anyone from all those years ago would even care now."

"Secrets are terrible things. They grow faster'n, bigger'n, an' stronger'n weeds. Somethin' ten years ago that might 'ave brought down one man, why now it might 'ave grown up big enough to bring down a whole town."

"You're a very wise man, Raisho."

Raisho grinned in the shadows of his cloak. "I 'ad me

a very wise teacher." He reached out and clapped Juhg on the shoulder. "We're doin' this, scribbler. Whatever else comes from it, ye know ye're doin' all ye can. Take some solace in that an' 'ave a little faith."

With the rain beating down on him, Juhg tried to take his friend's advice. But he couldn't help feeling scared and doubtful.

They were moving forward, much more slowly than Juhg would have wanted, but still forward. And now something from a thousand years ago—*something tainted with the evil of Lord Kharrion*!—was trying to reach out for them again.

They camped just before nightfall. Thankfully they'd reached the outskirts of the Deldal's Mills forest. If it ever had another name, it had been forgotten.

Raisho waited until full dark had fallen before he would allow them to start a campfire. Then, after he'd spent a long time searching for the lights of other campfires and listening for other riders, he built the fire himself, just big enough to seat the small cauldron they used to make a shepherd's stew in. They used some of the meat they'd brought and added in some of the wild vegetables in the area.

Once the stew started to boil, Juhg sat by himself and took out his writing kit. He worked in the rough journal he carried, bringing the entries up to date and adding images of the Steadfast River, the campsite, and the men who journeyed with them.

When the stew was ready, all of them crept close and ate out of wooden bowls, thankful for the heat. The meat was decent and the vegetables added extra flavor.

After he'd finished eating, Juhg took the first watch, wanting to get it over and try to get a full night's sleep. He fed oats to the horses tied to a rope they'd put up between two trees.

Raisho relieved Juhg after a couple of hours. The rain continued unabated and the river gurgled by constantly.

Juhg made his bedroll as comfortable as possible, grateful to be out of the rain. For a while he lay there, unable to go to sleep. Then, mercifully, his thoughts gradually unlocked themselves and let him fall through them.

"Wake up, Grandmagister Juhg. Wake up."

At first Juhg believed the child's singsong voice was a memory that had threaded into the dark dreams he had of Grandmagister Lamplighter's visit to the Cinder Clouds Islands all those years ago, and of Craugh's bloody disappearance. It was something that didn't belong but didn't overly concern him.

Then something wet and stiff and prickly touched his nose.

That was real! Juhg thought. His eyes popped open and he was staring into the garish face of a monster.

"Wake up, Grandmagister Juhg," the thin, whispering voice taunted.

The coals of the campfire had burned low, casting a soft orange glow across the scarecrow's face. Juhg didn't know if it was the same one from the cornfield he'd seen earlier or if it was one that resembled the other.

It had the same moon-shaped face made out of burlap. The eyes were charcoal-colored triangles over a red button nose and a black-stitched mouth. A hat that would have been otherwise comical sat atop its head. A bright purple kerchief was tied around its neck. It wore patched and faded blouse and breeches, both tarred so they would stand up to the elements. The clothing was stuffed with thick straw.

It held a hand scythe at the end of its right arm.

Juhg sat up and started to cry out.

The scarecrow moved quickly, shoving the sharp scythe

blade against Juhg's neck, pinning his head back against
the tree where he'd laid his bedroll.

"Quiet, Grandmagister Juhg!" the scarecrow warned. It
held its left arm to its stitched mouth, which never moved
despite the fact that Juhg heard the words it spoke. It didn't
have hands, just bunches of straw that stuck out the ends of
the shirtsleeves. Yet somehow it held onto the small scythe.
"I don't want to slit your throat if I don't have to."

Despite the fear that pounded through him, Juhg focused on the incredible creature holding him prisoner. He
knew the scarecrow wasn't actually alive. It was a simulacrum for a wizard somewhere. Probably not far away. He'd
seen things like the scarecrow before, but never so large.
Usually they were paper dolls or stuffed toys. Animating
a simulacrum was difficult work which became even more
of a struggle the larger the host object was.

"What do you want?" Juhg felt his Adam's apple bob
over the sharp blade. He thought he even felt a trickle of
blood running down his neck.

The stitched mouth tightened up into a smile. "To give
you a warning. If I believe you're taking my words to
heart, I won't kill you."

"Who are you?"

"Not someone you know," the scarecrow assured him.
"Not someone you wish to know."

"Did you take Craugh?"

"Craugh," the scarecrow grated, "has proven himself
something of a nuisance."

Has. Not had. The word choice wasn't conclusive, but
it was indicative.

Craugh escaped! The realization flooded through Juhg,
but he immediately wondered where the wizard had gone
and why he hadn't been in touch with them.

"Don't get your hopes up, halfer!" the scarecrow snarled.
"The wizard hasn't gotten away for long. There are others
tracking him down even now."

"What do you want?"

"I want to know what you're looking for."

"A book." Juhg hoped a book would be innocuous or so ominous that the wizard would abandon his efforts at threatening him. However, seeing as how a wizard animated the scarecrow, a wizard wouldn't be frightened of a book.

"What book?" the scarecrow asked.

Juhg silently wondered how much he could tell without giving away too much. Instead, he jerked his head to the side of the tree away from the scythe, went flat and brought up his knee. If the scarecrow had been a human, dwarf, or elf, Juhg would never have been able to dislodge it. But it wasn't. It was a scarecrow.

The enspelled creature went up and over.

"Raisho!" Juhg yelled as he rolled and got to his feet.

Only a few feet away, Raisho came up out of his bedroll at once. His hand closed over his dwarven-forged cutlass and the orange glow of the coals played over it. The young sea captain had always been a man of action.

"What is it?" Raisho demanded, looking around. His black hair was in wild disarray.

At that moment, the scarecrow pushed itself back up and came at Juhg, swinging the scythe in large pendulum arcs. Juhg dodged back, barely avoiding each swing.

Raisho cursed. By that time the rest of the camp was up, grabbing weapons. The two guards turned and came from their posts at dead runs. That gave Juhg some heart. At least the scarecrow hadn't seen fit to kill either of them.

Moving and twisting, Juhg stayed out of harm's way. Then Raisho stepped in front of him, handling his cutlass with superb skill. The scythe rang against the cutlass as they met, and sparks flew.

"I'll kill you all!" the scarecrow threatened.

Juhg knew that Raisho was superstitious. Most sailors were. But his friend was worse than most. Many of the tattoos he wore were wards against evil and ill luck.

Raisho stood his ground, though, and turned aside every attempt the scarecrow made to slash Juhg. The ship's captain cut and thrust at the scarecrow time and time again to no avail. The heavy blade passed though the scarecrow's straw body without harming it, scattering only a handful of straw and slicing the tarred clothing to ribbons.

Dodging back, thinking quickly, Juhg grabbed a lantern from their equipment, opened the oil reservoir, and emptied the contents over the scarecrow's back. Raisho kicked the scarecrow's feet out from under it, causing it to fall flat on its hideous face. Before it could get up, Raisho took out one of the long knives he habitually carried in his boots and brought it down hard into the scarecrow's back.

The knife blade passed through the scarecrow and into the earth below. Raisho left the knife there, pinning the creature to the ground, then rolling back to avoid the scythe.

"Listen to me, Grandmagister Juhg!" the scarecrow screamed, kicking and flailing like an insect pinned to a display board. "If you continue poking around into this, you're going to get killed! Your friends will get killed, too."

"Mayhap," Raisho growled, "but it's gonna take better'n ye to make that 'appen."

Juhg plucked one of the larger coals from the campfire with two wet twigs he found. With a flick of his wrist, the coal landed on the scarecrow's back. It took a little while, but the lantern oil caught and a gentle flame spread across the scarecrow's body.

Abruptly, the scarecrow started screaming and flailing with renewed vigor. It beat its handless arms and footless legs at itself but only succeeded in setting its extremities on fire as well. That was the negative aspect of the spell. The wizard's life was at risk as long as he maintained control of the scarecrow.

After another moment, the scarecrow gave out a final scream and relaxed. No one moved until the fire had consumed the scarecrow, leaving only a husked-out mass of ashes and burned straw.

Raisho looked at Juhg. "What was that about?"

"You heard it," Juhg replied, kicking the scythe from the unmoving thing's arm. "It was a warning."

"Why didn't 'e just slit yer throat while ye was sleepin'?"

"Maybe it would have wasted the whole warning bit," Juhg answered.

"No reason to get snippy about it," Raisho said.

Juhg sighed. "I didn't mean to. I just . . . did *not* expect anything like that." Now that the violence was past, adrenaline flooded his system. He sat down weakly. "But Craugh's still alive, Raisho. You heard the scarecrow."

"I did. Doesn't mean 'e didn't lie to ye an' Craugh's lyin' somewheres done fer."

"Maybe we could be a little bit more positive."

Raisho kicked the remnants of the scarecrow's body. Charred straw scattered over the wet ground. "At least we ain't dead. That's about as positive as I care to be right now." He recovered his knife and replaced it in his boot. Then he caught the three pieces that remained of the scarecrow and hauled them over to the campfire.

Juhg joined his friend at the fire as the flames jumped up greedily to consume the straw. The renewed wave of heat washed over Juhg, taking away some of the chill that had soaked into him. He held out his hands and was surprised to see that they were shaking.

"Did ye know who it were?" Raisho asked.

Gazing around at the darkness, Juhg shook his head. "No."

Raisho stirred the burning straw with his cutlass. Embers leapt up into the night sky. "Well, that's not good," he grumped.

Juhg silently agreed. "I can stay up for watch duty. I don't think I'm going to be able to go back to sleep."

With a grim grin, Raisho looked around at the sailors. "I don't think none of us are. If'n we don't, that'll be fine. But them that 'as watches will be up. Ever'body else can get sleep if they want it." He spoke for the benefit of the men.

A couple of the more seasoned veterans went back to their bedrolls and covered up. Juhg didn't know if they were actually sleeping or only easing their bones after the long, unaccustomed ride.

Returning to the tree where he'd set up his bedroll, Juhg took out his writing supplies from his pack. He lit a single candle, drove a needle into the tree above him, then speared the candle onto the needle so it would burn levelly. Opening his journal, senses alive to the night and the raindrops sounding like footsteps all around him, he concentrated on his work, focusing hard enough that the fear could no longer touch him.

In the morning, they rose with the dawn and saddled the horses.

"I 'alf expected to find the 'orses with their throats cut," Raisho admitted as he finished saddling his mount. "With us all 'uddled up close to the fire, they'd 'ave been easy targets in the dark. An' walking to Deldal's Mills would be a lot 'arder than ridin'. Not to mention 'ow vulnerable it would leave us."

"You thought of this just now?" Juhg asked, irritated with himself for not thinking of it. He was cold and stiff in the morning, not rested at all from the brief sleep on the hard ground he'd managed or from the hours he'd labored on the journal. Toward dawn he'd finally managed a little more sleep, but it was interrupted by nightmares of what had happened to Craugh, and by the maniacal scarecrow's face shoved against his.

"I thought of it last night." Raisho swung effortlessly up into the saddle. He raised the hood of his cloak over his head.

"And you chose to do nothing?"

"Didn't want to spread out our forces too thin."

Juhg leaped up against the horse, managed to snare the saddle horn, then pulled himself up high enough to get a foot in the stirrup. Horses weren't made for dwellers and dwarves.

The horse whickered, stamped its feet and blew.

As Juhg looked at Raisho, he realized how much his friend had grown and learned in the past eight years. The Raisho of old would have been more concerned about missing a night's sleep or trying to figure out if there was any way to find gold through the scarecrow.

Sometimes Juhg missed the Raisho of old, and it saddened him to think that one day he would miss him altogether.

Your thoughts are too dark, he told himself. So he forced a smile and said, "I'm ready when you are."

"Oh," Raisho said, "I've a feelin' ain't neither of us ready for what Craugh 'as involved us with."

Shortly after midday, though the rain never relented and Juhg never felt the passage of time through a forest that constantly dripped from unending rainfall, they reached Deldal's Mills.

"Looks quiet enough," Raisho commented as they followed the well-worn trail toward the town.

Juhg didn't comment.

"'Course, a quiet place is where bandits and assassins works best out of." Raisho eased his cutlass in the sheath he wore down his back.

Out on the Steadfast, the ferry between the two banks of the town bumped over the rolling water. Mule teams drew the ferry either way across the river, taking passengers as well as cargo. At noon it made a delivery every working day to the mill workers, supplying lunches that the mill owners paid for then charged the workers for.

"Where are we goin' once we reach town?" Raisho asked.

"The Wayside Inn." Juhg adjusted his hood to keep the light rain out of his face.

"This Minstrel Ordal will be there?"

"In all likelihood. If not, we can send word or meet him somewhere." Juhg's body ached with the constant motion of the horse. He looked forward to sitting by a roaring fireplace.

"Minstrel Ordal?" The tavern owner looked over Juhg's head. Juhg had to tiptoe slightly to look over the counter in the Wayside Inn. "I haven't seen her today, but she should be along with the evening crowd."

" 'She'?" Raisho repeated.

The tavern keeper was a portly man with a beard and a wandering eye. He'd introduced himself as Fhiel, but most of the other patrons seemed to call him Jolly. Juhg assumed it was because the tavern keeper laughed at all the jokes he was told, no matter how old those jokes happened to be.

Fhiel nodded and looked a little confused. "She. That's right. Haven't you met Minstrel Ordal?" Suspicion hardened his features.

"No," Raisho said.

"I have," Juhg replied. "But it has been a few years. The last Minstrel Ordal I saw was a man."

A broad smile split Fhiel's face. "Ah, well then, kind sir, you're in for a treat, you are. No one quite plays the harp the way this Minstrel Ordal does."

Juhg paid for ales for Raisho and his men, then got a tankard of hot mulled cider for himself. "We'll wait for Minstrel Ordal. If you'll just let her know we're here." He put coins on the countertop.

With a practiced move, Fhiel scooped the coins away. "Perhaps you'd like something to eat while you're waiting."

"No, thank you," Juhg answered. "We'll eat when we buy supper for Minstrel Ordal."

"Good, good." Fhiel rubbed his hands together in anticipation. "I'll make sure the bread's baked fresh by then, and that we have plenty." He ran his good eye over the group of sailors with renewed appreciation. "You look like a hungry bunch. Nothing like cold rain to bring up an appetite."

Juhg took his mulled cider to one of the tables near the large fireplace. Logs blazed in the hearth as he shed his cloak and hung it from a coat tree in the corner. Sinking into one of the big, stuffed chairs, he sipped the cider and let out a contented sigh. Once more among civilization, in front of a fire and with a warm drink in his hand, the fight with the scarecrow seemed far in the past.

Raisho sat across from him. "I thought ye said Minstrel Ordal was a man?"

"I did," Juhg agreed. "In my experience, he always has been in the past. But I guess things change."

"How did Minstrel Ordal change from a 'he' to a 'she'?"

"Minstrel Ordal is an hereditary title," Juhg explained. "Usually it's passed on from father to son. I guess this time there was no son to carry on." He sat staring into the fire for a time, then got out his journal and started working.

It didn't take long before his actions drew the attention of the inn's guests.

"Halfer," a thick, bull-necked man bellowed across the room. "What do you think you're doing?"

"Writing," Juhg answered. *It feels so good to be able to say that!* But some of the old fear stirred within him.

"Writing?" The bull-necked man stood. He looked like a logger, his arms and back big and strong, and his hands marked with scars from knives and axes. "Is that a book?" He said it like an accusation.

"Yes." Juhg looked up. "It is a book." He took pride in that fact.

"Are you stupid?" the man bellowed. "Are you trying to bring the goblinkin down on us? If they find we've got a book here, they'll likely burn the town down around our ears." He started across the room. "I don't know where you got that, but you need to toss it into the fire. Toss it into the fire right *now*!"

"No," Juhg replied.

"Then I'll do it for you." The man came at Juhg.

Casually, stretching smooth and quick as a great cat, Raisho shot out a foot and tripped the man. By the time the man hit the floor, the sea captain had his cutlass out and the point resting against the big man's throat.

The big man froze at once.

Three of his companions shifted in their seats and started to get up.

Immediately, Raisho's men loosened their blades in their scabbards.

Tense silence filled the tavern.

"I wouldn't," Raisho said in a carefully measured voice, "was I you. We've come a far piece under 'ard times, an' we didn't come 'ere to be 'andled like rough trade."

The men stood for a moment, obviously trapped by their pride. They didn't like being bearded in their own tavern.

"This 'ere's me friend," Raisho declared. "A learned friend who knows more'n any of ye will ever learn if'n ye devote the rest of yer lives to it. I'm not in the 'abit of lettin' me friends go unaided, an' I won't see 'is position disrespected. 'E's a Librarian. The Grandmagister of the Vault of All Known Knowledge. An' if'n ye 'aven't 'eard of 'im yet, ye will."

One of the men looked at the others. "What's a Librarian?"

Both his companions shook their heads. Still, confronted by the hard-eyed sailors from *Moonsdreamer*, they resumed their seats.

"Books ain't nothin' to fear no more." Raisho took the cutlass from the logger's throat. "They're good things. Things worth respectin'. And I won't stand fer it to be any other way." He glared back at the man on the floor. "Do we 'ave us an understandin' then?"

The man shot silent resentment at Raisho for a moment. Then he grudgingly nodded. "Yes."

"Ye can get up, then." Raisho caught Fhiel's eye at the bar. "We didn't come 'ere for no trouble, but we've 'ad some what give it to us on the trail 'ere." He nodded to the loggers' table. "Set 'em up with a round on me." Reaching into his coin purse, he took out a silver coin and flipped it to the barkeep. "Let 'em drink that up."

Looking somewhat relieved, Fhiel pulled ale from the cask behind the bar. "Yes sir."

The logger on the floor got up but didn't look at Raisho or Juhg. He returned to his table and the free ale. The men talked in low voices. Juhg overheard "Grandmagister" three times. He was aware of being the object of covert scrutiny.

"Do you think that was wise?" Juhg asked in a voice that carried only to Raisho.

"No, 'twasn't wise at all." Raisho grinned. "We're 'ard-lookin' men, scribbler. 'E should 'ave 'ad 'imself at least twenty more men afore 'e come over 'ere a-threatenin' the way 'e did. They're loggers, not trained warriors."

Juhg sighed. "That's not what I meant. I was talking about making an announcement about me being the Grandmagister and about the Vault of All Known Knowledge."

Raisho laughed. "I thought ye were in Shark's Maw Cove to convince all them people they should be a-buildin' schools."

"I was."

"An' ye were talkin' about the Library."

Frowning, Juhg said, "You know I was."

Grinning under the shadow of his hood, Raisho looked

around at the inn's patrons. All of them quickly looked away rather than risk accidentally meeting the sea captain's fierce gaze.

"Don't ye think they'll be talkin' about ye after ye're gone from 'ere?"

Juhg's cheeks burned.

Raisho laughed at his discomfort in good-natured humor. "They'll be talkin' about ye."

"I'd rather they didn't equate violence with an education."

"Really?" Raisho shifted, obviously enjoying himself. When they'd lain fallow onboard *Windchaser*, Raisho had often instigated arguments just to draw conversation from Juhg. The fact that he possessed a canny mind and a quick facility for learning had always made him a worthy opponent. "Wasn't it Baomet Sunkar that attributed much of education to invadin' armies what brought new learnin' back to both countries?"

In disbelief, Juhg looked at his friend. "You *have* been reading."

Shrugging, Raisho said, "It's a way of easin' long voyages."

Smiling in deeper appreciation of his friend, Juhg returned his attention to his journal. The cheery fire warmed him.

"Grandmagister Juhg."

Startled, Juhg looked up from his journal. A young woman with long red hair and her father's honest brown eyes regarded him. Her smile was open and friendly. She wore a yellow blouse with alabaster fringe and tan breeches. A feathered red cap sat on her head at a jaunty angle. She carried a pack over one shoulder and a small harp in one hand.

Gladness touched Juhg's heart and momentarily lifted the grave doubts and fears that his work on the journal barely kept at bay. He closed the journal, capped his ink-well, and put them both into his pack. He stuck the quill he'd been using behind his ear.

"Yurial!" Juhg exclaimed as he got to his feet and opened his arms. The young woman came to him eagerly, but he was surprised again at how tall she was. She had to kneel to take him into her embrace.

"I'll be Yurial to you," she said, "but to everyone else, I'm the Minstrel Ordal."

"Of course, of course." Releasing her, Juhg stepped back and looked her up and down. "You've grown."

Yurial laughed in delight. "I have. There was no alternative, I'm afraid."

"You were just a girl when I last saw you." Juhg waved her to one of the overstuffed chairs.

"That was twenty years ago, Grandmagister."

Juhg thought about it. Keeping timelines of outside things—dynasties, science, and other fields of study—was simple, but his personal timelines often blurred. One year seemed to leap headlong into the next.

"Twenty years brings about a lot of changes," Yurial said.

"It does. And don't call me Grandmagister. You're my friend."

"You have that title of office," Yurial said. "I wouldn't take it from you through casual address."

"Forgive me oafish friend," Raisho said, stepping forward to introduce himself. "I'm sure that sooner or later 'e would've remembered I were 'ere." He doffed his cloak to bare his head and smiled. "I am Captain Raisho, Master of *Moonsdreamer*, currently in port—"

"—at Calmpoint," Yurial said. "It's a pleasure to meet you, Captain Raisho."

"Ye seem to find out things pretty quickly," Raisho observed.

Yurial smiled. "Generally, if it happens in Calmpoint, Deldal's Mills, or a dozen other towns around here, I know about it." She sat in the chair Juhg had waved her to.

"We came straight from Calmpoint," Raisho said.

In that moment, Juhg realized why Raisho was being so inquisitive. "Raisho, Yurial didn't have anything to do with what happened to us last night."

"Then 'ow did she know *Moonsdreamer* was in Calmpoint?"

Yurial raised an amused and inquisitive eyebrow. "For one, Captain, you can't very well sail a deep sea ship up the Steadfast River. For another, a group of miller's men were returning to Deldal's Mills when you arrived, and they carried the news of your arrival. Then there are the horses outside that carry Ganik the blacksmith's mark. Another indication that you hadn't brought your ship upriver." She smiled again. "Unless you've some magic that allows you to fold your ship up and put it into your pocket."

"No," Raisho growled.

Juhg knew from experience that the young sea captain was embarrassed.

"I meant no disrespect," Raisho said, directing his gaze to Yurial as well as Juhg. "I just don't want nothin' to 'appen to the scribbler 'ere."

"So I judged," Yurial said, "from the reports of the near altercation in here earlier." She sat back calmly, her fingers plucking quiet notes subconsciously from the harp in her lap.

"Where's your da?" Juhg asked, hoping to steer the conversation away from the last few minutes.

"He's dead." Sadness touched Yurial's brown eyes.

"I'm sorry for your loss," Juhg said.

"As am I," Yurial said. "He was taken by Torlik's Fever three years past. One of the logging camps deep in the forest came down with it. Da went there because he couldn't bear the thought of those women and children dying without the all too brief happiness of stories and songs to tell them good-bye. So he went." She paused. "Da had been around Torlik's Fever on three other occasions. Survived it himself once. He thought he would be safe. He wasn't. We had to burn his body there with the others. But I placed a headstone for him in the graveyard. It gives me a place to go talk to him."

"You still have his songs," Juhg told her. "All those he taught you, as well as the ones he wrote."

A smile lightened her features then. "I know."

"I didn't know he was gone," Juhg apologized. "Otherwise I would have visited."

Yurial plucked sweet, sad notes, but she smiled. "I know you would have. You and Grandmagister Lamplighter. And since Wick's not here, am I to assume that something has happened to—"

"No," Juhg said. "Grandmagister Lamplighter abdicated his position to go off on a most remarkable journey." He didn't know how else to describe his mentor's disappearance with *The Book of Time*.

"Hopefully, Wick will return soon to us with marvelous tales of where he's been and what he's seen," Yurial said. "There's never been a talespinner like him."

"Never," Juhg agreed. "I wish he were here now to advance the idea of starting schools to teach reading and for the building of Libraries."

"From what I hear," Yurial said, "you've been doing well."

"Changing opinions is hard and slow."

"You're combating a thousand years of fear. That won't be an easy task."

"But if people could only understand what the Libraries have to offer," Juhg said, "they would take to the idea more quickly."

"All they know right now is that books may draw the goblinkin to them. The goblinkin still sack towns. Especially in the south near Hanged Elf's Point."

Juhg knew that. One of his Librarians was assigned to assessing the growing threat of that situation. Several of the leaders he'd talked to were afraid another goblinkin war was brewing. He couldn't discount that possibility.

"But enough of that," Yurial said. "What has brought you here when you have so many other important things to do?"

Juhg waved the innkeeper over to bring fresh drinks all around, then he proceeded to tell the tale.

"Craugh wants to ferret out the betrayal that happened at the Battle of Fell's Keep?" Yurial sat back in her chair and delicately strummed the harp. The music was hauntingly familiar. Juhg was certain he'd heard it before, probably played by her father, but Yurial had made it her own.

"Yes."

"Why?"

"Because, as he insists, the world—or at least the mainland—is getting smaller. The goblinkin activity in the south has bunched up the northern empires, kingdoms, and port cities. The populations there have increased, so trade and travel have become more important. It's hard enough to work out those things without the mystery of who betrayed who at the Battle of Fell's Keep standing in the way."

Yurial nodded. "I agree with that."

"As do I," Juhg said.

"But what brings you here to Deldal's Mills?"

"Grandmagister Lamplighter left a book at the Vault of All Known Knowledge detailing his search for the traitor. I finished translating the code only a few days ago. At the end of that book, he left a clue to the location of the second book."

"There are two books?"

"There are three in all," Juhg said.

"Is the third with the second?"

"I don't know."

Yurial thought for a moment. Her quick mind instantly provided an answer to the question she hadn't even asked.

"You came here to see me because you think I know the location of the second book."

"Because Grandmagister Lamplighter said Minstrel Ordal did."

Yurial shook her head. "He never gave me a book. Or my da. We helped Wick find a couple."

"Actually," Juhg said, "the Grandmagister said asking Minstrel Ordal a question would unveil the location of the second book."

"What's the question?"

A wave of nervousness passed through Juhg. The Grandmagister had been referring to Yurial's da, a man who had dealings with Edgewick Lamplighter on a personal level, swapping stories and humor and songs. Even though one Minstrel Ordal passed on all his knowledge to his apprentice, that didn't mean everything was handed down.

"The question is, 'What rides in on four legs, stands on two legs, and stumbles away on three legs'? I thought at first it might refer to the ages of a man. Crawling on four legs as a babe, walking as a man, then with the aid of a staff when he's bent with age."

Yurial smiled. "That's a good guess. Except it doesn't explain the bit about riding. Babes don't necessarily ride on four legs."

"Do you know the answer?"

"Of course I do. It's an easy question to answer if you knew Wick and my da."

"It escaped me."

Yurial stood and slung her pack and harp once more. "Come with me and you'll get your answer. Let's take care of Ganik's horses first. They look sad standing tethered outside."

"We don't need them?" Raisho asked.

"Not unless you intend to leave tonight."

Thinking about the scarecrow they'd encountered in the forest, Juhg shook his head. "We'll take rooms here tonight."

"You're welcome to stay at my home." Yurial looked at the sailors, who were also getting to their feet. "Of course, it will be crowded."

"We'll be fine here." Despite her status as Minstrel Ordal and the respect she had in the community as such, she had only a small house and was of modest means.

Together, after reassuring Fhiel they would return for supper, they departed.

Later, after the horses had been safely moved to the livery, Yurial led them through Deldal's Mills, through the shops and trade stores. Farther back, following a winding path between some of the older buildings in the town, they reached a small building that Juhg remembered.

It was three stories tall and narrow, a seeming clapboard building that was part shop and part residence. Though old, it had stood the test of time and looked solid enough to stand for several more years. Lights burned in the first floor.

An empty pottery jug painted with a sunburst (even though in the darkness that had fallen over Deldal's Mills Juhg couldn't see it) hung from the chain over the front door. It was the only advertisement, and it was all that was needed.

Evarch's Winery and Spirits was a legend along the Shattered Coast.

"I should have remembered Evarch's," Juhg said.

"You had a lot on your mind," Yurial told him as they walked up the tall wooden steps to the vintner's. She knocked on the door.

"Who is it?" an irritable voice demanded from within.

"Minstrel Ordal," Yurial answered, "Grandmagister Juhg, and friends."

"Go away. It's late."

"I know it's late, Evarch. I wouldn't be here if it weren't important. Come on. Open up."

"Tomorrow."

"Grandmagister Juhg is here."

"I heard you the first time. He can—" Evarch caught himself. "Did you say Grandmagister *Juhg*?"

"I did."

A moment passed as a shadow appeared on the curtained window. Locks ratcheted. Then the door opened. Evarch stuck his head out. Moonslight gleamed on his gray hair and beard. His leathery face was seamed with wrinkles.

"What happened to Wick?" Evarch demanded. "You didn't go and let something bad happen to him, did you?"

"No," Juhg answered. "Grandmagister Lamplighter is off on an adventure."

"Another one, huh?" Evarch shook his shaggy head. "I swear, Wick has never acted like any halfer I've ever known." He narrowed his eyes at Juhg. "You neither."

Juhg didn't know how to respond to that so he didn't.

"I suppose you're to blame for the interruption to my evening," Evarch accused.

"I am," Juhg admitted. "Grandmagister Lamplighter told me to come see you."

"He did, did he?" Interest flickered in the old man's eyes then. "Before he left?"

"The Grandmagister left the Library eight years ago. I was working on a book he'd written. There was a passage in there that sent me to Minstrel Ordal."

"Then to me?"

"Yes."

Evarch scratched his chin. "How did you come to me?"

"The Grandmagister sent me."

"Yes, I understand that. But how did you get the message? Did he just tell you to come see me? And you waited eight years to get around to it?"

"No."

"Because I can see that happening with you halfers.

Dwarves and elves, too. You act like you have all the time in the world. But there are those of us who count days more dearly."

"It was in the passage in the book," Juhg said.

"What book?"

"One of Grandmagister Lamplighter's journals about the Battle of Fell's Keep."

"When he went seeking Master Blacksmith Oskarr's battle-axe Boneslicer in the Cinder Clouds Islands?"

Juhg nodded.

"What did this passage say?" Evarch asked.

"I was to find Minstrel Ordal and ask him—"

"Not a *him* this time around," Evarch said.

"—and ask *her* the answer to the following question, 'What rides in on four legs, stands on two legs, and stumbles away on three legs?' "

"You should have known the answer to that," Evarch said. "Without Minstrel Ordal's help. Then again, you never had the same interest in razalistynberry wine that your teacher did."

"No."

"Still not as interested?"

Juhg shook his head. "Sorry." He'd never developed a taste for wine or pipeweed.

"Oh spare me from the uncultured palate. At least Minstrel Ordal was able to guide you to my door. The answer to your teacher's question is obvious. A thirsty man rides up on his horse's four legs to Evarch's Wine and Spirits, stands on his own two legs while he drinks his fill, then stumbles back using every lamppost along the way as his third leg."

It made sense to Juhg, but he knew he wouldn't have gotten the answer without Yurial's help. *Well, I might have even if Yurial hadn't been here*, he told himself. *Knowing the answer was in Deldal's Mills might have been enough. Once I'd started thinking clearly.*

"If that riddle led you here," Evarch said, "then you've come about the book."

"The second book of the trilogy?" Juhg asked.

"I don't know anything about that." Evarch stepped back and waved them into his house. "Years ago, Wick delivered a book to me for safekeeping and told me that one day his apprentice would show up for it. He claimed that only his apprentice would be able to read it."

Juhg followed Yurial through the door into the house. Nothing about Evarch's house smacked of business. It was a home first, and as such the first room was large and spacious, filled with decanters, tankards, and glasses from everywhere in the Shattered Coast.

Evarch waved them to comfortable furniture. There was room for all of them with space left over. Evarch sometimes entertained large numbers of guests, which belied the curmudgeonly persona he displayed.

"Juhg, light a few of the lanterns," Evarch directed. "We'll need illumination."

Juhg used the flames in the fireplace to light the lanterns. Soon, the room was cheery and bright. The flames reflected off the glass, stone, and metal containers arranged on the shelves around the room. The windows held stained glass images of grape fields and decanters, a concoction as audacious as the man who lived there.

Evarch returned in a few minutes with a large book in his hand. The blue cover caught Juhg's eye immediately. It was a reptile hide of some kind, and it immediately made him remember Rohoh.

"Before I give this book to you," Evarch said, "even though I know you, I want to abide by Wick's wishes in this matter."

"Of course," Juhg answered.

"He said whoever came for this book would know how to read it. He said that not even every Librarian he knew would be able to do that."

"Because he invented a code to write it in," Juhg said.

"Yes." Still a little hesitant, Evarch handed over the book. "I will know if you can read this."

Juhg opened the cover of the book with the reverence

Edgewick Lamplighter had taught him to have for books.
The code in this book was the same that had been used in
the last. After days of translating the other book, Juhg
could read the code with a little speed.

" 'Read this passage to Evarch the Vintner to prove
that you know how to read the code.' Signed, 'Second
Level Librarian Lamplighter.' " Juhg took a breath and
deciphered the next section. " 'Evarch, obviously the situation I pursued regarding the Battle of Fell's Keep and
Lord Kharrion's Wrath has become worse than I had
imagined. Some old secrets never go away, and fear remains just as sharp for those that have done wrong. Please
rest assured you have carried out to the best of your abilities the favor I have charged you with. Drink that bottle
we set aside to seal this agreement in good health.' "

"Then he is truly gone." Tears showed in Evarch's eyes.
"I'm going to miss that little halfer. I have known few
friends like Wick."

The old man's emotion touched Juhg and made him
more aware of his own loss. "I don't know that he is gone
for good, Master Evarch. Only that he has been gone these
eight years."

Evarch sat in one of the overstuffed chairs. "Eight
years. I'd feared something had happened to him. In the
whole time that I've known him, I've never known more
than two or three years to pass before I saw him again. I
knew too many years had slipped by this time, but I continued to hope that I would see him once more."

"You may still yet," Juhg said, but he knew he was
hoping that more than he believed it. The power wielded
by *The Book of Time* was incredible, and Juhg could only
guess at the number of worlds it had opened up to Grandmagister Lamplighter.

"The book will help you?" Evarch asked.

"I think so," Juhg said. "There's still a lot to learn." He
flipped through the pages, glancing at the pictures Grandmagister Lamplighter had drawn all those years ago when
he was a Second Level Librarian. "While Grandmagister

Lamplighter was in the Cinder Clouds Islands, he crossed the path of a thieves' guild called the Razor's Kiss."

"They operate out of Wharf Rat's Warren," Evarch said. "I've heard of them."

"So have I," Yurial said. "They're very dangerous."

Thoughts of the scarecrow that had attacked them the night before and of the bloodstains that were all that remained of Craugh aboard *Moonsdreamer* collided within Juhg's head, worrying at him. He wanted to get up and get moving, get back to Calmpoint and return to the ship. But Grandmagister Lamplighter's words—even across the years—seized his attention once more and pulled him into those events that had happened so long ago.

1

Wharf Rat's Warren

act like a thief, he says, Second Level Librarian Edge-wick Lamplighter thought crossly as he trod the icy streets of the city of thieves, murderers, assassins, brigands, thieves, cutthroats, cutpurses, thieves, burglars, thieves and—*I'm repeating myself. That can't be good.* He snorted in disgust. *Act like a thief, indeed. As if I know anything about being a thief. Why Craugh should—*

A howling wind from the Great Frozen North ripped through Whisper Street and distracted him. Out in the harbor, where a handful of ships sat sheltered in the Whip-crack Sea, so named because the sea had a tendency to freeze over with the sound of a whip cracking and crush ships mastered by unwary captains, rigging popped and rang against masts.

Wick pulled his black cloak more tightly around him and tried to remember the last time he'd felt his feet. They were frozen blocks at the ends of his legs that might as well have belonged to someone else.

As a dweller, he didn't really have a need for foot-wear. Generally his feet were tough enough for any task he had ahead of him. Today, however, he wished for a pair of boots just his size. Still, his discomfort was only an errant thought. The ruse he had yet to play consumed his thoughts.

He'd never before had to play the part of an assassin. Or was it a thief? For a moment, near frozen from his trek over the Ice Daggers, the small mountain range south of the city, and famished from not eating for what seemed like hours, Wick truly couldn't remember what part he was supposed to play.

He was supposed to be a thief or an assassin. He was pretty sure about that. The whole thing was Craugh's idea, which Wick had thought to be dumb from the beginning but hadn't had a better idea (or wanted to risk being turned into a toad by saying that), so he'd agreed to subterfuge. That had been onboard *One-Eyed Peggie*, though, and there'd been a meal waiting.

And he'd actually thought Craugh or Cap'n Farok would have become inspired and come up with something much better by the time they actually reached Wharf Rat's Warren.

He'd expected a hot breakfast that morning, too. Instead Craugh had roused him from his hammock, ordered him into his clothes, and marched him out to the little village where they'd dumped him.

Walking through the screaming wind, feeling the icy teeth of winter gnawing him all the way to the bone, Wick nearly tripped on his trousers again. The legs were several inches too long. Craugh had chosen to overlook that and told Wick he could simply keep them rolled up. Rolling them up hadn't lasted long. As soon as they'd gotten wet in the snow, they'd promptly unrolled and been a nuisance ever since.

He pulled the pants legs up again and felt the cold material slapping against his legs. The numbness seemed to be spreading. He had to pinch his ankles to discover that he *could* feel them even though he hadn't expected to.

To make matters worse, the donkey he was using as a combination mount and pack animal was becoming increasingly rebellious. Wick had to lean into his effort to bring the donkey along, and every now and then his efforts caused him to trip on a slippery spot and end up face-first in the snow. He didn't have a stitch of clothing that wasn't gunked up with mud.

When he fell again, Wick spat the dirty snow from his mouth and wiped it from his face. He was so cold that the snow actually felt warm against his skin, which was another bad sign.

I'm going to get frostbitten all over, he told himself. *If I somehow make it back out of here alive, Craugh and Hallekk are going to carve my toes, fingers, nose, ears, and other pieces off me.*

He turned to the donkey and stared the animal in the eyes. It was refusing to move again and strained at the end of the reins. Of course, since it outweighed him nearly ten times, the donkey didn't have to strain hard.

"Come on with me, you great lummox," Wick ordered. "You've got the easy part. At least all you have to do is act like a donkey."

The donkey swiveled its ears toward Wick as if it were listening intently. When he tugged again, it pinned its ears back, pulled its lips back in a big grin, and brayed donkey laughter. Then it sat on its haunches.

"I've got a mind to sell you to a renderer to be made into glue," Wick threatened. He set his feet and pulled with all his might.

Suddenly, laughter punctuated the howling wind.

Startled, Wick stepped back into the donkey's larger bulk for protection. He wasn't ready to start pretending to be a master assassin yet. Or thief. Whichever it was.

"Havin' trouble with your donkey, halfer?" one of the three men in front of the Tavern of Schemes asked. He was a tall human with a florid face and a big nose.

"No," Wick said, straightening to his full three and a half feet minus in height.

"You looked like you were having problems with him," the man continued.

Glaring, hoping the effect was both chilling and an

expression of warning, Wick patted the donkey's neck. "No. Not any problems. This is where I wanted him to sit."

"In the middle of the street like that?" The man looked at Wick doubtfully. "Someone will steal him."

Let them, Wick thought. *If they can get him to move when they want him to, they can have him.* After all, the donkey wasn't part of his assassin's disguise. Or thief's. He could gladly spare the stubborn beast.

"I'm toughening him up," Wick replied. "Having him sit in near-frozen mud puddles increases his endurance and strength. It's part of a training process."

The donkey yawned, smacked its lips, and stood, looking anything but trainable. Unbidden, it tramped toward the livery next door to the Tavern of Schemes, obviously smelling the hay and grain inside. The animal's sudden movement yanked Wick into motion and he stumbled along after it. Maybe he looked ridiculous, but at least he hadn't fallen on his face again. Still, looking in command of himself while being dragged by the donkey was impossible.

"And now I'm done punishing him," Wick said with feigned authority and confidence, falling into step with the donkey because he found the length of rope he'd tied around his wrist wasn't going to loosen up. "He knows who's boss."

The men laughed again at him, shaking their heads and going on with their business.

The donkey headed straight into the livery and Wick went with the animal, grateful to be out of the wind.

"How long are you going to be in town?" the dirty-faced young boy asked as he took the donkey's lead rope from Wick's wrist.

"I haven't decided yet." Wick gazed around the livery,

surprised at how clean it was. Wharf Rat's Warren wasn't known for its cleanliness.

"The charges are daily or by the ten-day," the boy said.

"By the day," Wick said. "For now." Craugh hadn't been overly generous about funding his present mission despite Wick's protests. The wizard had insisted that Wick couldn't very well play the part of a thief looking for work if he was flush with gold. The little Librarian didn't want to spend what meager amount he had on caring for the cantankerous donkey when it might mean he'd have to skip meals himself.

The boy lifted his thin shoulders and dropped them. "Whatever. If you're late on a day's pay, though, my da will sell the donkey for whatever he can get."

"All right." *This could work out all the way around*, Wick thought. He wasn't looking forward to dragging the donkey back over the Ice Daggers.

Several horses stood in the paddocks, munching hay and oats, and snorting and stamping. A few coaches and carts occupied the far end of the livery. Wick didn't think the wheeled vehicles were often used. The streets in Wharf Rat's Warren were filled with potholes and covered only in oyster shells and loose shale.

Ryman Bey and the Razor's Kiss thieves' guild have Master Oskarr's battle-axe, though, and I can't allow that to continue. Especially since Wick blamed himself for losing the weapon while on the Cinder Clouds Islands. (Actually Craugh blamed him for it, and there was no arguing with the wizard once he became convinced of something.)

Bulokk was still recovering from his wounds during the battle against the Razor's Kiss. Upon discovering that Wick was about to leave *One-Eyed Peggie*, Bulokk had asked the little Librarian to promise him that he would do everything in his power to recover Boneslicer.

Wick, even though he hadn't wanted to promise such a thing, hadn't been able to say no. Of course, he'd envisioned he'd have someone at his back to do all the heavy lifting and sword-swinging that accompanied such promises. Bulokk would have been better off asking one of his warriors. Then again, maybe he'd asked everyone.

The other dwarves had volunteered to accompany Wick, but Craugh had forbidden that. Craugh insisted that Wharf Rat's Warren was primarily a human dwelling, albeit a lawless one, and that having a party of dwarves in their midst would alert the Razor's Kiss. There were dwarven bandits and thieves, of course, but they didn't live in Wharf Rat's Warren.

Reluctantly, Wick had admitted the wisdom of that. So, with the Cinder Clouds Islands dwarves and *One-Eyed Peggie*'s dwarven crew removed from the board, there had remained only two possibilities for the position of spy.

Craugh had quickly pointed out that no one would ever see him as anything less than a wizard. Wick had guilelessly (the threat of being turned into a toad always persisted when talking to the wizard) presented the opportunity for Craugh to pass himself off as a *thieving and selfish* wizard, and suggested that the role might require Craugh to do a lot of acting, but it wasn't beyond the realm of the imaginable.

Craugh had only given Wick one of *those* looks, and the little Librarian knew how things would go. Two days later he'd found himself at the small village of Bent Anchor and equipped with an ill-tempered and stubborn donkey.

Outside in the wind, Wick debated his choices. Twilight was coming on and snow was starting to fall again in thin white flakes.

He shivered, wishful of a warm fire, a good book, and a pipe. Maybe a pint of razalistynberry wine. That was the only way to properly enjoy weather like this.

Grimly, knowing that time counted and he'd lost days while traveling across the Ice Daggers, Wick headed for the Tavern of Schemes.

Like all of the other buildings in the city of thieves, murderers, assassins, thieves, etc., the Tavern of Schemes was heavily weathered by exposure and neglect. Windows were boarded over, the glass panes unreplaced, but space had been left for crossbowmen to take aim. Wick knew the place only because it was next to the livery.

The Tavern of Schemes was one of the most used buildings in the city. It was there that devious plans were hatched, daring robberies planned, and assassinations bought and paid for all along the Shattered Coast. The Tavern of Schemes wasn't the only such place to sell those services, but it was the only one in Wharf Rat's Warren.

Wick tried the door.

It was locked.

So what is an assassin—or a thief—supposed to do in this instance? Is this a test?

Wick gave the dilemma some thought. Finally, he reached into the small bag he carried and took out his thief's lockpicks. He'd just opened the kit up and set to work when he heard someone clear his throat behind him.

"I wouldn't do that if I were you," someone said.

2

Quarrel

Looking up and back, Wick saw a slim young man standing behind him. The young man wore heavy outer clothing and a thick fur cap. The hilt of a rapier jutted over his shoulder. A long knife was scabbarded at his right hip. His eyes were pale blue and the brows sharply arched. A scarf masked his lower face but his breath still blew a fog in the cold.

"Hello," Wick said, not certain what he was supposed to do.

"Hello," the young man replied.

Looking at the innocent-seeming blue eyes, Wick couldn't help wondering what the young man did as a vocation. Most of the other men the little Librarian had encountered while trudging through Wharf Rat's Warren had hard, selfish eyes.

These eyes seemed genuinely amused. And maybe a little suspicious.

"What are you doing?" the young man asked in a soft voice.

"Picking the lock," Wick said, gesturing with his pick. *There's no sense lying about it. Besides, this is the city of thieves, murderers, assassins, thieves, etc. It's not like they're going to call the watch to lock me up. Such be-havior is expected here.*

"Why are you picking the lock?"

"Because the door's locked."

"Of course it's locked," the young man said. "This is the Tavern of Schemes. They don't just let anyone in. Saves them from getting surprised by any Watch members who come here looking for revenge or justice."

Wick could understand how the criminals of Wharf Rat's Warren would see that as a defense. Several of the residents there had prices on their heads all along the Shat-tered Coast.

"But if you pick the lock," the young man went on, "you'll probably get a crossbow bolt between your eyes for your trouble. Utald rarely misses when he sets his sights."

Wick thought about that for a moment, then put his lockpicks away. "Well, that's not something I look forward to." He faced the door and spoke more loudly so that anyone who might be listening behind the door could hear him. "Sorry. Picking locks is a force of habit. I'm a thief." *Or an assassin.* He shrugged as nonchalantly as he could with the promise of a crossbow bolt between his eyes star-ing him in the face. "I find a locked door, I just naturally reach for my lockpicks." He forced a chuckle to break the tension, then looked at the young man again. "You know how it is."

"No," the young man said, "I don't." His eyes narrowed in irritation. "I'm not a thief."

"Oh." *That obviously leaves murderer or assassin.* Wick wasn't sure if either of those left him more com-fortable than the other.

The door remained closed.

Feeling foolish, Wick jerked a thumb at the door. "Are you certain someone's on the other side of that door?"

A frown lowered the young man's arched brows. "Is this your first time here?" he asked.

"Yes." Wick stuck out a hand. "Righty Lightfingers at your service." *Should I have said that in a gruffer voice?* he wondered. *The thieves in Drelor Deodarb's tales always seem to be a scrofulous lot.* He made his voice deeper and added a hint of bravado. "I mean, the name's Righty. Righty Lightfingers."

"I see. But weren't you picking the lock left-handed?"

"A ruse," Wick said, thinking fast. *Why do I always get the ones with falcon's eyes?* It was enough to make him think being clever was not intended for him. Being intelligent, he'd found on several life-or-death situations, was decidedly different than being clever. Intelligence just didn't turn away axe blows and arrows with the same sort of success craftiness did. Intelligence involved learning, and sometimes learning was a direct application of the trouble he got into. "If I used my right hand, I'd give myself away."

"Most people," the young man stated, "are right-handed."

"Oh." In his hurry to cover his gaff, Wick had forgotten that. Being intelligent also wasn't a great defense when the other person was intelligent, too. Suddenly he felt like he was being taken to task just as he was by Grandmagister Frollo at the Vault of All Known Knowledge.

"Don't you know the secret knock?" the young man asked.

Wick blinked. *Secret knock?* "What secret knock?"

"The one that gets the guard to open the door."

"No."

The young man let out a breath of disgust that fogged the cold air for a moment.

Wick held his head up even though he wanted to drop it and turn invisible. "I did say this was my first time here," he reminded.

"So you did." The young man regarded him even more intently.

"I came here looking for work. Lots of thieves come to Wharf Rat's Warren looking for work."

The young man just looked at him.

"What's wrong?" Wick asked.

"You're the strangest thief I've ever met," the young man admitted.

"Maybe you haven't met many thieves," Wick suggested defensively.

"This is the place for meeting thieves," the young man pointed out. "I've met any number of thieves. After all, this is the city of thieves, murderers, assassins—"

"And thieves." Wick sighed.

The young man frowned. "I was going to say liars. There are a *lot* of liars here."

He said that as if Wick should take note that he knew all about liars.

"Of course," the young man went on, "lying doesn't pay as well as any of the other work. And *everybody* comes to hate you because once you start lying it's a hard habit to break. Once you start, you just sort of tend to forget you're doing it." The young man paused. "But it will get you just as dead. You might want to keep that in mind."

Wick gulped, but kept that reaction hidden. He hoped.

"Are you sure you want to go in?" the young man asked.

Actually, Wick was certain he did *not* want to enter the premises. One of the rumors he'd heard about Wharf Rat's Warren was that the Tavern of Schemes had a pit beneath it that allowed the disposal of bodies by way of an underground chute that led to the coastline only sixty yards away. Liars, cheats, and spies left the tavern with their throats cut and were given an impromptu burial at sea.

"Yes," he answered, and hoped that the young man didn't hear the momentary quaver in his voice.

The young man stepped to the door and banged on it with heavy-handed authority. The rapid syncopation of blows was answered from inside. Wick memorized both rhythms at once, in case he managed to emerge alive and ever had to go back to the Tavern of Schemes.

Then bolts slid and crossbars were lifted. The door opened and a huge troll shoved his blocky head through the space. He peered out with eyes large as a horse's and with sickly yellow irises. Nearly eight feet tall, the troll stood half that across, looking surely too broad to fit through the door. His skin, visible on his face and massively-thewed forearms, was the color of butter fat, pale and putrid with a hint of an ochre undertone. His hairless head was as square as a tree stump slapped into place atop his short neck. Pig's ears twitched atop his head, and the resemblance was carried out in his thick snout as well. Tusks in his lower jaw reached up past the outside corners of his eyes. He wore clothes fashioned from gray sealskin.

"Who is it?" the troll demanded in a voice even louder and deeper than a dwarf's.

"Quarrel," the young man announced. "You know me, Krok."

Quarrel fits you, Wick thought, surveying the young human. *Straight and sleek, no room for nonsense.*

The troll leaned down over the young human and blew out his breath in a great gray fog that enveloped Wick.

Wick almost threw up. Trolls smelled bad anyway, but whatever this one had been eating had been truly noxious. The little Librarian clapped his hand over his mouth and used his thumb and forefinger to pinch his nostrils shut.

Quarrel remained standing, arms folded over his chest. *He's got to be holding his breath*, Wick thought desperately. *There's no way he can stand that stench.*

"I know you," Krok admitted. "You can come inside." He moved sideways and Quarrel slipped through easily. Then the troll turned his attention to Wick and blocked the way again, halting Wick in his tracks. "And *you.* Who are you?" He thrust his face forward.

With the troll's features only inches from his own, Wick removed his hand from his mouth, but he forgot to let go of his nose. His reply, "Righty Lightfingers," came out sounding high-pitched and nasal.

"*Righty* Lightfingers, huh?" Krok glared at Wick.

Realizing that he was gripping his nose with the wrong hand, Wick changed hands. He was pinching his nose again, still sounding nasal, when he answered, "That's right. I'm Right, er, Righty." He removed his hand and tried not to breathe.

"So what do you do, Righty Lightfingers?" Krok asked.

"I'm a thief," Wick said. "And a master assassin." He added the last quickly.

The troll regarded him with fascination. "Is that so?"

Still not breathing, Wick nodded.

"A halfer who's a thief and an assassin." Krok smiled. "This should be fun." He shot out a big, three-fingered hand, grabbed Wick's cloak, and yanked him inside.

Wick had time for one strangled, "Eeeep!" before he was yanked into the dark interior of the Tavern of Schemes.

"Lookit what I found at the door!" Krok roared as he held Wick up and carried him through the tavern in one big fist.

"A halfer," a man with an eye patch exclaimed in delight.

"Entertainment," a man with badly fitting wooden teeth added. "Didn't know there was going to be a sideshow tonight." His teeth clacked as he spoke.

Another man rubbed his hand and hook together enthusiastically. "It's been long enough since we had a halfer for sport. How many pieces do you want to cut him up in?" He leered in anticipation.

With the fear flooding him, thoughts of the cold water out in the harbor awaiting his body, Wick didn't mind the troll's stench so much. Actually, it wasn't that he didn't mind the stink, because he did, but it suddenly seemed like the sour odor was the least of his problems. He fought against the troll's grip but couldn't manage to get away.

"Don't get caught," Craugh had admonished Wick

before they'd dumped him out of *One-Eyed Peggie*. *"Don't do anything to raise suspicions. Do your best not to get noticed in any way. Slink. Skulk. Sneak. Act like a thief."*

Well, that wasn't working out. And, at the moment, Wick would have preferred getting turned into a toad to ending up in chunks for the monsters out in the harbor. Toads still got to eat and had warm beds.

Krok thumped Wick onto the scarred bar at the back of the tavern. Gazing around the room, the little Librarian got the feeling he'd stepped right into the pages of one of Drelor Deodarb's crime romances. Only Wick didn't feel like one of the tough mercenaries or thieves or assassins Deodarb wrote about.

At least twenty men were in the room. All of them sat in shadows at tiny tables scrunched in between high-backed booths. Single candles barely illuminated the harsh features of the men seated there. All of their faces carried lines formed of misery and cruelty. Scars and missing limbs were in abundance. The reek of desperation swirled through the room.

Wharf Rat's Warren divided the residents there quickly into winners and losers, with a subdivision of losers who died and those who survived with scars to show how close they had come. There were two other trolls and four goblinkin. With the darkness lurking in the room, the tavern seemed small. The low ceiling maintained that image.

"What you got there, Krok?" one of the trolls asked.

"Going to find out," Krok answered.

Not knowing what else to do, Wick sat on the counter. He blinked and tried to think of something to say. If he'd been one of Deodarb's antiheroes, he'd have pulled out hidden stilettos and pinned both Krok's hands to the counter for him. Or a hidden short sword and lopped off one of the henchmen's heads.

Even if he'd had stilettos, Wick couldn't have found it in him to pin Krok's hands to the counter. He didn't care for violence at all. Despite that, sometimes violence seemed to follow him around. Most of the time, it chased him, waving a weapon or baring fangs, and threatening the most awful things.

"Says his name is Righty Lightfingers," Krok said. "He's supposed to be a thief and an assassin. Anybody heard of someone by that name?"

A chorus of "nos" ran around the room.

Looking back at Wick, Krok growled, "Nobody's heard of you, halfer."

"A thief and master assassin isn't supposed to have a reputation," Wick said in a small voice. "Except by those looking to hire him." Thankfully he managed to say that without quavering. He tried to look fearless, but doubted he pulled that off sitting contritely like he was in Grandmagister Frollo's study to accept a verbal drubbing. "Does anyone here want to hire a thief or an assassin?"

The tavern patrons broke out in laughter. It was undecided whether "A halfer thief!" or "A halfer assassin!" got the greatest response.

"Maybe he offers *low* prices!" someone else chortled.

"Or he specializes in *little* jobs!" another cried.

"In those hard-to-get-to places!"

Wick's hopes of survival dwindled.

"Do you know how many people would want to hurt me if they suspected I was a thief or an assassin?" Wick asked, trying to find some way to excuse his anonymity. "I can't just go around letting everyone know who stole the king's crown or who poisoned an important merchant."

Krok scratched his head thoughtfully. "That's true."

"And people I've stolen from don't want to admit it. Who wants to admit they've had a fortune stolen by a dweller?" Wick went on.

"That's true, too."

"Or had someone they were supposed to be guarding assassinated under their very noses by me?"

"Of course it was under their noses. He's a halfer."

"You've done that?"

Wick started to say a dozen times, then thought the tavern crowd might not believe that and considered lowering the number, then figured he really needed to impress and—hopefully—throw a little fear in them. "Nearly one hundred times," he declared, thinking that surely that was a respectable number of victims.

3

The Assassin's Résumé

Laughter filled the tavern immediately.

"No way," a grizzled mercenary said. "A little pipsqueak like you couldn't have killed nearly a hundred people."

"I didn't do it with a blade," Wick said. "They had to look like accidents. That's what I specialize in. Trip wires on stairs. Snakes in beds. Death by horse—"

"Death by horse?" a man asked. "You hire the horse?"

"No," Wick said, finding himself curiously drawn to his stories, which were lifted from various compendiums on assassinations he'd read. Grandmagister Frollo hadn't exactly been thrilled about finding those on Wick's personal reading list, either. Grandmagister Frollo wasn't of the opinion that all knowledge should be saved. "You can put a burr under a horse's saddle. Or poison it so it temporarily goes mad. Then you can just talk them into killing their riders."

"Talk to horses?"

Too late, Wick realized that he'd selected a means that didn't come readily to anyone other than elven warders. "I was taught the trick by an elven assassin."

"An elven assassin?" The doubt was evident in the sailor's voice. "Elves don't take easily to that trade."

"Not easily," Wick agreed. "But sometimes the best

solution to a problem is one corpse taken quietly so that ten others don't need to be taken." He paused. "Of course, the best tool of the trade is poison. I know how to make hundreds of poisons."

"Poisons," Krok repeated.

"Yes." Wick tried to act nonchalant. "I once walked into a banquet room with an incense shaker and spread invisible poisonous dust over the meals of eight men whose deaths I'd been paid for. The first one was dying as I walked out of the room." He shook his head. "Still, it was a near thing. The poison had acted much more quickly than I'd wagered."

Silence filled the tavern, and most of the patrons pushed their unfinished plates away.

"Is this true?" Krok asked.

"Of course it's true," Wick replied, warming to the hope that he could emerge with a whole skin. He tried to act calm and detached.

In the corner, a quiet smile flirted with Quarrel's lips. It appeared that the young man didn't quite believe Wick's tales. Thankfully, it seemed he was the only one who didn't.

"Mayhap the halfer's telling the truth," someone suggested.

"We'd have heard of him here," one of the men said. "We get to know everyone in that line of trade who come through here."

"This is my first time here," Wick said. "I didn't want to be known to so many." He paused. "I wasn't exactly given a choice here today."

"How did you keep us from hearing about you?"

Wick thought quickly and snatched at the first idea he thought was believable. "I'm really good at, uh, thievery and assassinations."

Silence hung in the tavern for a moment, then the thieves, murderers, assassins, thieves, etc. started laughing. They slapped their legs and thumped on the table.

"*Nobody* is *that* good," a slim man in black and purple

clothing stated. He stood and touched his chest, filled with pompous pride. "I'm Dawarn the Nimble. Perhaps you've heard of me."

"You're a burglar," Wick replied instantly. "There's a price on your head up in Kelloch's Harbor, a job waiting for you in Hanged Elf's Point if you decide you want it, and merchants in Drakemoor, Talloch, and Cardin's Deep want you dead. Well, maybe not Merchant Olligar in Cardin's Deep because he doesn't think the warehouse fire was truly your fault, and it worked out for him. Oh, and the captain of *Wavecutter* still wants you to pay off on the percentage he was supposed to get for helping you in Bardek's Cove."

An instant hubbub of conversations started around the room.

Then, "You never paid off on that percentage to Cap'n Huljar?" someone demanded.

Dawarn instantly lost some of his pompousness, throwing up his hands to the crowd that suddenly bristled against him. "Hey! Hey! Stop snarling and snapping like a pack of wolves! I was going to pay him! I still am!" He frowned. "Things in Bardek's Cove just got . . . *complicated.*"

"So complicated you stiffed Huljar?" someone said. "You don't stiff Huljar. You're lucky you're still walking around breathing through your nose instead of your neck."

"I'm not the one under suspicion here," Dawarn pointed out, taking his seat again, no longer wanting attention. "It's him!" He threw a finger toward Wick.

"Okay," Krok snarled, turning back to Wick, "so you know Dawarn, and you even know some of the work he's done. Including stiffing friends." He threw a sidelong glare at the offending burglar. "That doesn't mean you're who you say you are."

Wick gave the accusation consideration but didn't see an immediate answer.

"Test him," someone said.

Heads turned, all of them focusing on Quarrel. The young man sat at a table by himself. He'd unwrapped his face, revealing smooth-shaven, youthful features.

"He came in with you, Quarrel," Krok said.

"No," Quarrel replied. "He's not with me." He paused. "*You* let him in, Krok. If you want to make anyone responsible for his presence here, you have to take it. You could easily have left him outside."

Krok scowled. "Anybody else here want to get identified?"

No one volunteered.

"Just because he knows faces and names," Quarrel said, "doesn't mean that he's a clever thief or an assassin." He regarded Wick. "You should test him."

I hope you're caught in whatever your next endeavor is, Wick thought. Anxiety thrummed through him.

"All right then," Krok said. "A test. What kind of test?"

Wick thought he saw a way clear. He crossed his arms and looked as defiantly as he could out at the crowd. He was glad he was in baggy pants and not standing, because he didn't know if he'd be able to stand on his shaking knees.

"Pick someone for me to poison," Wick said, feeling certain that no one would be brought forth. Even if someone was, he could concoct something that would put a victim into a coma for several days. Provided the victim wasn't buried or thrown out into the harbor, he would recover. By then, with luck, Wick would be long gone from Wharf Rat's Warren.

"He doesn't just claim to be an assassin," Quarrel reminded. "He also says he's a thief. Let's see if he's as good a thief as he claims to be an assassin."

I really don't care for you, Wick thought.

"That's right! See if he's truly a thief," a man with a peg leg suggested. "Have him pick Utald's safe."

"A safe!" Wick cried, feeling instant relief. At the Vault of All Known Knowledge he was in the habit of tripping mousetraps so none of them would get hurt. He also kept the cats fed when no one was looking. "That's easy enough!" After all, he'd read several books on the manufacture of safes and lock-picking, which went surprisingly hand in hand in a lot of areas. *Surely they can't come up with anything I'm not familiar with.*

His enthusiasm, however, seemed ill placed. Evidently no one had expected quite that reaction. Everyone stared at him with increased suspicion.

Wick quickly realized that none of Deodarb's characters would have reacted in quite the same manner. He deepened his voice. "I mean, bring it on, you mutton-heads." *There. That's tough enough, isn't it?*

" 'Muttonheads,' is it?" Krok slapped his big hands on the counter on either side of Wick, emphasizing the fact that he could crush him if he wanted to.

"I was talking to the muttonheads," Wick said weakly. *Was that too tough? It had to have been too tough.* "Not to you. You're not a muttonhead. I wouldn't ever call you a muttonhead." *Maybe a cold-blooded killer. Maybe stinky, but never to your face. Maybe—*

"Utald," Krok roared. "The safe." He fisted Wick's cloak and blouse in his big hand again and lifted him from the counter.

The barkeep, who until this point had been a silent spectator to the action, walked to the wall of bottles behind the counter and slapped a big hand on the wall. Tall and overweight with sloping shoulders and long gray hair, the barkeep looked like a mercenary who'd gone to seed.

At the end of the series of slaps, a section of the wall popped open. The barkeep grabbed the hidden door and swung it wide.

"My safe," the barkeep said. "Nobody gets into *my* safe."

It was impressive looking, Wick thought. The safe was a contraption of hammered metal plates, springs, gears, wheels, and levers. None of the safes Wick had ever seen had looked quite the equal of this one. When it came to safes, this one was a dreadnaught.

"There she is." Utald slapped the safe's side with obvious affection. "I call her Lusylle. She's the best of the best."

"No one's ever beaten Lusylle," Krok said. "There's a lot of thieves who have tried."

"They all call her 'heartbreaker,' " Utald said.

"Well," Wick said grimly. "We'll see about that." (He said that with much more confidence than he felt.) "If you'll put me down."

Krok looked at Wick dangling from the end of his arm. "Oh. Okay." He opened his fingers.

Unceremoniously, Wick plopped to the ground and landed on his posterior. After all the slips and falls with the donkey, that region was already overly sensitive. He pushed himself back up. His lock-pick kit fell to the floor and scattered.

"Say," one of the men said, peering over the counter, "isn't that a Gladarn's Lock-picking Kit Number Six?"

"It's a Number Nine," Wick said. "It's acid-proof."

An appreciative *ooooohh* came from the thieves in the audience. At least, the ones that were above the regular cut-and-slash or thump-and-run caliber.

"Acid-proof," one old man said. "Now I could have used some of those when I went up against Thomobor's Forbidden Chest. Took me three days to get inside his fortress and two shakes of a lamb's tail for me to lose my lock-picks." He shook his head. "I never got that close again."

Wick set himself before the lock. As he considered the problem before him, all his fear seemed to drain away. The only thing that seemed to exist in his world was the conundrum of the safe.

"Little halfer's got his work cut out for him," someone murmured.

"Where did Utald get that safe?"

"Don't know. He's always had it here."

"Ever seen it open?"

"Nope."

Spinning the dials, Wick worked the springs and plates, pushing and shoving as he tried to find the rhythm of the safe. The safe was like a living, breathing organism, and everything had to be in perfect balance.

Snikk!

"That was the first lock," a man whispered.

"Has anyone ever popped the first lock?"

"Langres," Krok said. "But that's been two years or more."

"Four years."

"I said 'or more,' didn't I?" Krok asked irritably. "Four's more than two."

Ignoring them, captivated by the challenge of the safe, Wick kept searching for hidden pins to the second lock. After reading the books on lock-picking, he'd practiced on locks around the Vault of All Known Knowledge, until he'd locked himself into a closet and couldn't get to the lock. He hadn't noticed that fact until he was standing in the dark. Grandmagister Frollo had found him still standing in the dark a few hours later, looking for a monograph Wick was supposed to complete on sail design of the Silver Sea merchant ships. After that, Grandmagister Frollo had taken away Wick's lock-picks and forbidden him to lock himself in anything again.

Claaa-aaack!

The second lock popped.

"He's got a *second* lock!"

"How many more to go?"

"Three, I think. Hey, Utald, how many more locks?"

Wick glanced up at the barkeep, who continued to stand there impassively, arms crossed over his chest.

Utald shook his head. "Let the halfer find out."

The third lock wouldn't surrender its secrets. Wick used thin silver wire to snake out the confines of the mechanism, but had trouble picturing the device in his mind. Every time he almost had the pins in place, they dropped back into locking position.

Finally, he concentrated on feeling his way through the lock, easing each of the five pins into place. They fell again.

"Arrrggggghhhhhh!" the crowd gasped.

"What is it? What happened?" the mercenaries, murderers, and assassins asked.

"He can't get past the third lock. Keeps dropping the pins," the thieves answered.

I got past the first two locks, Wick thought plaintively. *No one has done that before. Surely you can believe I'm a thief now.*

But he knew they wouldn't. He wasn't that lucky.

"Ready to give up, halfer?" Krok grinned.

"No." Wick rubbed his hands together to warm them. Working on the cold metal of the safe for so long had left them chilled and leaden. *If I give up, I might as well just jump into that chute out to the harbor.* Besides, the problem of the lock had intrigued him.

He leaned into the safe again. This time he worked on each pin as it came free. On the third pin, he found a hole that shouldn't have been there. Going back to the first and second pins, knowing what to look for now, he found holes in them as well.

Wick smiled. *Clever. Clever, indeed.*

"He's smiling! The little halfer's smiling!"

I am, Wick thought, *because I know the secret of this one.* Using the wire, working by touch because he couldn't see into the lock, he searched for a hole on the front of the lock. When he didn't find one there, he searched from the back. After he found it, he ran the wire through the lock, threading the pins each in turn.

This time all the pins stayed in place when he pushed them back. He grabbed the lock lever, pushed a lever, and stretched two of the springs.

Kha-chunk!

4

Inside the Safe

"The third lock! He's got the third lock!"

Resting his cramping hands, Wick looked up to find an umbrella of faces peering down at him. The animosity was gone from them. It felt like they were all on the same team, all sharing the same expectations.

Unless I fail, Wick thought. *Then it's the chute for sure.*

"Hey, halfer," the man with the eye patch said, "let me buy you a drink. You can't keep working at that so hard without a drink. Utald, it's on me." He flipped a coin into the air.

Utald unlimbered an arm and snatched the coin from the air as effortlessly as a falcon taking a dove. He tested the coin between his teeth, then shoved it into a coin purse.

"What'll you have, halfer?" the barkeep asked.

"Razalistynberry wine," Wick said, grateful to have the drink.

"That's a sissy drink," one of the big mercenaries grumbled. "You should get you a shot of busthead. That'll settle your nerves just fine."

"Just the wine, please," Wick said. Then he thought about the response he should have made. He frowned and glared up at the mercenary. "Who are you calling a sissy?

I'm not just a thief. I'm an assassin, too. Maybe you want to remember that before you go to sleep tonight and don't wake up in the morning."

The tavern's patrons broke out laughing, and slammed their fists against the counter.

"He's got you there, Jolker!"

Quick as lightning, though, Jolker pulled his sword and had it tucked under Wick's chin.

"You might have a care there, halfer," the mercenary growled. He jabbed Wick hard enough with the sword to make him step back. "Won't be any trouble to snuff you out with the candle before I got to bed tonight."

Wick froze, leaning uncomfortably back.

"Jolker," a calm voice said.

Heads turned toward the voice.

In the lantern light, Quarrel stood there with a bow drawn. The arrowhead nocked on the bow gleamed.

"Sheath that sword," Quarrel said.

"And if I don't?" Jolker asked.

A thin smile curved Quarrel's mouth. "At this distance, this arrowhead will split your head like a melon." He paused. "I won't miss."

But people on either side of the big mercenary drew back. Just in case.

"You're taking a part in this?" Jolker asked. "Normally you don't involve yourself in anything that goes on here outside of a job."

"One," Quarrel counted evenly. "Two." The arrowhead never wavered.

Cursing, Jolker took his sword back. He grabbed up his tankard and abandoned the counter.

"You just made a big mistake, Quarrel," Jolker snarled. "A *big* mistake!" He left the tavern.

Trembling, Wick accepted the mug of razalistynberry wine from Utald. He tried to drink without spilling it all over himself, and for the most part managed that. As he put the mug on the bar, the little Librarian wondered what

Quarrel thought he was doing, and why the young man had taken part in the argument. But Wick was already starting to not think so badly of Quarrel.

"Go on then, halfer, let's see if you can defeat Lusylle," Utald challenged.

Taking a deep breath, Wick turned back to the safe. In seconds, he'd worked through the fourth and fifth locks. Neither had been anything special, and there had been no further tricks.

Click!

Ratchet!

Covered in sweat despite the chill that pervaded the room, Wick gripped the final lever and shifted the last spring.

"He's done it!"

"The halfer's done it!"

"Utald, whatever you've got hidden in that safe will never be safe again!"

A look of unease pulled at the barkeep's face. He took a step forward just as Wick gripped the doorframe and set himself to pull.

"Wait!" Utald commanded.

"Wait?" Wick echoed.

"Wait!" Utald repeated, stepping back.

That's not a good sign, Wick thought, stepping back himself.

"Why wait?" Krok asked.

Utald was silent for a moment. "Because the safe may be booby-trapped."

" 'May be?' You don't know?"

Scratching self-consciously at the back of his neck, Utald shook his head. "No."

"Why don't you know?"

"I don't know what's in there. It's not my safe. I stole it."

Wick looked at the big man in disbelief. "What?"

Utald shrugged. "I wasn't always a barkeep. I used to be with a group of bandits. We attacked a caravan and took everything they had." He nodded toward the safe. "That was one of the things they had."

"When was this?" Krok asked.

"Twenty-seven years ago. More or less." Utald looked at the safe. "I just kept it around, you know, in case I ever found someone that could open it."

"But you put it in the bar."

Utald nodded. "It made a good conversation piece, didn't it? Besides, I figured that sooner or later I would learn its secret."

"Do you know who the safe belonged to?"

"Could have been the caravan master's."

"I never heard of no caravan master carrying a safe like this," someone said.

"Or it could have been a wizard's," Utald said.

The tavern crowd drew back. "There could be anything in there," someone said. "Maybe even something the wizard wanted to get shut of. Maybe a monster. Or some undead thing that kept following him around."

Tense, the crowd took another step back.

Wick was suddenly aware that he was standing there alone. He slid his fingers around the doorframe, no longer prepared to swing it wide, but rather to slam it shut.

"Open it," Krok commanded.

"It is open," Wick insisted.

Krok drew a heavy two-handed sword. He gestured toward the safe. "Pull the door open."

Wick leaned on the door, hoping that if anything was inside it was dead or didn't know it had been released. He shook his head.

"Do it, halfer," Krok commanded.

"I'm a thief," Wick said. "Not a warrior."

"You're an assassin," the troll said. "If something bad comes out of there, assassinate it."

"Assassination, a good assassination," Wick insisted, "takes time. Something done in the heat of the moment, that's murder. I'm not a murderer. Any unskilled person can do that."

Utald scrambled over the bar, distancing himself from the safe.

"You've been curious about this for twenty-seven years," Wick said, feeling somewhat angry that the barkeep wasn't doing the door chores himself. "Haven't you wanted to see what you stole all those years ago?"

"Sure," the barkeep said, drawing a pair of long knives from somewhere on his person. "Open it up and let's have a look."

Wick fidgeted, trying to think of a way to escape opening the safe.

"Do it now, halfer," Krok said. "We're growing old waiting."

Closing his eyes, terrified of what he was going to find, Wick swung the door wide. He let the iron door carry him with it, hoping to use it for cover, and closed his eyes tightly.

"Bless me," Utald whispered in the stillness that followed, "for I am a rich man."

Since he hadn't been struck dead (by lightning, fire, or a death bolt) or mauled to death (by a gargoyle, a dragon, or a banshee), Wick grew curious. Across the bar, the patrons stepped forward again and looked inside the safe in amazement.

"I've never seen one of those made out of gold," one of them said.

"It looks comfortable," another said.

"Do you really think it's worth a fortune?"

"You melt that gold down, if it's pure enough, and it'll keep Utald living easy for the rest of his life."

"I don't know about that. You know how Utald is when he gets deep in his cups and gets around women. It's like closing your fist in a pool of water."

"Or slow horses. Utald stays an inch away from the poor house because he has an eye for slow horses."

Krok grinned. "Maybe you should charge to let people use it before you melt it down, Utald. Won't hurt the gold. I'll be your first customer."

"No!" Utald leaped the counter with the vigor of a much younger man. "Nobody's sitting on that! Or doing anything else either! It's mine! I've dragged it around for twenty-seven years, and put it up here at the Tavern of Schemes!"

So curious he could no longer stand it, Wick looked around the door and into the safe. At first he thought the safe held a chair. Then, since it was made out of solid gold and encrusted with a few gems, he guessed that it was a throne. Hypnotized by the deep yellow luster of the gold, he peered more closely.

On deeper examination, he discovered that the chair had no seat. Well, actually, it only had part of a seat.

"It's a privy," Wick said.

"Not *just* a privy," Utald corrected. "It's a solid *gold* privy. *My* solid gold privy."

Most of the people in the Tavern of Schemes broke out into laughter at Utald's good fortune, twenty-seven years in the making, and others cursed him for it. The barkeep didn't care. Overjoyed, Utald bought the whole tavern a round.

Later, mostly accepted into the fraternity of thieves, murderers, assassins, thieves, etc. that frequented the Tavern of Schemes, Wick drank razalistynberry wine and speculated on how the golden privy had gotten into the safe, and whom it had been intended for. No one knew for sure, and too many years had passed for Utald to remember whom it had been stolen from.

After they'd flushed the subject of the privy from their minds, the tavern's patrons told tales about past jobs and past employers. Wick listened to the stories the men told. Of course, being the storyteller he was, Wick was soon telling them of his own adventures as a thief and assassin.

He told them about the time he'd stolen King Iakha's magic mirror that kept him from aging (a story borrowed from Hralbomm's Wing), and the way he'd tricked Northern Giants into letting him know where their lair was (from an unfinished story he'd started working on with Taurak Bleiyz as the main character), and how he'd assassinated a dragon by destroying its magical heart.

By the time Wick had walked the tavern crowd through the lava-filled antechamber of Shengharck's lair (Wick actually renamed the dragon and his own purposeful destruction of it, as well as working in a vengeful king who'd hired him to do the deed—not mentioning, of course, that the deed had been accomplished through sheer accident and not design), many of the men were sleeping at their tables or in their chairs.

Wick walked along the countertop much as he had back in Paunsel's in Greydawn Moors when he'd first gotten involved in the search for what had truly happened at the Battle of Fell's Keep back during the Cataclysm. He was slightly tipsy from the wine, for it was a good vintage, but not so much off his game that he wasn't already wondering where he should spend the night. Particularly since he wanted to wake up in the morning.

Then the door opened and four hard-eyed men walked into the tavern. All four of the men wore the open razor tattoo on their cheeks that marked them as members of the thieves' guild Wick had come to Wharf Rat's Warren to scout.

Quietly, the little Librarian walked to one end of the counter and made himself as invisible as he could. He didn't look at the thieves, but he kept track of them through his peripheral vision. He also noticed that Quarrel was keeping watch over them as well.

The Razor's Kiss guild members bellied up to the counter and ordered. "Hey, Utald. Where'd you get the privy?"

"Oh, this old thing?" Utald asked, jerking his hand back toward the privy in the safe. "I've had it for a long time."

"I've never seen one before," the tallest of the men said.

"They're rare and unique things, Vostin," Utald agreed.

A sleek shadow slunk along the counter bottom beneath Wick's feet. The cat was huge, with tortoiseshell coloration and startling gray eyes. Just past Wick's feet, the animal sat on its haunches and gazed up at him in the way that only cats could.

Then, with a lithe leap, the cat jumped up to the counter next to him.

"Hello, kitty," Wick said. He reached to pet the cat.

The animal turned to him and hissed a warning. One paw lifted and filled with sharp claws.

Hastily, Wick drew his hand back. He didn't want to risk injury to his fingers because that would affect his ability to write. In the past, he'd hurt his hands and fingers, and the time he'd been unable to write had been almost unbearable.

"Not the friendly sort, are you?" Wick turned his attention back to the four Razor's Kiss thieves as they made small talk.

"What are you doing in here?" Utald asked.

"Meeting a man," Vostin said.

"Business?"

"Yes." Vostin tossed back his drink and looked hard at the barkeep. "None of it yours."

Wick's ears pricked up. Craugh was of the impression that someone had hired the Razor's Kiss guild to steal Boneslicer. As far as Craugh and his contacts in the city could ascertain, Boneslicer hadn't left the hands of the Razor's Kiss.

Sipping his drink, Wick wished his head would clear.

Nearly an hour later, after a dozen men came and went through the tavern, a new visitor walked through the door. He hadn't known the secret knock, which had marked him instantly as someone from someplace else, but he'd produced a marker of some sort that got him past Krok.

Wick watched with interest. Beside him, the cat yawned, pink tongue rolling out for a moment before curling back in.

The new arrival was a man of indeterminate years. He wore dark clothing against the cold, and carried a long-sword at his hip. After an almost casual glance around, the man settled on the four Razor's Kiss thieves. He tapped his cheek.

Vostin nodded and hooked a chair from another table with his foot. The man came over to sit.

After a brief conversation with the new arrival, the thieves got up from the table and headed out the door. The mood inside the tavern lightened almost immediately.

"I suppose they're not exactly popular around here," Wick observed to the man next to him.

"Razor's Kiss," the big mercenary muttered. He was deep in his cups and his gaze was a little slack. "Think they're something special here in the Warren." He took another sip. "They're not. Just thieves." He shrugged. "Thieves that will slit your throat as soon as look at you, though. Better to stay away from 'em."

"I will," Wick said, and wondered if he'd be able to. He had no intentions of—

"Follow them," a woman's voice ordered.

Wick looked down at his feet. He thought that was where the voice had come from. It was hard to imagine, though, because he hadn't seen any women in the tavern.

Only the cat lay there.

"Did you say something?" the mercenary asked.

"Not me," Wick said.

"Coulda sworn I heard a woman." Looking around, the mercenary pulled at his beard. "But I don't see any in here."

Okay, Wick thought, *we're imagining the same thing.*

He was just thinking how strange and improbable that
was when—

"Follow them."

The tone was more insistent this time. It also wasn't
finished.

"Get up off your duff, halfer, and get moving."

Now there was no mistaking *who* the voice was talking to.

5

"Is That *Your* Talking Cat?"

Wick was distracted by Quarrel as the young man got up and departed the Tavern of Schemes. Movement erupted at his side. When he turned back to the counter, he found the cat sitting there staring at him with those large gray eyes. At the moment, those eyes looked particularly intelligent.

And angry.

"Get up," the cat said, baring her fangs. (Wick was suddenly certain the cat was a she.) "Get up and get moving. This is what you're supposed to do. If you'd made it to the meeting, you'd have known that."

Meeting? Wick thought rapidly. Now that he considered everything that Craugh had told him, he did seem to recall some mention of a meeting. But he'd thought that wouldn't take place until he found Boneslicer.

The mercenary leaned in from the other side. "Is that your cat?"

"Noooooooo," Wick answered cautiously. He was fairly certain that talking animals would not be well received in Wharf Rat's Warren. With all the paranoia prevalent throughout the outlaw town, the animal would doubtless be hung as a spy. Or drawn and quartered. Or simply thrust into a bag with a brick and tossed out into the harbor.

The chances were also good that anyone with the cat would receive the same treatment. At his size, Wick thought it was possible he would fit in the same bag as the cat.

"Move it," the cat yowled. She struck at Wick with extended claws.

Wick barely got his hand out of the way. The claws sliced neatly through the sleeve of his cloak.

"Did you hear that?" the mercenary asked.

Looking innocent, Wick said, "I didn't hear anything."

"You didn't hear that cat talking?"

"No." Wick shook his head.

"You did," the cat insisted. She stood and stretched, arching her back and moving closer. The threat was evident. "Now get up."

The mercenary raised his glass and peered into it. "Utald must be forgetting to water his drinks. They don't usually have this much kick."

The cat swiped at Wick's arms again, chasing them from the counter. "Let's go. You need to find out where they're going."

Wick stood.

Moving with ease and grace, the cat dropped to the floor. Her tail flicked imperiously. She stopped and waited, clearly not happy about Wick's reluctance.

Jerking a thumb toward the door, Wick said, "I'm going to let the cat out."

"You'd better," the mercenary said. "She sounds really upset with you." He drained his drink and banged the empty glass against the counter, signaling for another.

Wick went. Now that the tavern's patrons were pretty drunk, none of them seemed to care that he was leaving. Seated near the door, Krok looked up at Wick.

"The cat," Wick said, pointing.

The cat waited impatiently at the door.

Krok nodded. "Who let it in?"

"I don't know."

"Filthy beasts," Krok growled. "Always carrying in vermin."

"Look who's talking," the cat hissed. "Is that your head? Or did your neck throw up?"

"What?" Krok roared, pushing up unsteadily.

"I didn't hear anything," Wick said.

"Get the door, halfer. You're losing ground."

"Is that *your* talking cat?" Krok demanded.

"No." Wick shook his head. "Definitely not."

"Then why are you taking it outside?"

"Because . . ." Wick thought furiously, "I'm tired of listening to it. I can't get it to shut up." That was the truth. "But it's not mine."

"You're going to be polite to a troll," the cat accused, "but you can't listen to me?"

"See?" Wick said, smiling as inoffensively as he could. "Get it out of here."

Wick opened the door and followed the cat out. He thought just for a moment of staying inside the tavern. But he'd been fortunate enough the first time to survive the encounter. Besides, now that the cat had mentioned it, he did remember that Craugh had given instructions about some meeting with someone named—

"Alysta," Wick said, looking down at the cat.

Regal and confident, the cat sat on her haunches and gazed up at him with gray-eyed command. "I am. You are the Librarian."

Wick glanced around to make certain no one had overheard the cat. Full dark filled Wharf Rat's Warren's streets, leaving thick shadows everywhere.

"I am," Wick admitted. "Second Level Librarian Edgewick Lamplighter."

"Second Level Librarian?" The cat, Alysta, looked displeased. "Craugh couldn't have arranged for a more *experienced* Librarian?"

Wick drew himself up to his full height. He was certainly taller than a cat, had opposable thumbs, and didn't cough up hairballs. How much experience could a cat have at spying?

"I'm the most experienced available," Wick said.

"None of the other Librarians have ever been to the mainland."

"So you're out on an island, are you?" The cat smiled.

No more information, Wick thought. Evidently the cat didn't know as much as he'd thought. And now it had one more piece of information about the Vault of All Known Knowledge.

"I'd thought the Librarians were based deep in the interior."

Wick refused to answer.

"And what does Craugh think?" Alysta demanded. "Just because you can read and write doesn't mean you're suited to find the lost sword."

"Reading and writing," Wick said, "are the two most important—" He stopped, suddenly realizing what the cat had said. "What sword?"

"Seaspray."

Wick racked his brain. For a moment, he couldn't place the weapon. Then it came to him in a rush. "Seaspray? Captain Dulaun's Seaspray?"

The sword was one of legend, just as Boneslicer was. Captain Dulaun of the Silver Sea trade empires had fought at the Battle of Fell's Keep a thousand years ago with Master Oskarr. In his own right, before the Cataclysm, Captain Dulaun had helped defend the Silver Sea holdings against the encroachment of goblinkin and anyone else that dared raise sails against them.

"It wasn't always Captain Dulaun's," the cat said.

"How do you know this?"

"You're not the only one that can read and write."

Wick was amazed. "You can read and write?"

"It's not that difficult," Alysta said. "I taught my daughter to read and write."

The image of a mother cat teaching her kitten to read filled his mind and seemed very strange. Wick was so captivated by that image that he didn't realize the cat was speaking to him again.

"What?" he said.

The cat hissed angrily. "You're wasting time. When we finish this, I'm going to tell Craugh exactly what I think of him for pairing me up with you."

You're not the only one, Wick thought.

"Now come on." The cat took off.

Reluctantly, Wick fell into step. "Where are we going?"

"To follow the Razor's Kiss thieves, of course." The cat leaped over a wide hole filled with freezing water, broken ice, and mud.

Wick saw the hole too late and nearly fell in. "Why are we following them?"

"Because they know where the sword is."

"You don't?"

The cat shot him a reproachful look but kept moving. "If I knew where the sword was, we would go there. Now be quiet. If those men find out we're following them, they might choose to kill you."

Then following them at all is a bad idea, Wick wanted to say.

The four Razor's Kiss thieves added six more to their number when they reached the livery.

Trailing after the cat, Wick circled around behind the livery to the back door. It wasn't locked. Alysta squeezed through the gap and disappeared inside. Wick sipped a breath of cold air that bit into his lungs. The odors from inside the livery hit him, too. After a moment, he eased through the door.

"Quiet," the cat admonished, like she was talking to a child. "And get down so you can't be seen."

Wick hunkered down behind the stalls. In the romances from Hralbomm's Wing, Deodalb's antiheroes and Decarthian spies managed to escape certain death all the time and never once doubted their skills. He was terrified to the point of being fumble-fingered. The happy buzz he'd enjoyed in the Tavern of Schemes was now a thing of the past.

Horses snorted and stirred in the paddocks. The sharp scents of oats, barley, and hay tickled Wick's nose. He caught himself right before he sneezed.

"Don't you dare," the cat hissed.

Wick held a finger under his nose. He needed to sneeze so badly that his eyes watered. Only the threat of painful death kept him from succumbing. Gradually, the pressure in his head went away. He let out a tentative breath.

Easing forward again, he joined Alysta and crouched at the end of the paddock. Peering around the corner, he spotted the Razor's Kiss thieves saddling horses while the livery boy looked on.

"You can't just take my father's horses," the boy whined.

One of the thieves turned and slapped the boy down. After he hit the ground, the boy stayed there. Tears streamed from his eyes as he looked at the thieves.

"Be glad it's just the horses we want," one of the thieves said. "Another word from you, and your father will come here in the morning and find he has to bury you."

The man who had hired them stood nearby. He wasn't saddling a mount. "How long will this take?"

The thief who had slapped the boy down turned to their employer. "As long as it takes, Captain Gujhar. Not one moment sooner."

In a crowd, the thief would have faded from view almost at once were it not for the distinctive tattoo on his cheek and the burn scarring over his right eye that pulled at that side of his face. In the cold, the scarred flesh was almost white as paper against his dark skin.

"That's not an acceptable answer, Flann," Captain Gujhar replied. He stood with military erectness.

Looking at the man, Wick now recognized the bearing and self-discipline. He was a man of authority, used to being obeyed.

So why is Captain Gujhar in Wharf Rat's Warren dealing with thieves? Wick wondered.

At the corner, the cat watched with supreme concentration, like she'd spotted prey. Her tail coiled and uncoiled behind her with methodical slowness. She looked ready to pounce.

Flann led his mount toward the livery's door. "I'm here to achieve results," the thief said. "If you think you can do it any sooner, then I suggest you be about it." He paused, waiting.

Captain Gujhar stood silent and still for a moment. His hand toyed with the hilt of the longsword at his hip.

Even with the odds ten against, he's thinking about fighting them. Wick was amazed. The man was either foolhardy or very good. Wick was curious as to which it was, chiefly because it was likely they were going to be enemies, or—at the very least—competitors for Bone-slicer.

"No," Captain Gujhar replied.

"Then let me be about my business," Flann suggested. "That way we can both keep your employer happy. We handled that situation on the Cinder Clouds Islands the way you wanted us to and it very nearly cost us when that other ship appeared."

"I don't know how the dwarves found out about Bone-slicer," Captain Gujhar replied.

"Or how they happened to have a fighting ship at their beck and call that night," Flann said. He grinned. "Seems there's a lot you don't know. You'd be better off letting us do what your master paid us to do."

The captain said nothing.

The cold wind howled through the open door and sucked what little warmth there was out of the livery. The horses whinnied and stamped in displeasure.

"Going to wish us luck then?" Flann smiled.

"Good luck," the captain said.

Flann pulled himself into the saddle as the horse reared and bucked, evidently in no hurry to get out into the freezing weather. Leaning forward, the thief seized the horse's ear and bit it, hanging on till it stopped fighting.

The other thieves quickly mounted as well, then they thundered down the street, heading back into the Flowing Mountains at the other end of Wharf Rat's Warren.

Captain Gujhar watched for a moment, then left without a word. The door slammed loosely behind him.

Still crying a little, the livery boy got up and closed the door. He cursed for a while and promised death to the thieves if he ever saw them again.

Wick started to move.

The cat pressed herself back against him. "Wait," Alysta said.

Before Wick could ask why, movement in the rafters caused him to sink back against the paddock wall. Then Quarrel dropped from the rafters into the area between the paddocks by the front door, startling a scream out of the livery boy.

"It's all right," Quarrel assured the boy. "I've come for my horse." He fished a coin from a small leather purse.

Always alert for details, Wick spotted a curious symbol stamped onto the leather purse. It was small and artfully done, a rose clasped in the thorny embrace of a vine.

The livery boy caught the coin in the air and made a fist around it.

Moving quickly, Quarrel saddled his horse, negotiated the price of a bag of apples for the horse, and led the animal outside. With his cloak wrapped around him, Quarrel galloped out after the thieves.

"All right," the cat said.

"All right what?" Wick asked.

"Now we follow them." Alysta walked out into the walkway between the paddocks.

Wick had been afraid the cat was going to suggest that. "Shouldn't we stay here? Until Craugh and the ship arrive?"

"Why should they come? You haven't found anything of importance yet."

"We're following those thieves."

"Yes, and that trail may lead us nowhere. We don't know yet."

"Doesn't Craugh know what we're here looking for?"

"That man," the cat replied. "Captain Gujhar."

"Why?"

"Because he's from *Wraith*."

"*Wraith*?"

"The ship that took Boneslicer from the Cinder Clouds Islands."

"Is Boneslicer still on the ship?"

"I don't know."

"Shouldn't we try to get the battle-axe back?" Wick still clung to the hope that he'd end up in a warm bed for the night.

The cat turned around and looked up at Wick. "All right."

Wick halted and looked back at the cat. "All right?"

"As in, 'All right, we'll steal the battle-axe back from a ship of armed guards before we follow that pack of thieves and see what they're up to.'"

Wick almost sneezed again. He lifted his fingers to his nose. "Armeb guarbs, huh?"

The cat gave a solemn nod.

Removing his hand from his nose, Wick said, "Maybe we could follow the thieves. At least for a little while."

"Splendid idea," the cat said.

"Sarcasm really isn't an endearing trait," Wick stated.

"Are you talking to that cat?" the livery boy asked. He stood in the walkway, a rag shoved up against his nose.

"No," Wick said.

"Yes," Alysta said. "We've come for the donkey."

The boy looked at Alysta. "I've never seen a talking cat before."

"I wouldn't say a word," the cat said, "if I thought the halfer could handle this on his own. Let's have the donkey. Come on. Quick now."

Dazed and befuddled, Wick joined Alysta at the

paddock that held the donkey. Inside the paddock, a feed-bag covered the donkey's lower face. He munched contentedly, but without any real interest.

Before Wick knew what was about to happen, the cat pounced on him, landing on his shoulder, then springing to the paddock.

"Well," the cat asked, "what have you got to say for yourself?"

Initially, Wick thought Alysta was talking to him. Then he noticed that her attention was on the donkey.

"The fact that we're behind schedule is partly your fault," the cat went on.

The donkey locked eyes with the cat. "It's not my fault," the donkey said. "Have you seen how dense the halfer is?"

Wick couldn't believe it. He leaned heavily against the paddock door. The livery boy gawped beside him.

"You can talk, too?" Wick whispered.

The donkey rolled his eyes, looking even more comical because the feedbag made him look like he was wearing a veil. "Do you see what I have had to put up with? He's not exactly the brightest candle in the bunch."

"You knew where the rendezvous was supposed to be," Alysta said. "You could have gotten him there."

"It was cold," the donkey said. He shivered and flicked his tail. "It's still cold."

"Doesn't matter," the cat told him. "We've got a job to do."

"We can wait till morning," the donkey suggested. "It'll be warmer in the morning."

That sounded good to Wick, too. He deserved at least one night in a warm bed.

"No," the cat said. "We're leaving. *Now*." She flattened her ears against her skull and eyed the donkey with dark-eyed threat. "Or perhaps you'd care to be a toad again instead of a donkey."

The donkey sighed. "All right, all right." He shifted his attention to the livery boy, who was staring in wide-mouthed astonishment. "Give me a refill on the feedbag. I'm taking it with me. Put it on the halfer's tab."

Minutes later, equipped with a replenished feedbag for the donkey and enough supplies for a few days, Wick mounted up. The cat leaped onto the donkey's haunches, who complained that they could—and should—both walk.

Outside the livery stable, Wick took up the chase of the Razor's Kiss at a sedate pace. He wrapped himself tightly in the cloak. At least this time he was riding instead of nearly dragging the donkey. Overall, he had to admit that it was an improvement. Except for the fact that it was so cold, so dark, and that he was probably headed straight into trouble.

6

Caught

Falling snow blew through the air. The howling north wind picked up more dry, white powder from the ground and mixed it with the new flakes. Wick felt them touch his face, brief moments of icy cold, then a stinging numbness that lasted just a short time.

After hours of riding, Wharf Rat's Warren was a collection of lights in the distance amid the foothills of the mountains. Wick had also begun to doubt the luxury of riding the donkey. In the beginning, he'd rather liked the idea of controlling the animal. Or at least having the illusion of controlling the animal. The donkey claimed to be an expert tracker, one of the many talents he professed to owning, and didn't have any problems cutting the sign of the Razor's Kiss horses.

Wick knew about tracking, too, and was confident that the donkey was on the right track. He was so cold he was miserable, even under the heavy folds of his traveling cloak. If he could have just closed his eyes for an instant, he felt certain he'd have fallen asleep.

Do that, he thought again, *and you'll be abandoned by the cat and donkey. They'll leave you lying, and since there's no true spring thaw up in the Great Frozen North, no one will ever find your body.*

Dropping the protective wrap of the cloak from his face, Wick peered forward. With all the snow blowing, it was hard to see, but the road was clearly defined between the trees. Going any other way was out of the question because the deep snowdrifts covered treacherous terrain. Traveling that way in the dark would have meant a broken leg for a horse. As it was, even with the road fairly well traveled, the donkey had a hard time pushing through.

"How much longer?" Wick asked.

"Oh, please shut up," the donkey snapped. "I'm the one doing all the work here."

Wick had to admit that was true. But it also sharpened the question of *why* the donkey and the cat were helping the wizard seek out Boneslicer. And now Seaspray. The cat, if she knew and Wick thought she did, wasn't talking. Even for a talking cat, she acted strangely preoccupied.

He turned his attention once again to the histories of the dwarven and human weapons, and to what he recollected about the Battle of Fell's Keep. Nothing new came to mind. Craugh claimed that his only goal was to settle the old injustice against Master Blacksmith Oskarr and prove that he wasn't a traitor to the brave warriors of the Battle of Fell's Keep, but Wick no longer believed that. Craugh had some ulterior motive in mind. Wick just didn't know what it was.

Scanning the skyline again, Wick tried to remember what was up in the mountains. He'd read about the area, but he would have liked to have read more. Primarily he remembered what had been written about the port city and the thieves, murderers, assassins, etc. who lived there. There were even a few outlying towns and villages that did a little business with Wharf Rat's Warren, bartering food and wood for trade goods such as cloth and farming equipment the pirates brought in from cargo ships they took.

Wick hadn't read anything about what lay beyond. Whatever it was, though, he felt certain they were headed there.

Sometime later, a pale glow took shape in the darkness ahead. It grew larger as they got closer.

"Stop here," Alysta ordered.

The donkey stopped and swung his head around. "This isn't the best place to spend the night."

"That's a campfire up ahead," the cat said. She uncoiled from Wick's back and stretched, arching her back and working one leg at a time. "We're not going any closer."

Wick gazed around wildly, not believing what the cat was intending. "We're going to spend the night here? *Here?*"

"Yes." With a lithe vault, the cat sprang from the donkey's backside and grabbed hold of a low-hanging limb on a massive spruce tree. Snow fell thick as fog for a moment from the branch, then thinned out.

"But we'll freeze," Wick protested.

"No you won't." The cat sat in the crook of the tree. Her head turned to watch the silent flight of a passing owl.

The donkey turned and lumbered into the open space beneath the spruce. He pressed up against a pile of boulders and rock that had been shoved there by the road builders all those years ago. Earth had washed down the mountain and formed a berm that splashed up over the boulders.

"Get off me," the donkey ordered.

Without a word, Wick slid off. *I should be the one giving orders*, he thought. *Craugh sent me to do this.* But that only made him think that the wizard should have been trekking up the side of the snow-covered mountain, not him.

Sheltered by the boulders from the wind, Wick rummaged through his supply pack. He took out a bundle of kindling.

"What are you doing?" the cat asked.

"I'm going to start a fire," Wick explained.

"No."

Grudgingly, Wick looked up at the cat. "If I don't have a fire, I'll freeze."

"Sit close to the donkey."

"He stinks," Wick said.

"Hey," the donkey replied, "you're not exactly an apple blossom yourself."

Wick realized that was probably true. He'd been on the road for several days, and there had been no way he was going to bathe in a freezing stream or pond. Still, he was certain he smelled better than the donkey.

Wick was determined not to sit next to the great, smelly donkey. He took an additional blanket from his pack and pulled it over himself as he sat in a spot he hollowed out in the snow. Despite his best intentions, though, he slid over close to the donkey, acting like he was falling asleep. Then, after a moment, he started feeling warmer and he went to sleep.

"Hey."

The voice woke Wick. He clawed through the blanket for a moment to peer out.

Quarrel sat hunkered down in front of him. The young man held his bow and a nocked arrow in his hands. In the moonslight reflected from the snow, he was smiling.

"What are you doing out here?" Quarrel asked.

The donkey came awake beside Wick and swung his big head around to survey the situation. Instead of being concerned, the donkey only yawned and smacked his lips.

Glaring up into the tree, Wick saw Alysta sitting there on the branch. Evidently the cat had gotten caught sleeping as well. She stared down with baleful eyes.

"I got a job," Wick explained.

"Awfully fast work," Quarrel commented. "When I left the tavern, you were still telling stories."

"That's how it goes sometimes. Unemployed, then you're employed."

"By who?"

Wick remembered a line from the Spymasters of Darcathia romance. "If I told you that, you'd have to kill me."

Quarrel looked at him as though he were odd. "You *are* the strangest thief and assassin I have ever met."

"I meant," Wick said, realizing that he'd gotten it wrong, "that *I'd* have to kill *you*."

Grinning again, Quarrel nodded. "I thought that's what you meant. It's just as well. Knowing that you would do me harm if you had to makes what I'm about to do even easier."

What you're about to do? Wick sat up a little straighter. "Maybe we could talk about what you're about to do."

"I'm going to let the thieves find you," Quarrel said.

"Thieves?" Wick swallowed, peering over Quarrel's shoulder at the forest. Shadows seemed to slip among the trees.

"I got too close to the camp," Quarrel explained. "My mistake. I was overzealous, I suppose. But it's nothing I can't fix now that I found you."

Wick heard the snow chuffing under footsteps then. Someone was closing in on his campsite. He tried to stand up but got tangled in the blanket and his cloak and couldn't get up.

"I do hope they don't kill you," Quarrel said. "Good luck with it." Then he sprang over Wick's head and ran with sure-footed grace up the pile of boulders. He was out of sight before Wick realized that he should be running, too. He made another attempt to get up and succeeded.

The chuffing sounded closer.

"Some watchdog you were," Wick growled at the cat as he staggered through the snow. He grabbed the donkey's harness and tried to urge the animal to his feet.

"I'm not a watchdog," Alysta protested. "I was sleeping up here." She craned her head around and kept her voice soft. "Too late, halfer."

Abandoning his efforts to move the donkey, Wick turned and tried to run through the chest-high—on him—

snow. His feet twisted and slipped beneath him. Before he got three steps, an attacker came up behind him and hit him at the base of the skull. He remembered seeing the snow-covered ground coming up to meet him, but blackness swallowed him before he hit.

Captured, he thought morosely, his thoughts swimming in pain. *I hate being captured.*

"Anybody recognize him?"

Someone grabbed Wick by the hair and flopped his head around. He tried to resist, but he was still too groggy. The headache exploding inside his skull seemed to be doing just fine, though.

"I think I saw him," someone else said. "Back at the Tavern of Schemes."

"Are you sure?"

"How many halfers do you think there are in Wharf Rat's Warren?"

"Not many," the other voice admitted.

"And even fewer of them with red hair like this one."

Forcing his eyes open, Wick found himself bound hand and foot and lying on his right shoulder.

"He's awake," someone said.

Instantly, a sword swooped down and rested heavily against Wick's throat.

"Have a care there, halfer. I'll split you open as soon as look at you."

Wick believed the speaker. The Razor's Kiss had gotten their name first from the method they'd employed to rob their victims: slitting open the fat purses of merchants and letting the contents drop into another bag. But the thieves' guild had slit a fair number of throats, too. He lay still.

"He's not dead, is he?" One of the thieves leaned in for a closer look. "You hit him a pretty solid knock on the noggin, Flann."

"He's not dead." The grizzled veteran holding the sword squatted down beside Wick. "I've hit plenty more a lot harder. Besides, everybody knows halfers has got thick skulls. Takes a lot to get through one of 'em. Or to break one."

Pain rushed through Wick's thoughts, so violent and fierce that he thought he was going to throw up. Then, horrified, he realized he was going to. "I'm going to be sick," he croaked. He made gagging noises.

Reluctantly, Flann took back his sword.

Wick turned over and threw up. He felt immediately embarrassed, which was exceedingly strange because he should have been frightened for his very life. Then he realized he was still scared as well. He felt very confused.

After a while, his stomach was empty of the wine. Worn out, chilled to the bone, he slowly rolled over to look at the Razor's Kiss members.

"Who are you?" Flann asked.

"Nobody," Wick said hoarsely. The taste in his throat threatened to set off another wave of sickness.

Flann prodded him with the end of the sword. "I'll have your name, halfer, or I'll bury you here without one." He raised an arched eyebrow. "Which is it going to be?"

"Tevil," Wick croaked. "My name is Tevil Bottleblower."

"Bottleblower?" one of the thieves repeated. "That's a strange name."

"I'm a glass blower by trade," Wick said. "I make . . . well, bottles."

"Bottles of what?"

Wick blinked at that.

"Bottles of what?" the thief asked again. "Ale? Pickles? Spices?"

"Just . . . bottles," Wick replied. "I don't put anything into them. I make them so that other people can put things into them."

"And you can sell an empty bottle?" The thieves marveled at that idea.

"Yes," Wick said. "Some bottles are worth hundreds of gold pieces."

"Really?"

Wick clung to that. If they thought he could make bottles worth hundreds of gold pieces maybe they wouldn't kill him out of hand. "Yes."

"How do you make a bottle?" one of the thieves asked. "I've always been curious. I thought maybe you might chip them out of glass, but I don't see how you can do that without breaking them."

"You don't chip them out," Wick said. "You cook glass, make it out of sand and other things, and heat it till it's molten. When you get it right, you scoop some of it up on a pipe and you . . . blow it."

"Ah," another thief said. "That's why you sometimes see bubbles in the glass. I always wondered about that."

"Enough about bottles," Flann growled irritably. "I want to know what you're doing following us, halfer."

Wick thought for a moment. "This, uh, is the *only* road out of town."

"He's right there," one of the thieves said.

"I wasn't following you," Wick insisted. "We just happened to be headed in the same direction."

"In the middle of the night?" Flann narrowed his eyes in suspicion.

"I had to get out of town," Wick said, thinking quickly.

"Why?"

"I picked the wrong pockets back in the Tavern of Schemes."

"That's him!" one of the thieves exclaimed, pointing at Wick.

For a moment, the little Librarian feared that the man was going to say, *That's him!* As in, *That's him! The halfer from the Cinder Clouds Islands!* But he didn't.

Instead, the man said, "That's the halfer who picked Utald's safe."

"So you're a thief, are you?" Flann asked.

Wick shrank back from the sharp edge of the naked blade. "Yes."

"Were you planning on thieving from us? Is that what you were doing in our camp?"

"I wasn't in your camp," Wick said. "I was here. Asleep."

"You weren't asleep when we got here."

"I was. I swear. Right before you got here."

"You heard us coming?"

Wick nodded. The back of his head squeaked against the snow.

"You didn't hear us coming," Flann said. "Hearing you even suggest that makes me want to gut you right now."

Being gutted wasn't a pleasant prospect. Several medical and history books in the Vault of All Known Knowledge had pictures of such barbaric procedures. Wick swallowed and gagged on the vile taste at the back of his throat again.

"So how did you really know we were coming?" Flann asked.

"Quarrel told me," Wick answered.

"Quarrel's your partner?"

"No," Wick said, wanting to be as truthful as he knew how. "The cat is my partner." He pointed up into the tree. "Or I'm her partner. I'm not sure exactly how that works. But I really think she's supposed to be my aide. She just takes far too many liberties to be a proper aide, though."

Alysta spat at him from the tree branch and flattened her ears in annoyance.

"The cat?" Flann repeated.

Wick nodded.

"You have a cat for a partner?"

"It wasn't my idea," Wick said honestly.

"The cat's name is Quarrel?"

"No. The cat's name is Alysta."

"Then who's Quarrel? Another partner?"

"No. Quarrel's a mercenary I met at the Tavern of Schemes. He's not my partner. You can't trust him." Wick had trouble reconciling the young man's actions in the tavern to save him and his recent betrayal.

"He was out here?"

"Yes."

Flann waved four of his men into motion. They quickly drew their swords and eased through the brush.

"Do you have any other partners I should know about?" the thief leader asked.

From the tone in the man's voice, Wick knew he had to be as completely honest as he dared. "I think maybe the donkey can be considered a partner. He talks, too. Not as much as the cat, but he's stubborn."

"Talk, do they?" Skepticism wrinkled tight lines through Flann's face.

Wick nodded.

Flann sighed in disgust. "I'm through talking to you, halfer. You lie every time you open your mouth. Make your peace."

Wick blinked. "You're going to kill me?"

Nodding, Flann said, "Don't worry. I'll make it quick and painless. We aren't enemies, after all. You were probably just following along, intending to rob us—which isn't the smartest thing you could have done. But I can respect that."

"Why are you going to kill me?"

"I can't very well have you following us around, now can I?"

"I could promise not to."

"I wouldn't believe you."

"Well, that's hardly fair. You don't really know me enough to make that judgment."

"Fair's only good in checkers," Flann said. "And that's only if you keep both eyes on the board." He waved a gloved hand. "Now hurry up with it. I can still get a few hours' sleep."

You can just kill me and go back to bed? Wick couldn't believe it.

"Flann," another thief spoke up, "don't kill him yet."

Anger showing on his face, Flann looked at the speaker. "Why not?"

"You weren't in the Cinder Clouds Islands," the other man said. He was young and intense. "I was."

"So?"

"While I was there, some of the goblinkin talked about a halfer they'd caught. A little red-haired halfer. Talked a lot, they said. Like this one. He was supposed to cook for them."

I'll never, Wick moaned to himself, *live that down. Even if I live through this. It will pursue me forever.*

"The dwarves rescued him," the younger thief went on. "Later, he was at the buried foundry. He was with the dwarves that found the axe we were sent for."

You were sent for the axe? That interested Wick intensely. Was it just happenstance that the subject of the Battle of Fell's Keep had arisen that night in Paunsel's Tavern, or was there something more diabolical afoot? His native curiosity weighed in heavily against his fear.

Flann regarded Wick. "Were you there, halfer?"

For a moment, Wick was torn, not knowing which way was the safest to answer. *Saying* no *in this instance,* he believed, while looking at the sword in Flann's hand, *is probably a . . . dead end. Or a life-altering one at best.* He took a deep breath and let it out. No brilliant ideas came to him and he was decidedly disappointed.

"I don't have all night," Flann said. "Tell me the truth, and I'll know it when I hear it—"

Wick had serious reservations about that statement since the thief leader didn't believe him about the talking cat and donkey.

"—or you'll never wear a hat again," Flann finished.

"I was there," Wick answered. Then he set himself to be as coy as he could. *They won't get any more answers out of me! I'll die before I tell them anything that will make them think they can kill me immediately.*

Without a word, Flann lifted his sword and slammed the hilt against Wick's forehead with a dull *thunk*. Blinding pain consumed the little Librarian and he dropped once more back into darkness.

7

Krepner the Goblinkin

The whole world moved as Wick swam up through the cottony darkness. *I'm alive!*

Of course, that discovery wasn't as inviting as it might have been if he'd been certain he was out of the hands of the thieves' guild and had woken up instead in his bed at the Vault of All Known Knowledge. At first, he didn't move—he was sure of it—but the sensation of moving stayed with him. Nausea wormed through his stomach.

Then he felt rough wood against his hands instead of snow. He also realized that he was no longer wearing his travel cloak. That woke him at once. His writing kit was secreted away in the cloak's hidden lining.

His journal was missing!

Cracking open an eye, Wick discovered that he was in a ship's brig. The heavy iron door rested awkwardly in its frame, and rust patches showed inattention. The interior of the brig stank of excrement and vomit. Not at all the kind of place Wick would ever hope to be. Although it had been exciting to "borrow" those places for a time in his reading.

Lantern light glowed on the other side of the iron door.

"Haw, haw, haw!" a deep voice boomed. "I beat ye again, Dolstos!"

"I swears, Krepner, ye're a-cheatin'! I know ye are!" The second voice was falsetto and angry.

"Ye can't prove I'm a-cheatin'," Krepner said.

"It's like ye're a-seein' me thoughts," Dolstos protested.

"Just pay up an' cease yer whinin'."

"Let's go again," Dolstos said. "Double or nothin'."

"Ye'll just end up owin' me double," Krepner warned. "Can't say I didn't warn ye."

"Ye can't be lucky forever, an' if'n ye're a-cheatin' I'm a-gonna catch ye."

Curious, Wick pulled himself up the iron door and looked around. He was on a ship. The gentle sway of the vessel resting at anchor told him that. The iron door revealed to him that he was down in the ship's brig. And the stench that even overpowered the stink of the brig, well, that told him he was being held by goblinkin.

Peering out into the brightness of the lantern light, lifting one hand to partially block the rays that seemed to pierce his head, Wick saw a lone goblinkin sitting at an uneven table. He wondered where the second voice had come from.

The goblinkin shook his right hand, stuck out two fingers, roared, "Even!" then chortled with laughter. "Haw, haw, haw! I beat you again! I'm a-tellin' ye, Dolstos, ye can't beat me!"

"Cheater!" the falsetto voice screamed. "Dirty, rotten cheater!"

The big goblinkin rocked back and forth as he guffawed. "I tell ye, Dolstos, doin' guard duty without ye to play with would be mighty borin'. Mighty borin' indeed."

"Nobody else will play with ye because ye cheat all the time," Dolstos accused.

Then Wick saw where the second voice was coming from. At least, he saw where the second voice was supposed to be coming from. He couldn't believe it. A shiver of fear rattled along his spine.

The goblinkin used his right hand to play the odds and

evens game, but he played it against himself. His left hand was dressed up in miniature clothing like another guard and a face had been drawn on it in charcoal. A worn piece of sheep's wool created a patch of hair on the back of the hand.

When the goblinkin, Krepner, wanted the other player to talk, he flexed the thumb like a lower lip and raised his own voice, then spoke out of the corner of his mouth. As Wick watched, the goblinkin played himself again, and beat the hand puppet once more. Krepner howled with glee and slapped the table with his good hand while his other hand thumped in agony.

"Cheater!" the falsetto voice shrilled. The high-pitched voice filled the brig. "I'm gonna kill you!"

Moving quickly, Krepner drew the long knife at his side and held it against the hand puppet's wrist, just under the fake lower lip created by his thumb. Where a goblinkin's neck would be if the hand puppet were another being. "Don't ye be a-threatenin' me, Dolstos!" he roared. "Ye knows I can't stands it!"

The puppet struggled against the knife. Krepner pinned his left hand against the top of the table. A thin line of blood trailed the knife blade.

A new wave of nausea rattled through Wick. He was certain the goblinkin was about to amputate his own hand for talking back to him.

"Don't."

The voice surprised Wick. It was even more surprising when he discovered it had come from him. He knew that when the goblinkin's head swung around and locked on him.

"So," Krepner said, "ye're awake. I thought for sure they'd kilt ye." He kept his knife at the hand puppet's throat.

"Yes," Wick said nervously.

"Ye saw him!" The hand puppet squirmed against the knife, trying to get out from under the blade. "Ye saw him a-cheatin'! Tell him ye saw him!"

Krepner glowered at Wick. "Are ye goin' to accuse me, too?"

"No," Wick answered. "I didn't see you cheating." *And I also don't see how you couldn't be.*

"He was a-cheatin'!" Dolstos yelled.

Losing interest in the shouting match, Krepner leaned back in his chair. He left the hand puppet lying on the table. "I'm here to watch ye, halfer. Don't give me no trouble an' ye'll live until they kills ye."

Oh, and that's so comforting, Wick thought, not relaxed at all. "Okay."

The goblinkin stared at Wick for a long time. Wick stood his ground on the other side of the iron door and looked at everything but Krepner.

"Want to play odds an' evens?" Krepner asked.

"No."

"What?" Krepner asked belligerently.

"No. Thank you," Wick added.

"An' why not? Do you think I cheat?"

Wick pulled back from the door. "I didn't say that."

"Well, ye'd best never—"

"You're a cheater," a woman's voice declared. "You're cheating Dolstos out of everything."

"What!" Krepner thundered. He vaulted from his chair and stood with his knife in his hand. The stacks of copper coins on the table behind him (most of them on Krepner's side and not Dolstos's) scattered in a tinkling rain.

Wick jerked backward and bumped into the back wall of the brig. "Nothing!" he said anxiously. "I didn't say anything!"

"I heard ye, halfer." Krepner strode to the brig. He thrust his knife through the iron bars of the door. "Ye best watch yer unkind tongue, or I'll have it from yer head, I will."

"You're a cheat. I'll say it again in case you didn't hear me with those pig-ugly ears."

Shaking his head, Wick said, "Not me. I didn't say that."

The cat lay curled up in the back corner of the brig. Her tail flicked lazily. "I said it," she announced.

"Ye better tell yer cat to shut her lyin' mouth, halfer." Krepner glowered at Wick.

"I can't," Wick pleaded. "She doesn't listen to me."

"Don't make me come in there."

"Why?" the cat demanded. "Do you think we're afraid of you?"

"Ye should be!"

"Because you cheat Dolstos?" The cat pushed herself up on her forepaws and wrapped her tail around herself. Her eyes glinted mockery. "Dolstos doesn't even have any arms to defend himself."

"What are you doing?" Wick demanded of the cat.

"Do you really want to die a slow death in the belly of this rat-infested ship?" Alysta asked.

"All right, halfer, I've had me about enough of ye an' yer blasted cat!" Krepner fumbled for the keys hanging from his hip.

Alysta turned to Wick. "Get ready," she said.

"Get ready?" Wick stared at the goblinkin, who was easily three times his size.

The cat got on all fours. "Keep your head, Librarian. It's only one goblinkin. Surely you can handle one goblinkin."

"No," Wick said, pretty certain that he couldn't. "I'm not a fighter. I'm a Librarian."

The cat spat in disgust. "We're all fighters when we have to be."

Not me, Wick thought.

"Just stay away from him," the cat said. "You've seen for yourself that he's not overly bright."

He talks to his hand, Wick thought desperately. *That's a sure sign that there's no mind lingering in that thick skull. How can you reason with a mad goblinkin?*

By then, amid curses and threats of bodily harm, Krepner opened and swung wide the heavy iron door. It clanged against the wall.

"I'll have the tongue from yer head!" the goblinkin roared.

"An' the tail of the cat as well!" Dolstos shouted in his falsetto voice.

Together, goblinkin and hand-goblinkin charged into the brig.

Krepner reached for Wick with his free hand, intending to grab his hair. Instead, the little Librarian ducked and rolled between the goblinkin's legs too fast to be caught.

By that time, the cat was in motion, springing from her haunches and launching herself up the goblinkin in a series of lightning-fast jumps that took her up the body of their foe. Then she sat atop his head and started clawing and scratching and biting Krepner's ears and nose.

Wick watched in stunned fascination.

"The keys!" the cat yelled. "Grab the keys!"

Krepner flailed at the cat, barely missing her as she sprinted over his head and shoulders. Her claws dug into fabric and flesh. Off balance, screaming in terror and anger, the goblinkin collided with the rear wall of the brig and the bars.

"Get the *keys*!"

Galvanized into action, Wick darted forth, swallowing his heart, which was pumping frantically in the back of his throat. His hand closed on the heavy key ring and yanked.

It didn't come off.

"Get the keys!" the cat yelled. The goblinkin's efforts to seize her got closer and closer.

In another moment Wick felt certain her foe would have her. Redoubling his efforts, Wick seized the key ring again and yanked with all his strength.

Cloth tore. The keys came away in Wick's hand, but the goblinkin turned on him at once.

"Ye done made a *bad* mistake, halfer!" the goblinkin growled. He stepped toward Wick, who shrank back at once. The little Librarian was certain that his life was at an end. He raised his hand before him, hoping to ward off any blows, but knowing that the knife would probably nail his hands to his skull.

Then the goblinkin's pants, torn loose by Wick's efforts to claim the keys, fell and tangled around his ankles. He tried to take another step, but he tripped. "I'm gonna—gonna—ulllllllppppp!" He crashed to the floor.

"Go!" the cat commanded. "While he's *ulllllppping!*" Lithely, she jumped over the fallen goblinkin.

Krepner flailed with his knife and reached for his pants at the same time. He yelled and screamed and cursed.

"Out!" the cat shouted, throwing herself at Wick.

Standing, Wick rushed out the door and threw it closed behind him. He fumbled with the key as Krepner got to his feet and leaped toward the door. The lock engaged with dull, grating clicks.

Krepner reached through the bars with the knife, slashing at Wick. "C'mere, ye terrible little beast! I'll rip ye to pieces an' gnaw on yer bones!"

All the more reason to stay away, Wick thought. He was glad he remembered to yank the keys from the lock.

Krepner continued to roar and rage. "Stupid, stupid halfer!"

"Who are ye callin' stupid?" Dolstos demanded. "Ye were the one that let him out!"

"I didn't let him out! *Ye* let him out!"

"He took the keys from *ye!*"

"It was ye supposed to be watchin' me back!" Krepner slashed at his other hand, but missed. The hand dressed up as Dolstos slapped the knife from Krepner's hand. Then it lifted and drove at Krepner and started strangling the goblinkin. Overwhelmed, Krepner went backward, tripping over his dropped trousers again.

That goblinkin is not *right in his head,* Wick told himself. He watched, hypnotized by the action as Krepner rolled across the floor of the brig fighting his own hand.

"Have you taken root?"

Yanked back into the danger that immediately surrounded him, knowing that he was in more danger outside the brig than in it because the goblinkin that discovered him free aboard the ship might decide to kill him at once and ask questions later, Wick glanced around the room.

"Let's go," Alysta said. She bounded toward the door that led to the hallway.

Instead, Wick turned his attention to searching the room. He ran quickly, fearing that at any moment a goblinkin might wander down from the upper deck.

"What are you doing?" the cat asked.

"Looking for my cloak." Wick sorted through the pile of outwear in the corner. Evidently a lot of the goblinkin crew dropped their cloaks and coats there.

Or maybe there were a lot of victims that had ended up in stewpots and no longer needed them. It was a sobering and chilling thought.

Exasperated, the cat said, "Grab any cloak. Better an ill-fitting cloak than fitting back inside that cage again."

"You don't understand." Wick kept turning cloaks.

"I'm not going to help you out of here again. It was hard enough sneaking onto the ship after you this time. I nearly ended up in a stewpot."

"It's not just my cloak," Wick said. "My book is in there."

That caught the cat's attention. "You brought a book from the Library?"

"Not a book. A journal."

"What's a journal?"

Wick didn't bother to explain. Two coats later, he found his cloak. Frantic, he felt through it and discovered that his journal and writing kit were missing. "No!"

"Let's go," the cat said. "That's your cloak."

Worried about the journal's absence, Wick pulled the cloak on. He'd written the journal in a special code that he'd devised, so reading it wouldn't be easy. But it could still be done. As a Librarian, he'd learned all codes were eventually broken.

Having no choice, Wick followed the cat. Perhaps the journal had fallen out when he'd been taken prisoner.

Thinking of the journal, made with his own two hands, languishing out in the snow pained him. His journal surely deserved a better fate.

Also, the journal had been carefully and craftily hidden within his cloak. It couldn't have easily fallen out. By the time they reached the ladder leading up to the waist, he was convinced that someone had to have removed it.

But who?

"Carefully here," the cat whispered when they walked through the ship's waist.

Wick nodded and followed slowly. The waist of the ship was low on a human or an elf, and would have caused any from either of those two races to have to bend over to proceed. Waist decks were sandwiched below the upper deck and above the cargo area. On the particular ship Wick found himself on, space was at a premium.

Throughout the whole vessel, the stench of goblinkin pervaded. Wick stopped breathing through his nose and breathed through his mouth. It helped a little.

Together, one after the other, he and the cat made their way through the waist, tiptoeing quietly past rooms where goblinkin slept in swaying hammocks. No one had roused to hear Krepner's shouts and curses. Then again, walking through the waist now Wick couldn't hear them. Of course, it was possible that Krepner had managed to strangle himself, though Wick hadn't ever heard of that being done.

The next ladder took them to the upper deck. At the top of the ladder, Wick slowly opened the hatch, surprised to see gray daylight instead of night awaiting him. But it made sense. He'd been brought in at night.

"I'll scout ahead," Alysta said.

"All right," Wick replied, opening the hatch wide enough to allow the cat through, then closing it back down once she was on the deck. He watched her through the slit he'd left.

Alysta walked back and forth, very much like a real cat would. Wick started wondering if she'd always been a cat.

She turned and looked at him with those big eyes. "Come on, then. Be quick about it."

Hating the fact that he had to put so much trust in the cat's talents, but knowing at least she wouldn't be noticed as much as a dweller hanging around on the main deck, Wick slid through the opening and closed the hatch behind him. He stood for a moment in the shadow of the main mast.

Wharf Rat's Warren lie spread out to port. Snowflakes swirled through the air, large and fat, but with plenty of space between. It would gradually accumulate, but it would take time.

Wick couldn't believe what he was seeing. He'd spent all that time, and he was farther away from his goal than he'd been.

"Let's go," the cat said.

Wick started forward.

The cat went ahead, bounding for the stern. Gazing up at the stern castle, Wick saw three goblinkin lazing around a bucket of coals on the deck. The smell of cooking meat lingered in the air. Wick didn't want to think about what was cooking.

Just then, the door to the captain's quarters swung open. Wick took advantage of the brief respite he had to clamber into one of the two longboats the ship had on the port side. He slithered up under the tarp while the cat kept watch.

8

Escape

The man who had come to the Tavern of Schemes the night before walked out onto the deck. As he passed by Wick's hiding spot, the little Librarian saw that the man consulted a book.

Wick's heart leapt for a moment as he believed the book to be his own journal. Then he saw that it was bound differently, and in another color. Still, it was a book and that was exciting enough. Before he knew it, Wick started wondering about other books that might be in the man's quarters.

That one, Wick felt strongly, *and any others he might have, belong in the Vault of All Known Knowledge so they can be preserved and protected.*

The man walked to the stairwell leading down to the galley.

The cat called for Wick.

Reluctantly, feeling overly exposed in the pale gray daylight, Wick climbed out from under the tarp and out of the longboat. He crossed to the port railing and looked out at the dock. Ice chunks floated in the water. The span was too far to jump, and the water was near freezing, assuring him of a quick, relatively painless death. He hunkered by the longboat, using it to shield him from sight of the goblinkin in the stern.

"Har," one of the goblinkin said. "I wonder if Krepner is still down in the brig cheatin' hisself at odds an' evens."

The other goblinkin laughed.

"One of these days," another goblinkin said, "he's gonna get tired of cheatin' hisself at odds an' evens an' kill hisself over it."

They all had a good laugh about that as they warmed their hands over the kettle of coals.

"Go," the cat said.

"Where?" Wick asked. Surely the cat couldn't be suggesting that he dive into the water. That would be the end of him. Even if he made it to shore, which Wick doubted, his clothes would be sodden and heavy. He'd never get away.

"The ship is tied up to the dock," Alysta said. "If we reach the stern, we can climb along the mooring rope."

"I'll be seen," Wick said.

The cat twitched an ear in irritation. "I'll provide a distraction. These goblinkin would love nothing more than to put me in a stewpot."

Except maybe a dweller for the stewpot, Wick thought but didn't say. He didn't want to get into an argument over who would provide a finer goblinkin repast.

"Now get ready. On my word." The cat bounded away, moving so quickly that she appeared weightless. She leaped and landed on the railing of the stairwell leading up to the stern castle. Quickly, she ran along the railing until she stood at the railing's center.

Then she meowed, loud and long, like a hungry cat standing outside the door and wanting in. It was, Wick had to admit, one of the most annoying sounds ever.

The sound caught the attention of the goblinkin immediately. The biggest one of them slapped the two others and shushed them. Like a pack of predators, which Wick knew they were, they stared at the cat with anticipatory gleams in their eyes.

Deliberately, the cat squatted on the railing and wrapped her tail around her paws. She meowed again, acting innocent and vulnerable.

Wick was really starting to wonder where the cat had been before she had appeared to help him. She was too arrogant—well, perhaps not. Cats, by their nature, tended toward arrogance and filled everyone's life whose path they crossed with demands.

"A cat," one of the goblinkin said, reaching for the knife sheathed on his hip.

"Stew meat," another goblinkin hissed. "Get him, Rido."

Rido slipped his knife free and drew it back to throw. Alysta meowed again, as if totally unaware of the danger.

Fearing for the cat, certain he was about to see her pierced by the knife and dead soon after, Wick watched helplessly. He slid a hand over his face to hide his eyes. But he found himself transfixed, unable to cease looking on.

With some skill (goblinkin were more accustomed to bashing and slashing and even gnashing things with their fangs rather than true ability), Rido flung the knife. It came with greater speed than Wick would have imagined, glittering through the intervening space.

Looking almost bored, the cat flicked out a paw as she dodged to the right and batted the knife away. The blade flew over the stern railing and clattered to the deck.

"Did ye see that?" one of the goblinkin asked. "That cat knocked the knife away!"

Alysta flicked her ears and meowed, sitting comfortably once more on the railing.

"Why, it's laughin' at ye, Rido," one of the goblinkin said.

Growling curses, Rido picked up a stone war hammer leaning against the back stern railing. "I can't promise ye stew meat after this," he stated as he hefted the huge weapon, "but ye'll at least get broth an' a few bones to suck the marrow from." He took up the hammer in both hands and moved slowly toward the railing.

Alysta continued sitting there and meowed again.

"Nice kitty, kitty," Rido rumbled soothingly. "Nice kitty. Just ye keep a-sittin' there. This'll be over in a bit." He kept slide-stepping forward, raising the hammer over his head. "Nice kitty, kitty."

The other goblinkin watched expectantly.

Wick almost couldn't bear to watch.

Then Rido swung the hammer with all his prodigious might. Alysta uncoiled from her haunches and leaped to the left, catching hold of one of the lines and clinging by her claws. Rido's hammer crunched through the stern railing and the sound of splitting wood filled the air.

"Oh, that's bad," one of the goblinkin said. "Cap'n Gujhar's gonna be pretty vexed at ye."

"Me? It was me ye sent after that blasted cat!" Rido drew the hammer back from the wreckage of the railing.

Alysta yowled, and the sound was almost laughter.

"Get that cat!" Rido roared.

The other goblinkin sprang to pursue the cat, drawing weapons. Alysta ran through the rigging, drawing them on down the starboard stairwell away from the stern castle. The whole time, she remained tantalizingly close to the goblinkin, as if she didn't have her wits about her and was running in fear and only just managing to avoid sudden death. That perceived luck only drew the goblinkin into a greater frenzy.

Taking advantage of the moment, Wick sprinted from hiding and ran for the other stairwell on the port side of the stern castle. The goblinkin were so intent on their prey that they never noticed him. But new goblinkin arrived from below, coming out of the stairwell amidships to see what was going on. They saw the cat, too, and immediately gave chase.

Afraid he was going to be seen, Wick ducked into hiding beside the stairwell instead of going up it. He sunk back and tried to become another layer of the wood as the goblinkin chased the cat through the rigging. The goblinkin threw knives, axes, and belaying pins at the cat, setting up all kinds of noise.

Even the man, Captain Gujhar, came up from below-decks to see what the matter was. The man held a finger in the pages of his book to mark his place.

That reminded Wick of his own missing journal. He wanted it back. Then he noticed that he stood next to the captain's quarters. He eyed the door latch. Before he knew what he was doing, his hand dropped to the latch and flipped it.

The latch opened.

In the next instant, Wick was inside.

The captain's quarters were cramped, much as they were aboard *One-Eyed Peggie*. Shelves and boxes and chests took up all the space that wasn't occupied by the bed. Light poured in through the stern windows. A small leather bag sat on one of the shelves. A quick inspection revealed that it held a handful of gold and silver coins.

But Wick's eyes were immediately drawn to the small desk built into the wall. Three books lay on top of the desk. One of them was his journal.

Before he knew it, Wick stood at the desk, his hands sliding over the books. He immediately tucked his journal into the cloak again, once more in its hiding place. Then he opened the larger of the two remaining books.

The volume was written in a human tongue, one of the old ones before the Cataclysm. He recognized it and the words came to him swiftly.

THE LOG OF THE WRAITH

Drawn by curiosity that overrode the fear clamoring at him, Wick turned the pages. The man who had penned the ship's log had an inelegant hand. It wasn't the language as much as the writing that inhibited Wick's almost instant translation.

Wraith had taken leave of her port home in Illastra deep within the Forest of Fangs and Shadows eighty-seven days ago. She'd been fully stocked with provisions and trade goods, and had a crew of thirty-two goblinkin that—

Someone banged on the door. "Who's in there?" a voice roared. "I saw you go in there! Come out at once!"

A crew of goblinkin that are even now banging on the door, Wick thought fearfully. He closed the book and ripped a pillowcase from the bed, fashioning a makeshift knapsack for the books. Thinking of the water he had to go over in the harbor, he wished he had better protection for the books.

But that couldn't be helped.

Knocking slammed the door in its frame again. "Is that you, dweller?" the man demanded.

First you have to save yourself, Wick told himself. He tossed the bag of gold and silver coins into his makeshift bag as well. Working quickly, he knotted the pillowcase, then tied the ends together to make a sling that he pulled over his head and one shoulder. Sliding the knapsack onto his back and out of the way, the little Librarian ran to the stern windows.

The beating resumed on the door. Captain Gujhar called to his goblinkin crew. "Stop chasing that cat! Get over here and break down this door!"

Wick opened the stern windows. If he'd been a normal-sized elf, dwarf, or human, he wouldn't have had room enough to escape. He stuck his head out. The stern window was almost twenty feet above the freezing harbor water. Wind plucked at his clothing and hair. The dock was thirty feet away, way beyond his reach.

Panic thundered through Wick in time with the pounding on the door.

"What are you waiting on?"

Hearing the cat's voice above him, Wick looked up and found her hanging headfirst on the anchor rope. "I'm trapped," Wick said.

"Use the mooring rope." The cat crept along the rope

herself, placing one paw neatly before the other with effortless grace.

For the first time, Wick noticed the rope that angled down from *Wraith* to the dock. The hawser rope was thicker than a dwarf's wrist. It would surely support his weight, but he wasn't as fleet as the cat, who he was certain could run along it if need be.

But he had an idea from one of the romances in Hralbomm's Wing. Turning, he opened the sea chest beside the bed and took out a leather razor strop. The wide leather band looked suitable for his purpose.

Wood split behind him. The door shoved inward a little. It wouldn't take much more abuse before it gave way.

Returning to the stern window, he slipped outside again. Standing on the narrow ledge of the window, he tiptoed in an effort to reach the hawser. His fingers were several inches short of his prize.

The door shuddered inward, falling in pieces inside the cabin. Goblinkin poured into the room.

"They're going to catch you!" The cat paused, already halfway to the dock.

Desperate, barely maintaining his balance on the gently bobbing ship, Wick held the leather strop in one hand and flipped it over the hawser. Jumping up, he caught the other end, gambling that he could catch it and not drop into the harbor.

His hand closed around the strop and he held on tight. Immediately, the smooth leather slid across the hawser, gaining speed. He shot toward the cat.

"Look out!" Wick yelled.

Voices rang out above him. Twisting uncontrollably at the ends of the razor strop, Wick saw that goblinkin lined *Wraith*'s stern, too. Several of them threw knives, hand axes, and belaying pins at him. Luckily, all of them fell short.

The leather zipped along the hawser and he was on the cat. Alysta cursed him soundly as she gathered herself.

Wick feared that she would be knocked from her precarious perch by the strop.

Instead, at the last moment possible, the cat leaped up from the rope and the strop passed harmlessly underneath. He expected to see her land again on the hawser, managing a child's trick of jumping rope. She came at his head, though, her paws flailing and her claws extended.

Wick couldn't help it. Instinct forced him to duck. The cat missed him with three of her paws but managed to hook him with her left foreleg. Her claws dug into his hair and his scalp.

Yelping in pain, Wick was distracted from the sudden stop waiting at the end of the hawser. The cat clung to him, digging all of her claws in deeply enough to draw blood. From the corner of his eye, Wick saw the piling ahead just before he slammed into it.

For a moment, he thought he'd knocked himself out. He'd knocked the wind out of his lungs and his senses spun dizzily inside his battered skull. Ice and water lapped at the piling below his feet. From where he hung, he had a clear view of *Wraith*'s prow. The ship's figurehead had been carved into the shape of a monstrous looking thing rising from the ocean. Wraiths took many shapes, Wick knew, but there was no doubting what that one was.

"Are you going to hang there all day?" the cat demanded.

No, Wick thought. *I'm going to hang here and listen to my heart stop.* He felt certain that was going to happen. Then he managed to take a breath as his lungs finally started working again. Unfortunately, that started an onslaught of pain.

The cat leaped from the top of Wick's head to the dock. At her urging, he managed to heave himself up and lay gasping on the dock.

Onboard *Wraith*, Captain Gujhar called out to the goblinkin. Some of them grabbed bows. Arrows thudded into the dock as Wick climbed with renewed enthusiasm.

Keeping his head covered with his hands, he ran down the dock amid cargo handlers who dove for cover.

"Avast there, ye blasted goblinkin!" a tall human yelled. Then he reached for his own bow and nocked an arrow. A heartbeat later, he seated the shaft in the chest of a goblinkin who squalled in mortal agony.

"This way," the cat called.

Wick ran blindly, trusting the feline even though he didn't want to. He turned to the right at the end of the dock, scattering a gathering of seagulls that took flight from the fish heads and entrails left by the morning fishermen. By that time, a proper fight had started between the goblinkin and the human sailors along the dock. In the next minute he was gone, lost among the twisting alley of Wharf Rat's Warren.

9

Seaspray

heart pounding and lungs burning, Wick couldn't go on anymore. He halted in the last alley they'd come to and leaned against the wall.

"Come on," Alysta said. She stood ahead of him, looking as cool and composed as if she'd just wakened from a nap.

Wick shook his head. "I can't go on any farther." He sucked in air, believing he was about to die.

"All right then," the cat said reluctantly, "rest. I'll go make certain we're not being followed." She ran to the front of the alley and peered out. Her tail twitched behind her, keeping perfect time.

Still trembling from the close call, not willing to believe that he was actually going to make good his escape, Wick held his arms up for a moment to let his lungs fill more easily. Then, before he knew it, he took the ship's log from the knotted pillowcase. His eyes moved restlessly across the pages, scanning information. As always, he got lost in the words almost at once.

"What are you doing?"

Wick ignored the cat and kept reading. "Getting information."

"What information?"

"About the people on that ship. *Wraith*."

"They want to kill us."

"Yes."

"There's not a whole lot more to know."

"Actually," Wick said, licking his thumb and turning the page, "there is. The man who hired the Razor's Kiss thieves here isn't just after Boneslicer and Seaspray. He's also after—"

"Deathwhisper."

Wick frowned. "You knew."

The cat turned over a paw, then sat and wrapped her tail around her feet. "Honestly, I can't believe you know so little."

"Craugh didn't tell me anything other than to come here. And that someone would be here to help me."

"Didn't you study the stories of the Battle of Fell's Keep?"

"I did," Wick said.

"Then you should have known what the people we're up against were after."

Wick suddenly realized what those prizes were. "Boneslicer, Seaspray, and Deathwhisper."

"Magical weapons are a rarity in this world," the cat confirmed. "Nothing like them has been made since the Cataclysm."

"I know," Wick said.

"And they were all present during the retreat from Teldane's Bounty. That was one of the reasons the defenders were able to hold out as long as they were." Sadness touched the cat's gray eyes. "If they hadn't been betrayed, maybe more of them would have escaped being overrun."

"How do you know about the Battle of Fell's Keep?"

The cat stood. "We need to be moving. You've got your breath back."

"Where are we going?"

"To find Seaspray." The cat started off.

"No," Wick said.

"No?" Alysta turned, and despite the fact that she was a cat, irritation showed in every line of her body.

"We can't go on alone. It's too dangerous."

"We're already nearly a day behind, thanks to your capture."

"I didn't get captured on purpose. But we should stay here. Craugh, Cap'n Farok, and Hallekk will be here soon."

"Do you think it's wise for *One-Eyed Peggie* to drop anchor in the harbor at Wharf Rat's Warren?"

Actually, now that he thought about it (in other terms than simply of his rescue), Wick thought maybe *One-Eyed Peggie* putting in to port at the city wasn't a good idea. She'd be set upon at once by several of the pirates who traveled to the city of thieves, murderers, assassins, thieves, etc.

"No," he sighed.

"Good, because I don't think Craugh would believe it was safe, either. You might wait there for a long time." Alysta got underway again. "Our time would be better spent finding Seaspray."

Reluctantly, Wick put the ship's log away and fell in behind the cat.

"You *sold* my donkey?" Wick stared at the livery boy in disbelief. Alysta had told him his captors had used the donkey to bring him back to town. They'd left it at the livery.

Cautiously, the livery boy stepped back. Bruises showed on his face where the Razor's Kiss thieves had hit him the previous night. It looked like he had a few new additions, so maybe his father hadn't necessarily believed his story about the stolen horses. "I told you when you left it here yesterday that if my da came in an' it wasn't paid for, he'd sell it. Those men didn't pay for it. So, he did."

"To whom?" the cat asked.

The livery boy hesitated. "To the . . . renderer."

"You knew he wasn't a normal donkey," Alysta protested.

Sullen, the boy said, "Let the donkey tell the renderer that, then. I tried to tell my da it could talk." He touched a painful looking bruise on his forehead. "I got clouted extra hard for that one, let me tell you."

"When did the renderer pick up the donkey?" Wick asked. He couldn't help thinking about the dreadful fate that awaited the donkey. In a few days, what was left of him could be made into pretty decent glue. *People need glue*, Wick thought. *It has to come from somewhere.*

"This morning," the boy answered. "He always picks up unclaimed livestock in the mornings."

"How quickly does he . . . does he . . . ?" Wick couldn't go on thinking about it.

"Is he already dead?" Alysta asked.

Pensive, obviously a little afraid of Wick even though the little Librarian was smaller than he was, the boy lifted his shoulders and dropped them. "I don't know."

"Where can I find the renderer's place?" Wick asked.

The livery boy gave him directions and Wick left quickly.

Outside, Wick hurried after the cat. The goblinkin searched through the city even now. If the boy knew that, if he went to the goblinkin, they would have time to intercept them.

"He won't tell," Alysta said.

Wick kept pace. "What makes you so certain?"

"He's afraid of the goblinkin, and of his father," the cat said. "He was even afraid of us."

Wick tried to believe that. He just hoped that the donkey wasn't sitting in little pots of glue already.

The renderer kept a small shop outside of town, not far from the trail that led up into the mountains. The little stone shack leaned against a hill of snow and ice, looking like it might blow over at any moment. Only a short distance away, a ramshackle barn bracketed by trees looked bowed under the weight of the snow on the slanted roof. A few horses and two donkeys stood listless in the corral out front. Gray breath plumed from their nostrils.

Seeing the animals there, knowing the fate that awaited them, Wick felt a pang of sorrow for them. *Concentrate on what you need to do*, he told himself. *It's the same as one of the chickens that end up in a pot, or a fattening pig.*

He trudged through the snow on his bare feet, which he—by some miracle—could still feel. The cat rode his shoulders, no longer able to break through the high drifts. Wick glanced hopefully at the steady stream of smoke pouring from the chimney against the slate-gray sky. Surely it would be warm inside.

A trail existed between the corral and the shop, and to the well out back, but there was no other. Wick made his way to the uneven porch and pulled himself up. Drifts covered the porch and the two rocking chairs that sat there.

Gathering his courage, Wick knocked on the door.

"Who is it then?" a voice called from inside.

"Wick of . . . of Meek's Crossing," the little Librarian said. Meek's Crossing was a small town outside Wharf Rat's Warren.

"What do you want?" the voice demanded.

"There's been a mistake," Wick said. "A terrible mistake." The stink from the corral hit him then, thick and cloying in the cold wintry air.

The cat leapt from Wick's shoulders to a window sill. She peered inside and her breath frosted the glass.

"I ain't made no mistakes. And I'll club the man that says I made one. When I make glue or paste, it's good. It'll hold anything you're of a mind to put together. That's my guarantee."

"There's no mistake about your work, sir," Wick said. "The livery boy made a mistake. He wasn't supposed to—"

The door opened suddenly and a shaggy old man stood there in patched-over clothing. His gray beard hung to his waist and looked wild and unkempt. Under an ill-made fur cap, he was bald. His pale, runny eyes didn't look in the same direction.

"You've come about the donkey, then," the man said. He extended his hand.

Almost overcome by the strong chemical smell coming from inside the shop, Wick didn't know what to do. He shook the man's hand. Heavily callused and covered in patches of glue that held horse's hair and other disagreeable things, the man's hand spoke of cruel strength.

"I, uh," Wick said, trying to figure out what was happening, "uh, I have. About the donkey."

The man grinned and the effort looked slapped on and forced. "Well then, it's good to see you. He said you might be coming by for him."

"He did?" Wick was astonished. "He told you that?"

The man nodded. "He did. I'm Rankle. Come on in."

Trepidation stirred within Wick. He didn't trust the renderer.

"Wick," the donkey called from inside. "It's all right. Come on inside."

Hesitantly, Wick followed the man inside the home. Shelves lined the walls and tables took over the open space in the center. Pots and bottles filled the tables and shelves. The chemical stink was even stronger inside the room, but it was warm.

The donkey sat on his haunches near the fireplace. He looked comfortable and rested, not like the other poor beasts out in the corral.

Alysta walked into the room with Wick.

"Is that your cat?" Rankle asked.

Wick waited for Alysta to answer, but she didn't. Obviously she didn't care to let the renderer know she spoke.

"Yes," Wick said.

Rankle scratched his beard and looked at Alysta longingly. "Are you particularly attached to it? Out here, with winter on us so fierce, it's just another mouth to feed. I could make you a good deal on it. Can always use cat guts for strings and such. And there ain't nothing quite as delicate as cat glue."

"Uh," Wick stuttered, at a loss.

Alysta hissed at him and flicked her tail disdainfully.

"The cat is mine," the donkey said, looking back over his shoulder.

"Yours, is it?" Rankle asked. He smiled and turned back to the donkey. "Well, Prince Dawdal, I wouldn't harm a hair on your cat's head."

"Prince?" Wick looked at the donkey.

The donkey nodded. He flattened his lips and grinned. "Yes. *Prince.*"

Wick hadn't even known the creature had a name. He couldn't be a prince. Could he?

Rankle waved to a chair in front of the fire. "Sit. Be comfortable. Would you like something to drink? To eat?"

Still dazed, Wick said, "Yes. Very much." Rankle pushed him into motion and the little Librarian walked to the chair and sat.

The donkey had a deep bucket of some kind of oat mash in front of him. Bits of apples and carrots showed in the mixture.

"Want some?" the donkey, Dawdal—maybe even Prince Dawdal—asked.

"No," Wick said. "Thank you." Even as hungry as he was, the bucket's contents didn't look appetizing.

"I've got oatmeal," Rankle said.

Minutes later, Wick sat with a bowl of warm oatmeal as the heat in the fireplace burned away the wintry chill he'd carried in with him.

"Prince Dawdal told me the whole story," Rankle said.

"He did?" Wick asked, anxious to hear the tale himself.

"Of course, at the beginning I didn't know he was a prince," the renderer said. "I got him this morning and was going to slit his throat out in the barn. Then he started talking." He shook his head. "In all my days, I never heard an animal talk." He lowered his voice. "You ask me, it's kind of unnerving the first time."

Wick silently agreed.

"Anyway, he told me about the curse," Rankle continued.

"About the curse?" Wick asked. He spooned up oatmeal, grateful for the simple meal. Rankle had also put out a loaf of bread and chokeberry jelly. The bread tasted fresh and the jelly had a sugary tang.

"The curse Wizard Hardak put on him," Rankle said.

"The one that turned me into a donkey," Dawdal said. "I told Rankle about how my father, the king, had put you in charge of finding me."

"On account of no one would suspect a halfer," Rankle said. He leveled a forefinger at Wick and grinned. "Clever plan, that one."

"Right," Wick said. "Clever." But he was wondering where the donkey got his imagination. During the days they'd shared together earlier, the creature had shown no sign of intelligence.

"I also told him about the treasure," the donkey said.

"You told him about the treasure?" Wick asked.

The donkey nodded solemnly. "I told him we were trying to find it because it had a cure for the curse that keeps me a donkey. I also promised Rankle a portion of it for sparing my life." He paused and looked at the renderer with sorrowful eyes. "It was the least I could do for his generosity."

"Yes," Wick agreed. "It was."

Only a short time later, once more fortified with supplies, Wick set out with the donkey and the cat. Rankle stood on his uneven porch, waved at them, and wished them well.

"Remember your promise, Prince Dawdal," Rankle called after them.

"I will," the donkey replied. Then he swiveled to face forward again and muttered, "When pigs fly."

Given what he'd seen the last two days with talking animals, Wick wasn't so certain that he wouldn't see that before his journeys were over.

"You're not really a prince, are you?" Wick asked.

The donkey looked at him. "What do you think?"

Wick gave the question serious thought. At the moment he wasn't getting to ride the donkey and was being forced to lead him. Perhaps appealing to the donkey's ego would get him up out of the snow.

"I think you are," Wick answered.

"Idiot," the cat snarled.

The donkey brayed with laughter. "You're not riding me. Those days are over."

As he trudged through the snow, Wick missed those days. Why couldn't Craugh have arranged for someone who would actually *help* him? Only the thought of tracking down Boneslicer for Bulokk drove him on. That and the certain knowledge that toads couldn't turn pages in a book or write with a quill and ink without a great deal of difficulty.

They headed into the mountains, once more taking up the trail.

Near nightfall, they reached one of the small outlying villages on the way down the mountains to Wharf Rat's Warren. No more than a dozen small structures jammed together with fifty or so houses scattered behind them, the village framed the road as it twisted to the east.

Candlelight burned soft yellow against a few windows. Only a few people were about on the street. They gazed curiously at the small group that wandered into their town.

Wick felt uncomfortable under the weight of the stares. During the last few hours of breaking through the new-fallen snow and staring through the flakes that continued to fall, he'd thought of nothing but the three magical weapons that had been at the Battle of Fell's Keep. He couldn't help wondering why Captain Gujhar was looking for them. Of course, the captain was working for someone else, but he'd purposefully not mentioned his employer.

What was it about the three weapons, though? Wick wondered. *Why were they so important after a thousand years?*

Nothing in anything he'd read offered a hint of that. In fact, he didn't know why Craugh had come to Greydawn Moors and been so interested. Though looking back on the situation, neither Craugh nor Cap'n Farok was the type to just go searching for the truth of a battle that took place during the Cataclysm on a whim.

So what weren't they telling him? The thought rolled uncertainly in Wick's mind. He didn't like thinking like that, but the truth of it stared him in the face. But even as he felt anger over being used, he knew that Cap'n Farok— and probably Craugh—wouldn't have gambled his life without good reason.

That could only mean that the danger he was walking into was even greater than he feared. Wick almost felt sick with anxiety, but curiosity drove him as well.

He stumbled tiredly down the street, knowing he had to have someplace to rest. Thankfully, there'd been no sign of pursuit from either the goblinkin or the Razor's Kiss.

A man with a sword stood on a porch in front of a tavern. "Greetings, stranger."

"Greetings," Wick said, bringing the donkey to a stop. Alysta popped her head out of the pack of supplies she'd been riding in. Wick hadn't seen her for hours and guessed that she'd been sleeping.

"What brings you to our village?"

Wick wondered if the place even had a name. Some of them were so small they didn't.

"I'm just passing through," Wick answered. "But I'd like a night's lodging if I could."

The man shook his head. "We don't have lodging here. Even this tavern's just for drinking and eating. Most that travel this road never stop here." He looked around. "There's a few who take in lodgers." Stepping out into the snow-covered street, he pointed out the houses. "Give 'em a try. Tell 'em Enil sent you."

"I will," Wick replied. "Thank you." He moved through the street, leaning into the harsh wind and the swirling snow.

The first two houses didn't even answer his knocks. The third offered lodging, but apologized, saying there was no room for the animals.

Back out in the street, Wick spotted another building that held a leather harness and an apron, advertising the shopkeeper was a leatherworker. Without a written language, shops did the best that they could to advertise what they were.

The detail on the apron, made large enough to nearly cover the expanse of leather, caught his eye. It was a rose caught in the thorny embrace of a vine. He remembered exactly where he had seen such a design: on the leather bag Quarrel had carried.

The leatherworker's shop had been one of the places the man at the tavern had pointed out.

Drawn by his curiosity, Wick went to the shop and rapped on the door. He felt encouraged because a lot of light came from inside.

A man in his middle years opened the door. "Yes?" He was lean and composed, dressed in a leather apron and a dark shirt and trousers. His face was hollow and tired.

"Enil said you might have a bed for the night," Wick said. "I can pay."

The man looked at the donkey and at the cat, who had her head poked up through the supply bag. "For the animals as well?"

"Please."

The leatherworker suggested a price that was fair and Wick agreed. The man said, "There's a small shed in the back. The donkey can stay there. The cat can come inside."

"Thank you," Wick said.

"I'll show you." The man pulled on a heavy coat. "I'm Karbor, by the way."

Wick introduced himself, again claiming to be a glassblower. Together, they took the donkey around back to the small shed and saw to his needs, then returned to the house next to the modest shop.

10

The Leather-Maker's Tale

Inside the house, Wick helped Karbor in the kitchen, setting out dishes for a small but scrumptious repast.

"I apologize for the meagerness of the meal," Karbor said. "I've not had company for a while, and I've been somewhat distracted of late."

"The meal looks good," Wick replied. "It's been days since I've eaten this well." He hadn't gotten to eat in the Tavern of Schemes, and there'd been no decent meal since he'd left *One-Eyed Peggie*. The renderer's oatmeal had been just enough to keep his stomach from meeting his backbone.

Dishes held venison, sweet potatoes, fresh-baked sourdough bread, and a canned vegetable medley with a pepper seasoning particular to the south.

"One of my affordable vices," Karbor grinned as he poured the glass jar of vegetables into a small kettle to heat in the fireplace. "I do like exotic flavors. Up here, usually it's potatoes or other root crops, things that the farmers can get this cold earth to give up in ready numbers. I have to warn you, though, if you're not used to peppers, they can burn."

"I love peppers," Wick assured him. The fragrance of

the peppers opened his nose and made his stomach rumble.

"Then you've been beyond Wharf Rat's Warren." Karbor put out a dish of honey butter.

"Several times," Wick agreed.

In minutes, everything had been heated and they set to at the small table. Wick ate with more than his usual appetite, devouring sourdough bread, cheese, venison, vegetables (which were even hotter than he expected), and sweet potatoes.

"You eat bigger than you look," Karbor observed. He dangled a piece of venison out for Alysta, who took it with proper disdain.

Embarrassed, Wick apologized. "I'll pay extra. I hadn't meant to. But, as I said, it's been a long time since I sat down to a meal like this."

Karbor waved the offer away. "It was just conversation. These are the winter months up here, and I'm not used to having company. During this time, I generally do a few commissioned pieces and put back others for sale in the spring when the traders start their regular trips back and forth across the mountain."

Curious as always, Wick talked to Karbor about the goings-on of the community. It was hard acting like he was knowledgeable about the area while at the same time trying to get an idea of what might have drawn the Razor's Kiss up into the mountains.

To cover his inadequacies, and because he didn't like silence at the dinner table without a book in his hand, Wick summoned up some of the old legends he knew about the northlands and spun them out in great detail. Most of them were about cursed pirates, shipwrecks bearing lost fortunes, and monsters that tore men to pieces high in the mountains. And a dragon or two. Dragons always made for some of the best stories.

"Are you sure you're a glassblower?" Karbor asked during a break while they retired to the fireplace to smoke their pipes.

"What do you mean?" Wick asked, at once worried that he'd somehow given himself away.

"You could be a storyteller." Karbor puffed on his pipe and stared into the flames. "You have a knack for weaving a tale."

"Thank you," Wick said. "You're too kind."

"No," Karbor said. "I know a good taleweaver when I hear one, and you're better than any I've ever heard." He puffed for a moment. "I only wish that my daughter were here to hear you. She always loved a good story."

"You have a daughter?"

"*Had,*" Karbor said quietly. "I lost her."

"I'm sorry for your loss."

"It was only a few months ago. She wasn't my daughter by blood, but I raised her from the time she was eleven years old. She's seventeen now. Her name was Rose." Karbor took down a piece of leather from over the fireplace. "She was gifted in leatherwork, though it wasn't her calling. She crafted the design I've been using for the last few years." He tapped the rose wreathed in the thorny vine. Smiling at the memory, he traced the imprint. "She did this as a lark. I chose to use it to mark our work. Not many do that, you know. Because the goblinkin see such a mark as writing."

"I know," Wick said.

"She was a precious child," Karbor said as he put the leather piece back on the mantle. "But sad. I never could get her past the melancholy that plagued her as a child."

"Why was she sad?" Wick asked, before he realized that he might be prying. He couldn't bear to leave a tale untold.

Karbor packed his pipe and got it going again. "Her parents, my good friends in younger and more profitable years, were killed by goblinkin. Rose barely got away. When I found out what had happened, I went down the Shattered Coast to see to her. She had no other family, so I brought her back here to live with me."

"The goblinkin overran her village?" Wick asked. That

wasn't an unusual tale. Goblinkin ferocity had been building across the mainland as the tribes turned outward to
work out their aggressions instead of fighting with each
other as they had in the past.

"No." Karbor's voice was soft. "As it turned out, the
goblinkin were searching for her family."

"Why?"

"Because they are the present descendants of Captain
Dulaun, the hero of—"

"The Battle of Fell's Keep during the Cataclysm,"
Wick said. Although the large meal had made him sleepy,
he was once more awake.

Karbor glanced at him with concern.

"I collect tales," Wick said. "The Battle of Fell's Keep
is one that remains on everyone's mind."

"It does." Karbor nodded. "Many people—humans and
elves—distrust the dwarves due to Master Blacksmith
Oskarr's betrayal of those brave defenders."

Master Oskarr didn't betray anyone! Wick curbed his
response with difficulty. "Your daughter was Captain
Dulaun's descendant?"

Karbor nodded. "She was. On her mother's side. I didn't
know it at the time. Rose told me that later. Her ancestor
wielded the sword Seaspray in a thousand battles, and he
lost his life there at the Battle of Fell's Keep."

"And the sword fell into goblinkin hands," Wick said,
remembering.

"Yes, and during the last thousand years, it was lost in
time. No one knew where it was. But there was someone
who believed he knew." Karbor puffed on his pipe. "In
fact, he felt certain Seaspray was somewhere in this area."

Wick's heart quickened. "In Wharf Rat's Warren?"

"No, but somewhere nearby." Karbor waved to the north.
"A dozen empires and kingdoms have risen and fallen in
the mountains. One of them, I don't know which, was
supposed to have found Seaspray."

"Was the sword found?"

Karbor shrugged. "I don't know." He sounded tired and old.

Wick felt sorry for the man then. Karbor was in the winter of his years, alone and without family. No one should have to die like that, he thought. Then Wick realized that he had a chance of doing exactly that while on the task Craugh had set for him.

Unless, of course, he was able to learn enough to save himself.

"They came here to find my daughter," Karbor said.

"Who came here?" Wick asked, fighting the fatigue that filled him.

"The goblinkin. Under the direction of a despicable man named Gujhar." Karbor scowled. "I was next door. In the shop where the hides are cured. I heard the sounds of a fight and ran outside. By that time the goblinkin already had Rose." Tears showed in his eyes and his hand trembled as he held his pipe. "She fought them. With tooth and nail, she fought them. I swear, you've never seen a girl who could fight so well. Her mother was a warrior, trained in swordcraft and hand-to-hand arts. A child was chosen in each generation to train so."

"Why?"

"In the event that Seaspray was recovered."

"Who trained your daughter?"

"Her mother, for a time. But even here she felt the need for more training. There's man in the village, a blind man who was once part of a king's bodyguard, that trained Rose in hand-to-hand techniques. And not far from here, I know another man who was once a sellsword. I bartered for lessons for her because she wanted so badly to learn."

"You don't know what happened to her?"

Karbor shook his head. "I went down to Wharf Rat's Warren and tried to spy on the goblinkin ship. I nearly got killed for my trouble." His voice broke. "But I learned enough to know not to hold out any hope for Rose."

"While I was in Wharf Rat's Warren," Wick said, "I

saw a man who carried a small bag with the rose emblem on it."

"A bag?" Interest flickered in Karbor's wet eyes.

"Yes." Wick looked around the room. "You make a lot of leather goods—gloves, blacksmith's aprons, and harness—but I don't see any bags or backpacks."

"I don't make them," Karbor said. "The communities I sell to are all working people. They don't have enough wealth for excesses. A leather bag when a cloth one would do is excessive."

"So you didn't make that one? I saw the emblem with my own eyes."

"I made one," Karbor said. "But only one. For Rose." His voice thickened. "Tell me the man's name. I'd like very much to talk to him if I'm ever given the chance."

"Quarrel," Wick answered.

"Was he human?"

Wick nodded.

"Part of Gujhar's group, no doubt."

"I don't think so," Wick said. "Why would Gujhar want your daughter?"

"Because Seaspray is ensorcelled," Karbor replied. "The magic inside the sword can't be wakened without one of the true heirs holding it. Only Dulaun's family can evoke that."

"Why would the goblinkin want her or the sword?"

"I don't know. According to the legend Rose told me, all three of the weapons—Master Oskarr's battle-axe Boneslicer, Captain Dulaun's sword Seaspray, and the elven warder Sokadir's mighty bow, Deathwhisper—were used to strengthen the wards protecting the defenders there at the Battle of Fell's Keep."

"How?"

"By tapping into the magic within them."

That was the first time Wick had heard such a story. He sat up a little straighter. "Rose told you this?"

Karbor nodded. "She did. Her mother told her the story,

though her mother never mentioned it to me. Only a handful of the defenders at that battle knew about that."

After a time, Karbor excused himself and went off to bed. He made up a pallet in front of the fireplace for Wick.

Despite a full stomach and not much rest, Wick found his mind was too busy to allow him to drift off to sleep. His thoughts kept chasing themselves inside his head. Instead, he'd taken out his journal and his writing tools and set about putting down the events of the day. The work went quickly by the firelight, even though he knew he would have to revisit it at a later date.

Still restless, he turned to the books he'd taken from *Wraith*. The journal detailed Captain Gujhar's progress in his search for Boneslicer and Seaspray, and even mentioned that Deathwhisper was rumored lost somewhere deep within what had been Silverleaves Glen. There was even a series of maps detailing the elven city of Cloud Heights and the environs as they had been and as they currently stood.

One of Captain Gujhar's notes said: *I have been told* (Wick noted that never once did *Wraith*'s shipsmaster acknowledge who might have told him) *that anyone with two of the weapons in hand will be guided to the third. With the successful location of Boneslicer, all I need is Seaspray to find Deathwhisper. The men among the Razor's Kiss that I've been dealing with swear they know where Dulaun's sword is. We will see.*

"You should get to sleep," Alysta said softly.

Blinking, Wick looked over at the cat. She hadn't spoken while Karbor was around, which was understandable, but she'd seemed aloof and lost in her own thoughts even after the man had gone to bed. He wondered if he'd done something to upset her and was afraid to ask.

"I will," Wick said. "I usually stay up far later than this at the Vault of All Known Knowledge."

"Not," the cat insisted, "after you escaped goblinkin earlier in the day, and after spending the night trying to stay warm in a snowdrift."

Wick studied the cat. "Are you worried about me?"

The cat glanced away. "No. But I'm not going to be blamed for your failure to escape early in the morning in case the goblinkin come here looking for you."

Wick didn't truly think that was likely, but that didn't mean it wouldn't happen. The cat's demeanor intrigued him. "You're worried about something."

Without another word, she rolled over and faced the other way, soaking up the heat of the fireplace.

For a while, Wick read but didn't learn much. Words escaped him and twisted inside his normally agile mind. After a bit, he put away his journal and writing kit, then hid the books as well. He made himself as comfortable as he could on the pallet, turned so that his back was turned to the flames. After a moment, he was warm and toasty, and he dropped right off to sleep.

In the morning, Wick set off again into the teeth of the blustering winds. Karbor added to his provisions, and he thanked Wick for his generous payment.

"There is one favor I would ask of you as you travel this road," Karbor said.

"If I can," Wick answered.

"If you hear any news of my daughter, if you hear any news of Rose, I ask only that you trouble yourself enough to let me know what you find out."

Wick nodded. "I will."

Then he set off, once more leading the donkey because Dawdal wouldn't allow him to ride.

Three miles up into the mountains, the trail Wick followed split out into a Y. He stood there for a time, not knowing which way to go. The cold pinched his face and his feet longed for a fire to be propped next to.

There was no clue as to which direction the Razor's Kiss thieves had gone.

Alysta roused herself, obviously put on notice by the halt of the donkey. "What's the matter?" she asked.

"I don't know which way to go," Wick replied. He walked back and forth in front of the two roads, trying in vain to find evidence on which to base an answer.

"That's why I came," Alysta said. She put her dainty nose into the wind. "To the left."

Wick looked to the left. That fork led more deeply into the mountains. On the face of things, there wasn't a better place to hide a magical sword than more deeply into the mountains. Still, the right fork might take them to an area where hiding such a thing was even easier.

That's assuming Seaspray is still in existence, he told himself. But he didn't have any doubts about that.

"How do you know it's to the left?" Wick asked.

The cat looked at him with her cool agate eyes. "I don't. I'm guessing."

"Guessing?"

"Yes. Guessing is much better than walking back and forth till you wear a trench in the ground."

Wick looked back the way he'd been pacing. It was true, he supposed, that he had been rather heavy-footed in his indecision.

He sighed. "I'd have much preferred a scientific basis for reaching that decision."

"How about a mathematical one?" the cat asked. "It's a fifty-fifty chance."

Unwilling to argue such a point with the cat, Wick started forward, taking the left fork. They would find out the truth of the matter soon enough.

At sundown, Wick stopped to make camp. He was cold and tired and scared. In his exhaustion, he was beginning to sense shadows flitting around him and imagining them as ravening beasts waiting to take him down and feast on his bones.

He went off the road for thirty yards or so, thinking to hide himself and his camp better than last time. The snow flew thicker now, gathering intensity again as if in the night it found a new strength.

The forest was thick around him, and it was alive with nocturnal creatures. He cut the trail of a fox and heard an owl pass overhead with a heavy *whoosh* of its wings before ducking down and spotting it only a heartbeat later. Thankfully he found no bears or wolves, which could have provided uneasy slumber at best.

He had a cold dinner of jerked meat and journeycakes and longed for the warm meals he'd enjoyed at Karbor's home. He thought again of the leather worker, how his daughter had been taken by the goblinkin and poor Karbor didn't know what had happened to her.

He sat under thick blankets with his back to the donkey, who munched contentedly on a feedbag of oats purchased from Karbor. The cold was kept at bay by thick woolen blankets. Alysta slept near the donkey, more vulnerable to the cold because of her small size.

Wick hated the darkness. It was too dark to travel any farther, but his mind wasn't yet tired enough to sleep despite his physical exhaustion. He needed a book. Not even a pipe or a glass of razalistynberry wine. Just something to occupy his mind. Unfortunately, it was also too dark to read, although the moon occasionally broke through the cloud cover for long silvery moments.

In the silence of the night, amid the calls of the nocturnal hunters and the wind, Wick heard the sound of a trickling stream. He'd crossed the stream once and been aware of its presence most of the day. It came down the mountain, clear and pure.

Grudgingly, he took the water bag from the pack the donkey had carried and went in search of the stream. He stumbled another twenty yards through the forest, push-

ing at the pines and getting the scent of them all over him
in the process before he found the stream.

The stream meandered through the forest, running between the trees and boulders. It wasn't any wider than six
feet across and was only inches deep.

Making his way through the snowdrifts, Wick tripped
and fell. As he pushed himself back up, irritated now
because he had snow all over him and would probably be
wet soon when the flakes melted back at the camp, the
clouds passed for a moment and moonslight touched what
he'd tripped over.

It was a body.

11

The Fortress

Pale, anguished features peered up from the snowdrift where Wick had inadvertently uncovered it. In life, the victim had been a young man, a human of few years, a man by their standards, though not long so.

Wick automatically thought of him as a victim because his throat had been slit. Getting to his feet, the little Librarian discovered that he was in the cold camp of the dead. Hypnotized, recognizing the lumps around him for what they were, Wick brushed away the snow and found six more people.

They'd all been humans, traders by the look of their rough clothes and some of the supplies that had been left in their packs. All of them had died by violence, not far from the cold, dead ashes of their campfire.

Wick knew they'd been killed only a short time ago. The scavengers hadn't been at them yet. He stood in numb horror, gazing down on the faces.

"There's nothing you can do for them." Alysta stood near a tree outside the camp.

Wick said nothing, but the howling wind made him feel near-frozen inside.

"Did you hear me?" the cat asked.

"I heard you," Wick mumbled.

"There's nothing you can do for them," Alysta repeated.

"A burial," Wick suggested.

"You have neither the tools nor the energy." The cat gazed solemnly at the scene. "And the earth is frozen solid." Her voice was quiet. "Better to leave them as you found them and hope that someone else finds them to give them a proper burial."

Stunned, Wick recognized the truth of the cat's words. He nodded.

"At least we know we're on the right track," Alysta said.

"What do you mean?"

"The Razor's Kiss thieves came this way."

Tearing his gaze from the dead men, Wick looked at the cat. "How do you know that?"

"The wounds," Alysta said. "Most of them were made by razors, not swords. These men, the majority of them, were murdered in their sleep. The razor is the chosen weapon of the men we're pursuing."

Wick knew that. "It could be another group of thieves."

"I doubt it. Thieves don't often come up into the mountains."

"That doesn't mean there *wasn't* another group of thieves."

"No, but common sense would dictate that we're following the men we trailed from Wharf Rat's Warren." The cat looked through the forest and slunk back as a great owl passed by. The predator's shadow almost found her in the darkness. "Fill the waterskins and come back to camp before you lose your way."

Wick stood frozen, peering down at the bodies and fearing that he might end up just like them. It was a wonder that he wasn't dead already. *I'm a Librarian*, he thought desperately. *Not an adventurer. Not a sellsword. Not one of those heroes like Taurak Bleiyz from Hralbomm's Wing.* He took a small, deep breath and tried to steady his spinning senses. *I'm a dweller, and I'm a long way from*

*home in a land that will kill me if the men I'm chasing
after don't.*

In the dark deep of the night, Wick wished only that he
could go home. Someone else could solve the riddle of
the Battle of Fell's Keep and who had really betrayed
whom out there. It had happened a thousand years ago.
Those events should have no bearing on what was taking
place now.

But they did. The arguments that took place in Paunsel's
Tavern back in Greydawn Moors. The loss Bulokk still felt
over his ancestor's battle-axe and Master Oskarr's good
name. The kidnapping of the girl, Rose, who was supposed
to be the descendant of Captain Dulaun. All of those things
had happened because of the Battle of Fell's Keep. There
were many who needed to know what had happened.

"Second Level Librarian Lamplighter," the cat called
with more intensity. "Do you hear me?"

Wick pushed away his fear. Fear clouded a person's
thoughts and killed him faster than an opponent's weapon.
"I hear you."

"Fill the waterskins or return to camp," the cat said
gently. "You can't spend the night looking at those men
you can't help."

I know. With an effort, Wick got himself started. He
went to the stream and filled the waterskins, made himself drink until he could hold no more, and headed back
to camp after the cat.

They had chosen the right direction at the fork in the
road. That had to mean something. But he was afraid that
it only meant he was walking to his death.

The fortress came into view by late morning.

Wick rode the donkey instead of walking now. Rags
wrapped his feet to stave off most of the chill. Dawdal
wasn't happy about being ridden and having to suffer

Wick's slight weight, but Alysta had given the donkey no choice. When Dawdal had pressed her for a reason for the change, the cat had declined to answer. She rode in front of Wick and he shielded her with his cloak.

The donkey saw the fortress first and had stopped. New-fallen snow, showing no signs of interruption, covered the narrow trail up into the mountains. When Alysta had demanded to know why they had stopped, the donkey had pointed his blunt nose at the fortress and told them where to look.

The building sat atop the mountain amid a thick copse of pine and spruce trees. The overcast sky didn't allow much sunlight to illuminate it.

The main structure was a tumbled-down wreck, and several buildings ringed it. Humans didn't build with the same care that elves and dwarves did. Their lives were fleet and filled with more violence than those of elves and dwarves, and even goblinkin. They had a tendency to build and abandon, seeking something new or different, or simply exhausting what the land had to give them in certain areas.

They also reproduced much more frequently than any race except the goblinkin. Elves planned each birth as a special event, and dwarves bore strong sons to help their fathers. The Old Ones had given the seas to the humans because the seas covered more space than the earth, which was given to the dwarves. The elves claimed the magic of the air, of the high and lofty places. And goblinkin had been birthed in fire.

As a result of the humans' proclivity for reproducing and moving around, the Shattered Coast and the islands were littered with abandoned homes and settlements. Few human cities lasted more than a few hundred years.

Upon viewing the fortress, Wick felt certain that it had been vacant much longer than it had been occupied. Fire had claimed the fortress at some point, burning away the wood and cracking the mortar. Piles of stone poured out into the snow, and most of those piles were covered by snow as well.

When it had been a place where people had lived, the fortress had four towers at the corners of the structure, flanked on both sides by guard towers. Now two of those towers had fallen, spilling across the fortress and the broken land that led up to it. Spruce and pine trees and brush had started to claim the area inside the broken fortress walls as well.

It was a place, Wick felt certain, that had been looted over and over again. Nothing could lay in that tangle of stone that hadn't been found. It wasn't possible.

We're on a fool's errand. Sickness twisted Wick's stomach and soured the back of his throat. *If Captain Dulaun's sword was ever here, it's surely gone by now.*

Smoke from three separate campfires curled into the leaden sky, mute testimony that someone was still there.

"The sword is still at the fortress," the cat said, as if guessing his thoughts.

"Do you know that for certain?"

"Why else would the Razor's Kiss thieves be here?" the cat asked. "Why else would we be here?"

Because we're idiots, Wick thought, but he refrained from saying that.

Turning away from the trail, hoping their arrival had gone unnoticed in the thick flurry of snow that continued to fall, Wick and his companions forged more deeply into the forest. Once they found a grade they could climb, Alysta and Wick left the donkey in a thick copse of trees that kept him out of the weather for the most part, and tied his feed-bag on for him. He was munching away, probably the only happy one of the group, when they headed up into the mountain.

The way was hard and made harder by the snowdrifts

that came as high as Wick's chest as he carried Alysta. But after a while, he broke through the last of them and made his way around to the cave Alysta had spotted on the western wall of the mountain.

The cave was small and shallow, more like a divot in the mountainside. It also smelled strongly of animal musk, indicating that it was sometimes a home for wild things. Thankfully, none of those were about at the moment.

Wick wanted a fire, but he knew the smoke would give away his presence. If the Razor's Kiss thieves hadn't already spotted him.

Instead, he tried to enjoy the relative comfort of the cave and tell himself that not having the wind blowing against him was good enough. For a while, he watched over the fortress.

The thieves kept a watch over the area, but it was too big for them to maintain properly. Also, they stayed busy poking about in the ruins.

There was no sign of Quarrel. Thinking about the young man, Wick wondered if he had been one of the victims he'd found last night. He regretted now not looking then, but then he hadn't wanted any more of those dead faces permanently painted in his memory.

"What are they looking for?" Wick whispered to the cat.

She sat beside him, her eyes busily watching the thieves as well. "Clams."

The reply jarred him. "Clams?"

The cat glanced at him with preening disdain. "What else do you think they'd be looking for?"

Wick grimaced. *You left yourself open for that.*

"Why don't you act like a Librarian?" the cat suggested.

"What do you mean?"

"You have Captain Gujhar's ship's log. Maybe you could *read* it and find out why the Razor's Kiss thieves are here."

Actually, Wick had been itching to read the books but hadn't thought Alysta would appreciate the effort. Rather than react to the sarcastic tone the cat had adopted, he reached into his pack and pulled out the book. Last night at Karbor's, Wick had labored through the man's crabbed handwriting (oh, for a raconteur who had been trained as a Librarian and could write neatly!) but hadn't been able to read too much in the weak light of the fireplace.

He'd started with the latest entries and worked his way backward. Most of those entries, though, had concentrated on Gujhar's search in and around Wharf Rat's Warren, mundane things. Before that, there had been the excavation by the goblinkin in the Cinder Clouds Islands.

In all, Wick decided that the captain kept rather good notes. But then, that was probably because whomever he represented demanded them that way.

He kept turning pages, leafing through narrative and illustrations. Alysta had come to peek over his shoulder as he sat on the cold stone floor on several occasions, but she'd walked away in obvious ignorance. Perhaps the cat had taught her daughter to read (a claim Wick still doubted somewhat), but she couldn't read the captain's hand or his language.

After a bit, he opened their provisions and ate jerked meat, feeding tidbits to Alysta without being asked. The cat didn't refuse the offerings.

Hours later, toward midafternoon, Wick found the answer they sought.

"After the Battle of Fell's Keep," Wick said, summing up what he had translated from the ship's log, "the goblinkin kept Seaspray for almost four hundred years. Then they lost the sword."

"To whom?" Alysta peered intently with her cat's eyes. Wick shook his head. "Captain Gujhar's narrative doesn't say. They only thing they were certain of was that Seaspray was taken by a man of Captain Dulaun's bloodline."

"But not his direct bloodline," Alysta said. "It was a descendant through another ancestor."

Wick looked at her. "You know more about this than you're telling."

"Keep reading," the cat said. "I would know more."

Closing the book, Wick returned the cat's measured gaze. Outside, the sky was starting to darken with twilight. "Tell me what you know."

"When I'm ready."

"No," Wick said, drawing on reserves of courage he hadn't known he'd had, "*now*." And those stores of courage evaporated even as he gave utterance to the word.

"*What?*" Alysta's ears flattened. Her furred face grew taut. She launched herself unexpectedly, catching Wick in the chest and knocking him backward. She remained atop him and unsheathed the claws on one paw. "Don't trifle with me, halfer! I would kill you for that!"

Wick lay stunned. He didn't know what to say, and he feared to make a move.

Alysta trembled. With a flick, her claws disappeared. "I'm sorry. I shouldn't have done that." Her tone carried contrite apology.

"No," Wick agreed. *You almost scared me to death.*

The cat walked off him, then sat and peered out the cave mouth. "I have been searching for that sword for a long time," she said in a voice barely above a whisper.

Cautiously, Wick sat up and picked up the book.

"I gave up more than you know, more than you could possibly comprehend, in the search for that sword," the cat went on.

"Why did you search for the sword?"

"Because finding that sword became entrusted to me. I'm of Captain Dulaun's bloodline, and my family is charged with returning that sword to his rightful heir.

There is only one out there now who can carry that sword and wield the magic in it. My granddaughter." Alysta's head rose proudly. "My time for it has past, but not my granddaughter's. She must carry the sword for us all."

Silent and eager, Wick listened and marveled at what was being revealed. Now that he knew this, he could guess at so much more.

"I swore upon my father's bedside that I would find that sword or die trying." Alysta shook her head. "Instead, it has come to this. I'm a cat."

"But you weren't always a cat."

"No. Once I was human. Once I was young and beautiful. But now . . . now I've grown old. And I'm no longer human. I gave up being a mother and a grandmother to pursue that sword."

"You taught your daughter to read," Wick said. "You told me that."

"I did," Alysta agreed. "But I never stayed to see if she taught her daughter to read. Then . . . then it was too late for all of us." She looked at Wick. "That's why the sword is so important. That's why I allowed myself a second life as a cat. So I could finish what I started. Or die trying. There's no other way for me to accept what I've done."

Wick thought about that, and he began to see the cat in a whole new light. "The man who stole the sword from the goblinkin—"

"Thango," the cat said.

"You're welcome," Wick said, thinking she was acknowledging his decision to reveal what he knew. "That man—"

"No," Alysta told him, "the man's name was Thango Enlark." She spelled it.

Wick took out his journal and wrote as he spoke, jotting down the gist of the information he'd distilled and guessed at. "Thango took the sword from the goblinkin down in the south, at a place called Pinanez Narrows."

"Where the Steadfast River flows out of the Forest of Fangs and Shadows," Alysta said. "I've been there. I'd even heard that Thango took back the sword there, but I couldn't confirm it."

"According to Captain Gujhar's notes, he did. The battle was bitter and bloody, and it took place over four days, a series of skirmishes that went up and down the Steadfast River." Wick drew illustrations of the river. He'd been to the Pinanez Narrows. The terrain came easily to hand, and so did the small figures engaged in battle. His craft with illustration was as good as his hand-writing. "Finally, though, Thango took possession of the sword."

"He always denied it," Alysta said bitterly. "My ances-tors, the true ones to whom the sword belonged, didn't believe him. But they couldn't prove elsewise. So they searched for him, and they searched for the sword. Given our destiny, our lives were always at risk."

The little Wick had read about the search for the sword bore out the truth of that statement.

"Soon there were more funerals than births," the cat went on, "till our line came down to just my father. He sired me and an older brother, then they were killed by goblinkin. I held my brother in my arms as he died, and on that day I gave up hunting for the sword for years. I met a man I could love, settled down, and had a daughter. I struggled not to feel that I was betraying my heritage, and I didn't tell my daughter or my husband who I truly was."

Wick turned the page and sketched the cat, drawn by the melancholy that clung to her. Her large eyes were pitiful.

"But then a rumor reached me," Alysta said quietly. "A whisper. Nothing more. But someone said the Razor's Kiss in Wharf Rat's Warren was searching for Seaspray, and that they knew where Boneslicer and Deathwhisper were as well. If all three weapons were being searched for, I knew something terrible was about to happen."

The wind stirred the snow outside the cave and chased it inside.

"I was old by that time. Truly too old to do what I did.

I'd buried my husband five years before that. Maybe if he'd been alive I would have stayed. You'd think that a daughter and a granddaughter would be enough to keep me."

"But it wasn't," Wick whispered. He made no accusation; just stated fact.

"But it wasn't," Alysta agreed. "My blood is drawn to that sword. I told my daughter and my granddaughter who we were, and what our legacy was." Pride glinted in the cat's eyes. "My daughter was afraid. She didn't want me to go. She said that a thousand years lost was forever. But my granddaughter—" Pride and pain thickened her voice.

Listening to her speak, knowing that Alysta was once more in those days in her mind, Wick felt tears in his eyes.

"My granddaughter was only a child, but she promised me that if I didn't find the sword, she would. If I had fallen, my granddaughter would have taken up the hunt. She never got the chance." The cat's voice broke. "The goblinkin killed her mother and father just a few years ago. She was lost. *My* granddaughter was lost." The pain echoed in her words. "And I'm here with you, hoping that you can lead me to Seaspray, that I can at least redeem myself that way."

"If there's no one in your bloodline left," Wick said, "what good will it—"

"Perhaps another bloodline can carry the sword now that my bloodline has ended," Alysta said. "I think that might be true. By the Old Ones, I *hope* that is true."

Silence filled the cave for a time, and kept even the wind and the cold at bay.

Finally, Wick could no longer control his curiosity. "How did you become a cat?"

"I got into a battle with a band of goblinkin near Hanged Elf's Point. I'd gone there to get information about the Razor's Kiss guild because I'd heard they made port there.

I'm old, and my body at that time had seen nearly all of its years after all the hardship I'd put it through."

After only begetting two generations? The thought struck Wick as odd until he remembered Alysta had been human. They were the only race that didn't live to see many generations of offspring.

"The goblinkin took me down and mortally wounded me," Alysta said. "I was near death when they closed in on me. I lay there helpless and dying, with nothing I could do to defend myself. They would have cooked and eaten me, except Craugh arrived."

"Craugh?"

Alysta nodded, and the response looked strange coming from a cat. "That was when I first met him." She paused. "I'd heard of him, of course. His name is spoken in all the dark places throughout the Shattered Coast, and there are many who fear him."

Not without reason, Wick thought.

"To my surprise, he knew who I was," Alysta said, "and he knew what I searched for. He slew most of the goblinkin, and those he didn't slay he drove away. He is fierce in battle, and he will neither give nor ask quarter."

Wick had seen the wizard in battle a few times. Alysta's assessment of Craugh was fair.

"Afterwards," Alysta said calmly, "he told me I was dying. Of course, I already knew that. He asked me what I was doing. I told him I was searching for the sword, for Seaspray. He told me that was a worthwhile cause, something that he had an interest in as well. When he offered to put me into the body of this cat, which was all he could do, I accepted."

"The cat died in your place?" Wick wasn't entirely happy with that possibility.

"No." Alysta hesitated. "Craugh made this body with his magic. Scooped up some earth and shaped it into what you see before you. I'm not flesh and blood, Librarian. I'm something else."

"And Dawdal?" Wick asked.

"I don't know what Dawdal is. Perhaps he's only a talking donkey. But once, he told me when he'd been eating fermented berries, he'd been a toad for a few years because he'd angered Craugh."

Wick absently drew a toad with incredibly long ears and a toothy grin. He thought it favored Dawdal well.

"Since that time I've hunted Seaspray." The cat stared out at the fortress. "I've never been closer to finding it."

Quietly, Wick said, "Seaspray is here."

"You're sure?"

"I am." Wick gazed out at the ruins of the fortress. "When Thango Enlark fled, he came here and built a small keep."

"Why?"

Wick tapped the book. "If Captain Gujhar knew, he didn't write why."

"That is Thango's keep?"

"No. Thango's keep is buried beneath those ruins. At least, his keep is beneath one of those ruins somewhere in these mountains. Since the Razor's Kiss has concentrated their efforts on that one, I would guess those ruins would be where Thango held the sword."

"Is Seaspray still there?"

"Captain Gujhar and the Razor's Kiss believe so. According to what I've read, Thango concealed the sword within a maze of hidden walls and secret passages."

"That explains the need for the thieves."

"Yes," Wick said, thinking of the tricks and deadly traps that probably lay in wait.

"Then we must go there," Alysta said.

A sinking sensation dawned in Wick's stomach. He knew the cat was going to say that. But he had to admit to some concerns himself. According to a few of the notes in *Wraith*'s ship's log, Thango had assembled a small library of books about arms and armament. He desperately wanted to find those and get them back to the Vault of All Known Knowledge.

"Tonight," the cat said, watching the thieves prowling through the ruins.

Glancing at the sun, Wick saw that the time was only a few hours off. He made himself eat, not knowing if he would find an appetite. But he did.

12

At Sword's Point

If they catch us there, they'll kill us." Wick hadn't said that once for all the hours he'd thought it, but he couldn't let it go unsaid any longer.

"Then," Alysta said calmly, "it would be in our better interests not to get caught."

Wick refrained from further comment as they made their way down the mountainside. Thankfully the trees stayed thick, but creeping through the snow was difficult, especially when it reached to Wick's chest. Even worse, when he looked back he saw that the trail he left was clearly marked.

The Razor's Kiss thieves kept guards stationed around the perimeters of the fortress ruins, but none of them ventured much past. Campfires lit the interior of the ruins and created long shadows that danced against the stone structures and piles.

The men talked in low voices.

Alysta leaped through the snow and occasionally fell through, but never for long. Dawdal had remained at their camp.

They stayed with the trees and went past the fortress, then hooked back around, following along the broken coastline till it met the outer perimeter wall. The stones hadn't been set flush, and the mortar had cracked and fallen away. There were plenty of hand- and footholds.

Swallowing the sour taste of his fear, steadying himself and hoping the night kept him in its shelter, Wick followed the cat up the wall. They climbed twenty feet up till they reached the top.

Wick hung by his fingertips, cautiously peering over the edge in case a guard had been stationed there. The way was clear.

"Come on," the cat hissed, barely audible over the wind that rushed in from the seaside. They had made their way back around to the coastline farther south where the keep had been.

Throwing a leg over, Wick pulled himself up and onto the top, then hunkered down in the shadows. During the climb, his hands had gotten cold. His bare feet had proven up to the task and to the chill touch of the stones, but he was always protective of his hands. The thought of losing his hands, even a finger, terrified him. There would be so many things he couldn't do.

He shoved his hands under his armpits to warm them, then crept around the wall till he could look down into the Razor's Kiss camp.

"Someone's coming," Alysta said.

From his vantage point, Wick saw a line of riders coming up the trail he and his companions had taken earlier. *Something important brought them out at this time of night*, he thought. He hid behind the low crenellation atop the wall and watched.

Two of the eight riders carried torches. The flames stood out hard and bright against the darkness. The men in the camp greeted the new arrivals and brought them into their camp.

Wick studied the men and discovered Captain Gujhar was among them. He also recognized another of the Razor's Kiss members. There was no mistaking Ryman Bey, the leader of the thieves' guild.

Ryman Bey was a lean man of medium height, with

nondescript features save for the ruined right eye he hid under a crimson leather patch embroidered with a straight razor. His long hair brushed his shoulders, and he wore expensive black clothing.

All it would take, Wick realized, was a change of clothing and the distinctive eye patch, and Ryman Bey would disappear in a crowd.

Bey and Gujhar talked to the men in the camp only for a short time, then disappeared into an entrance in one of the tumble-down buildings.

"What place is that?" Alysta whispered.

Wick pictured the sketches he'd seen in the ship's log. Gujhar had maps of Thango's keep as well as the later structures. "It was the main house. It was located almost directly over Thango's keep."

"There are piles of earth around that building," Alysta said. "Some of it is fresh-turned."

Wick noted the dark earth staining the new-fallen snow then. The cat's eyes were better than his. Several wheelbarrows stood nearby.

"They've been excavating," the cat said. "We need to get in there."

"The entrance is too well guarded."

"There has to be a way. We have to get in. They didn't bring Ryman Bey and Gujhar out here for no reason."

Fearfully, Wick followed the cat as she padded through the snow piled atop the wall. At least there were no footprints in the snow, no sign that anyone else had come this way. Hopefully that meant they wouldn't encounter a guard.

Several long minutes later, the cat found a set of broken steps leading down to the ground level. After a brief pause, Alysta headed down the snow-covered steps. Wick's breath blew out gray but the wind quickly tore it away. The snow made the steps slippery, but he took care.

On the ground, they remained behind broken piles of stone and went soundlessly. The Razor's Kiss thieves remained hovering around the hissing campfires under the thin shelter of oilskin tarps that kept most of the falling snowflakes from the flames.

Despite his observation of the thieves around their campfires, Wick got the distinct impression he was being watched. He halted in the inky shadow of a broken wall and listened. In the humid winter air, sound carried farther.

"I'll be glad when they finally find that sword," one of the thieves grumbled. "I thought they'd have by now for sure."

"I'm in no hurry to see it," another thief said. "The way I hear it, there's a curse on that sword. Anybody who touches it is doomed to die soon after."

"I'm not touching it," a third thief said.

"What are you going to do if Ryman Bey orders you to carry it back to Wharf Rat's Warren?" the first asked.

The man cursed. "I'll take my chances with the curse. Not with Ryman Bey. He carries more blades on him than the number of years he's lived."

The other two men agreed. One of them threw another piece of wood on the fire, starting a brief stream of sparks that leaped into the air.

"I just hope this new place they found doesn't have the sword, either," the first man said.

"That man Gujhar thinks it does, though."

Wick leaned against the wall at his back and kept his breathing slow. If the Razor's Kiss found Seaspray, they would take the magical weapon and go. He wouldn't be able to catch them or take the sword away.

He gazed around the snow-covered inner courtyard and saw three other entrances. He suspected there were more. But all of the ones he saw now looked like they hadn't been entered in weeks.

Except for two of them.

Wick's eyes narrowed as he studied the trail leading into those entrances. Had the thieves gone that way of late? Snow nearly covered the footprints. Before morning, they would be completely disguised again.

At that moment, a shadow stepped into view at the end of the wall. The man held a sword naked in his fist. When he saw Wick, he grinned.

Fear washed through Wick, leaving him more frozen than the weather for a moment. He'd been discovered.

"Well, well, halfer," the man taunted. "I cut your trail back there while I was headed to the privy. I knew somebody was out here. Wouldn't have thought it was you. Figured you'd be too smart to come here again."

Desperately, Wick looked around for an escape path. None presented itself. As soon as he ran, even if he proved more fleet than the thief in the snow, the others would run him down.

"Heard from one of our new arrivals that you'd escaped Gujhar." The thief took another step closer. "He wouldn't admit to it, but there was plenty who saw you. Too bad you didn't have enough sense to stay away from us." He gestured with the sword. "Get over now, or I'll kill you where you cower."

I, Wick thought, *am having no luck at all when it comes to staying concealed.*

Beside him, Alysta cursed and spat. She padded around him and headed for the thief. "Get ready to run," the cat said.

Wick slowly stood.

"You've got a talking cat?" the thief asked.

"A m-m-magical cat," Wick stuttered. "She knows spells."

"Then why is she a cat?" the thief asked.

Alysta chose that instant to spring for the man's throat, claws silvered by the moonlight. The thief swiped at her with his sword but missed. He staggered back under her attack, throwing up his free hand to protect his face as she scratched again and again. The thief screamed in fear and pain, crying out for assistance.

"Run!" Alysta shouted.

For a moment, Wick didn't know which direction to run. The wall seemed too far away, and hiding behind the broken structures of the inner courtyard would only delay the inevitable. He took two steps one way, then two steps in the other, and noticed that he was running in the direction of the thieves, who had left their campfires and were coming on the double.

"The wall!" Alysta shouted as she climbed on top of the flailing thief's head and kept slashing.

Wick yelled in terror before he realized he was wasting his breath and stopped. He devoted his energies to running. Glancing back over his shoulder, he saw two of the thieves drawing back knives to throw.

"Get down!" a voice ordered.

A foot darted out in front of Wick and tripped him, sending him sprawling through the snow. The throwing knives shot by overhead. He rolled and tried to get to his feet at once.

"Stay down if you want to live." Quarrel nocked an arrow to string while he stood behind a tall column, then turned and took aim at the rushing thieves. The young man had three other arrows fisted in his left hand holding the bow. As smoothly as Tongarian spidersilk, Quarrel released the first arrow, flipped the next around to the string, drew the fletchings back to his ear, and released again. In the space of a man's exhaled breath, the young archer had three arrows in the air.

All of the arrows hit their targets with meaty thunks. In quick succession, three of the Razor's Kiss thieves tumbled to the ground, hit dead center in their chests.

Wick was impressed. He'd seldom seen archery so swift and certain outside of elven warders.

The surviving Razor's Kiss thieves scattered, taking cover behind broken buildings, scattered piles of stone, and a few of the larger trees that had taken root inside the inner courtyard.

Thinking quickly, Wick felt confident that three of the thieves were either dead or dying. Originally, ten of the Razor's Kiss thieves had ridden out to the ruins. They'd been joined by seven more, including Ryman Bey. Gujhar made eighteen. That number was down to fifteen.

Even as he thought that, though, Quarrel put another arrow into the chest of the man fighting to get Alysta from his head. The man was dead before he hit the ground, and Alysta jumped free of the body as it fell. Immediately, arrows followed the cat but hit the ground well short of her.

Then an arrow fired by one of the thieves thudded into the snow-covered ground only inches from Wick's head. *Not good*, he thought.

"Get over here," Quarrel ordered. He knelt and whirled around the stone column, drawing and firing again effortlessly. His arrow just missed the man who'd fired at Wick.

Scrabbling through the snow, in truth staying under it most of the way, Wick joined Quarrel and hunkered down. Arrows from the thieves shattered against the column or whistled by.

"We can't stay here," Quarrel said.

Wick agreed, but he looked around. "Where did the cat go?"

"The cat?" Quarrel shrugged and peered around the column, then ducked back as an arrow glanced off, narrowly missing him.

"I had a cat with me," Wick said.

"Whatever for?"

"Because she wanted to come."

"Why couldn't you have picked a bear?" Quarrel asked. "A bear would be more of a deterrent than a cat."

"I didn't exactly have a choice in the matter."

Muffled voices reached their ears.

"They're going to surround us." Quarrel looked around, rolling to his right and drawing the fletchings back to his ear. He released and Wick saw one of the thieves drop to the ground.

More cursing suddenly filled the air. Shouts of promised revenge followed the dying man's last cries.

"We'll never reach the wall," Wick said. "Even if we did, they'd pursue us."

"I've no intention of leaving here till I get what I came for."

"Seaspray?"

Quarrel looked at Wick. The young man's eyes narrowed. He looked even younger with his smooth face. A beard or a mustache would have added more maturity.

"What do you know about Seaspray?" Quarrel demanded.

"Practically nothing," Wick lied.

Quarrel shook his head. "I knew I should have let the thieves kill you."

"Actually," Wick said, changing his mind when he thought it wouldn't be any trouble for Quarrel to boot him out into the open and use him for a distraction while he made his own escape, "I know a lot."

"What do you know?" Quarrel's gaze was filled with challenge.

"I have a map of the keep that was here before this fortress."

"Where?"

Wick took out the ship's log and tapped the cover. "Here."

"Give it to me."

Taking a step back, Wick hid the book once more in his cloak. "No. You'll leave me out here."

Quarrel showed him a thin-lipped smile. "Perhaps."

"Are the two of you going to stand here and natter all day?" The cat sat atop a heap of stones only a few feet away. She looked no worse for wear despite her fight. "Or do you think possibly you could avoid getting killed or captured?"

"A talking cat?" Quarrel asked.

"It's not as amazing as it sounds," Wick said. "And not nearly worth the trouble, I tell you."

"They're coming," Alysta said.

"Follow me." Quarrel turned and ran, staying low and within the shadows.

Wick trailed after the young man. They ran a zigzag trail through the tumbled buildings of the inner courtyard. Some of the statues of people and creatures startled Wick. He hadn't seen those in his earlier observations.

Quarrel cut across other trails, confusing their own tracks with those of others. He obviously had a destination in mind, but he took a circuitous route to it. Finally he headed into one of the doorways that opened a throat down into the earth.

With the dank moldering smell all around him, Wick couldn't help feeling he was descending into an open grave. Broken rock lay strewn about. Snow had blown in through the entrance and sat in heaps.

Inside the chamber, the thieves' voices reached Wick's ears more readily. They'd gotten confused and anxious, becoming more certain their quarry had somehow managed to escape.

"Did they get over the wall, then?" someone asked.

"If they'd gone over the wall, we'd have seen them," another answered.

"They're still here," another voice, more commanding in tone, announced. "They're hiding. Spread out and find them. I want to know who they are and what they're doing here."

"Ryman Bey," Quarrel whispered in the quiet of the chamber.

Wick had assumed that. "What are we going to do?"

Quarrel frowned at him. "I should have let them kill you."

"Perhaps they wouldn't have killed us," Alysta replied.

Quarrel snorted derisively. "They'd have killed you."

"Then you were a fool to interfere," the cat accused.

Ignoring the comment, Quarrel slid his bow over his

shoulder and drew his sword. He stared at Wick. "Let's have another look at that book."

Wick hesitated.

Quick as a wink, Quarrel placed his blade tip at the little Librarian's throat. "Now would not be a time to vex me, halfer." Even though his voice was soft, there was no lack of menace in it.

13

To the Dungeon

Swallowing hard, feeling the keen edge pressed up against his neck, Wick weighed his chances. Everything in him that was a Librarian (which was *everything* in him) screamed out not to surrender the book. It held clues to the person who had sent Captain Gujhar in search of the three magic weapons that had been at the Battle of Fell's Keep. The pages offered hints at where Seaspray was located.

And it might even tell what was at stake, why the weapons were being gathered after Lord Kharrion had fallen and a thousand years had gone by.

"Your word," Wick bargained in a croaking voice.

Quarrel stared at him in surprise over the length of sword steel between them. "What?"

"Your word," Wick repeated. "Before I give you the book, I want your word."

"On what? That I won't kill you?" Quarrel nodded. "Done."

Wick knew that was no trade. Quarrel had already risked his life to save his. He didn't think the young man would just as quickly take it. Even if he did have a sword at his throat.

"Your word that you will give the book back to me," Wick said.

Quarrel cursed. "You bargain too far, halfer. I could just as easily pluck the book off your dead body."

"And I could just as easily start yowling and draw the Razor's Kiss thieves down on you," Alysta said.

Silence stretched between them for an instant.

"Perfidious cat," Quarrel snarled.

Alysta sat on her haunches a safe distance away, her tail curled around her paws. "That's just one of my more endearing qualities," she replied. Her large eyes winked in amusement.

"Do we have a bargain?" Wick asked.

Quarrel didn't answer.

Alysta purred, on the verge of a yowl. "Don't mind me," she said. "I'm just tuning up my voice."

Heaving a great sigh, Quarrel dropped the sword from Wick's neck. "Old Ones preserve me, the two of you don't know what you're in for or what I've had to do to get this far." He gestured with his free hand. "Very well, you've got my word. Now let's have a look at that book."

Relaxing a little, Wick took the ship's log from his cloak and handed it over.

Quarrel sheathed the sword and took the book in both hands. "Where did you get this?"

"From *Wraith*."

"How?"

Wick related the story of the escape from the goblinkin ship (perhaps playing up the nearness of the escape and his amount of derring-do a little, but he felt entitled since it *was* his story) and his subsequent journey to the ruins. The cat hissed at several of the more fragrant points, but offered no comment. As he talked, Quarrel walked more deeply into the chamber.

Wick was grimly aware that the thieves could enter the tunnel at any time. He wondered how far back the tunnel went. As narrow and barren as it was, there didn't appear to be many places to hide. Defending their position was out of the question; all the thieves had to do was starve them out.

Two turns later, Quarrel stopped in a work area that Wick could barely discern in the low light. Quarrel, with only his human's eyesight, had to trail a hand along the tunnel's side to find his way. In the work area, a lantern hung on the wall. Using a tinderbox on a shelf near the lantern, the young man lit the lantern.

The soft yellow glow filled the work area.

Quarrel opened the book and leafed through the pages. "I can't read it," he admitted.

"You can read?" Wick asked, surprised when he thought he wasn't going to be any further surprised.

"Yes." Quarrel frowned at the pages as he continued turning them. "But not this."

"The halfer can read it," Alysta said.

Quarrel looked at Wick. "Is that true?"

Blabbermouth, Wick thought at the cat. He sighed. "Yes."

"How?"

"With my eyes," Wick said. He didn't mention that he could also read with his fingers, by scent, by sound, and even by taste. After all, he was in training to be a First Level Librarian.

"That's not what I meant." Quarrel looked exasperated.

"Oh."

"Who taught you to read?"

"Someone," Wick answered.

Quarrel shook his head. "Fine. Keep those secrets. But not this one. Can you read this?"

"Yes."

"What does it say?"

"I haven't read all of it. There wasn't time." Wick glared at the cat, indicating that lack was purely her fault. Alysta just winked at him in disdain and wrinkled her nose. If Quarrel caught the look, he gave no indication.

"But it talks about Seaspray?" Quarrel asked.

Wick nodded. "The text refers to Seaspray and Bone-slicer and Deathwhisper."

Quarrel frowned. "All of the weapons that were at the Battle of Fell's Keep."

"Yes." Wick was quietly surprised that the young man knew so much about the weapons. He wanted to ask how Quarrel had come about that knowledge, but he didn't dare.

"Why?"

"I don't know. The captain of *Wraith*, a man named Gujhar, was sent to retrieve them." Wick almost added that he'd been on hand when Boneslicer was taken.

"For what reason?"

"I don't know. Yet."

"Who sent him?"

Shaking his head, Wick said, "I don't know that, either."

"Perhaps the ship's log will reveal that."

"That's what we're hoping."

" 'We?' "

Wick pointed to Alysta. "The cat and I."

"How did you become partners?"

Alysta interrupted. "Do you think we really have time to talk about this now? The thieves outside aren't going to give up looking for us."

"She's right," Wick said.

Quarrel held the book closer to the light. Wick had to hold his tongue. In the Vault of All Known Knowledge, flames weren't used. Illumination was provided by lummin juice from glimmerworms. Several dwellers, Wick's father among them, raised glimmerworms.

The young man flipped the ship's log till he found the maps of the ruins. He studied them.

"The thieves gave up on this site," Quarrel said, "but I felt that something more was hidden here." He placed a finger against the map. "What's this?"

Wick peered at the page. The small picture at the edge of the old keep Thango had built was of a ship with full-bellied sails.

"It's a ship," Wick said.

"Here in the mountains?"

"Perhaps there's a cave at the bottom of the mountain that leads to the sea," Wick said.

"I've been there," Quarrel said. "I didn't see a passage to a cave."

"Maybe you didn't know what you were looking for," Alysta suggested. "In any event, staying here only makes us increasingly vulnerable. It's better if we put some distance between us and our foes."

Wick was antsy, too, eager to be moving.

"I'll take you to this spot," Quarrel stated. He handed the ship's log back to Wick. "Let's go."

Carrying the lantern, his sword naked in his fist, Quarrel led the way down into the ruins. Looking around at the layers of earth that had piled on top of the past structures, Wick was reminded of the caves in the Cinder Clouds Islands. How much history had been lost in the world even before the Cataclysm? At one time, writing hadn't existed. It troubled him to think of how many people's stories would never be told.

Down and down they went, following Quarrel and the swinging lantern. Soon, though, he halted at an opening.

"We'll have to go easily from this point on." Quarrel shined the lantern into the next section. "This leads to Thango's main house. To the dungeon area. There are a number of passages. They are in relatively good shape."

"Hold on." Wick opened the book, knowing from memory where the map of the pre-existing keep was. He studied the drawing for a moment, looking at the scale at the bottom of the page.

"The opening to the dungeon is ahead." Quarrel held the lantern closer.

Instinctively, Wick pulled the book back from the lantern's heat. "The dungeon wasn't filled in?"

"I don't think anyone even knew it was here before Gujhar and the thieves found it."

"You've been there?"

"I have."

"Did you see a ship?" Alysta asked.

"No."

"Was there a passage down to a cave at the bottom of the mountain?"

"There still is," Quarrel replied.

"Could that be the ship on the map?" the cat asked. "A reference to a hidden port?"

Wick thought about that. Several cities and keeps had smugglers' paths. Contraband existed everywhere, though it was generally goods that the sellers and buyers didn't want to pay heavy taxes on. He trailed a finger down the map, tracing the passageway marked on the paper.

If the passageway led to a secret port, why wasn't the ship drawn at the bottom of the passage rather than the top? That troubled him.

"There's nothing there," Quarrel said.

Wick read through the script under the picture. "According to these notes, Gujhar—or whoever he works for—is convinced that this room holds a secret of some sort."

"What secret?"

"It doesn't say."

"What's in that room?" Alysta asked.

"Nothing." Quarrel looked disgusted. "If Seaspray was ever in that room, it's long gone. That was probably the secret."

"Then why hasn't the sword ever been found since Thango brought it here?" Alysta asked.

"Perhaps Seaspray has been destroyed." Quarrel sighed.

The cat looked at him. "Do you believe that?"

Hesitation showed on Quarrel's smooth face. "I hope it's not true."

"Why?"

Quarrel's eyes narrowed. "Because I want that sword."

Alysta hissed in displeasure. "You can't always have what you want, boy."

"Let's go have a look at this room," Wick suggested, hoping to remind the others why they were there. "Provided we get out of here alive, I'll wager we don't get many chances to come back this way."

"Agreed," Quarrel replied.

The cat sniffed.

Quarrel turned back to the open area. "This excavation gives us a way to reach the dungeon entrance. After we enter that, the way becomes much more dangerous. Not all of the traps have been sprung."

Traps? Wick thought. *There are traps?* Then he sighed. Of course there were traps. There *had* to be traps. He wondered if Craugh and the crew of *One-Eyed Peggie* were near. He hoped that they were because the situation at the moment didn't look good.

The entrance to the dungeon was a hole in the floor set next to an excavation wall. Obviously the excavation had been done some time in the past because the wood was rotting. New braces had been set into place over the old ones, but nothing about it looked safe.

"Will it hold?" Wick asked nervously.

"There are no guarantees," Quarrel replied. He ducked down and climbed down into the dungeon.

When the light left with the young mercenary, Wick realized he was about to be left standing in the dark. He stepped into the entrance and followed Quarrel down.

Steps cut into the wall led down at least twenty feet. Wick judged that by the fact that the steps were each about eight inches high and there were thirty-two steps in all. The actual height was twenty-one feet and four inches, but he didn't quibble. It made for a solid shelf of rock overhead, even with the generous headroom.

"Carefully through here." Quarrel shined the lantern around, revealing the iron-barred cages set in the wall to the right.

Rats ran among the bones of the deceased. No flesh remained on the ivory underpinnings, but there were several insects that lived in the detritus left by those who had tramped through the dungeon looking for Dulaun's lost magical sword. They protested the invasion of the light with high-pitched squeaks.

It was obvious that those who had opposed Thango had met bad endings once they'd fallen in his hands.

Past the four prison cells, the torture room offered a glimpse into past horrors. Two iron baskets held skeletons. Other skeletons hung from chains set into the wall.

"I take it Thango wasn't the forgiving type," Wick commented.

"No," Alysta said. "By all accounts, he was a vindictive man even before his frustration with Seaspray."

"What do you know about the sword?" Quarrel asked.

"More than you do."

Quarrel grimaced, but thought better of saying anything. He turned and followed the lantern again. He stopped against a wall on the other side of the torture chamber.

"I found a secret passage here." Quarrel hung the lantern on a nearby hook, then put his hands on the wall and pushed on two separate stones. "The thieves had found it before me. They'd found more than a few of them, but they left some of them untripped and set to catch anyone who happened upon the way and wasn't wary."

Wick surveyed the map and saw that a passage did go on past the area on the drawing that he now knew to be the torture chamber. At that same moment, a section of the wall turned to a ninety-degree angle, swinging on concealed hinges. Grinding filled the room and echoed down the hallway ahead.

"It leads to the room with the secret passageway to the sea." Moving cautiously, Quarrel entered the passageway. He kept his sword at hand and moved with cautious speed.

Only a short distance ahead, a skeleton in tattered

clothing stood pinned against a wall, pierced by a long metal shaft. A callous later visitor had used one of the skeleton's eye sockets as a candle sconce. Melted wax filled the empty space and wept waxy tears down the cheekbone into the soundless scream of the mouth.

"Evidently Thango wasn't simply protecting his wine cellar," Alysta said.

The next trap was a yawning pit with sharpened metal stakes at the bottom. It was ten feet across, built so that an unwary man couldn't just stretch out and save himself as he fell. It also held a dead man at the bottom amid the other bones of past victims. The dead man had evidently been in that condition for months.

"Did you know him?" Wick asked.

"No. As I said, there have been a lot of luckless that came this way in the past."

"Oh." Wick tore his eyes away from the sight with effort.

Quarrel looped the lantern to his hip with a piece of rope, then made his way across by way of the pegs sticking out from the wall. He made the crossing look effortless.

Wick tucked the ship's log into his cloak and reached down for the cat. Alysta flattened her ears, raised a paw in warning, and hissed.

"Do you think you can navigate that climb unassisted?" Wick asked reasonably.

Grudgingly, the cat hissed again and lowered her paw. Instead of letting Wick lift her, though, she ran up his arm and spread herself across his shoulders.

"All right," she said.

14

Hiding Place

Wick stepped onto the first peg at his feet and reached for the ones well above his head. He was barely able to reach, and felt certain if the climb had been a long one he wouldn't have had the strength or endurance to manage it. The cat's weight across his shoulders further increased the difficulty.

Quarrel waited on the other side of the chasm, holding the lantern to better light the way.

Making the journey without incident, Wick stepped down onto the next ledge. Without a word, Quarrel turned and they went on.

Ahead, bones lay in scattered disarray beneath four axe blades that had swung out from both walls, the floor, and the ceiling. All of them had been set off by a weight-activated stone. Now the axe blades were heavily rusted and falling to pieces.

"Some of the traps sprung themselves over the years," Quarrel said, indicating a crumbled section of wall. He directed the light inside to reveal the rusty shards that had once been steel spikes. "The traps that relied on venomous snakes hold only dead things now, but there are some venomous spiders that have propagated down here and done well."

Suddenly aware of the cobwebs that lay against the back of his neck, Wick flailed at the webs and shivered.

"Also, the traps armed with acid and poison might have diluted over the centuries, but they can still poison you or make you sick." Quarrel went on.

Down and down they went, sometimes on inclined hallways and sometimes by way of corkscrew stairs. Evidently the dungeon had a few levels.

"I'm taking us to that room," Quarrel explained. "The one on the map. By the safest route possible. It's not necessarily the shortest."

Wick's legs ached from the effort of walking. With all the floor changes, he was reminded of the Vault of All Known Knowledge. A much gloomier version of the Great Library, to be sure, but just as serpentine.

Along the way, they passed several other victims of the traps left scattered throughout the dungeon levels. Many of them were scattered literally instead of merely figuratively.

Thango's trap designers were very thorough, Wick noted grimly.

Only a little while later, they reached the room that was supposed to have held Thango's greatest secret.

"Stay here," Quarrel said. "This room, more than all the others, continues to be dangerous." He held up the lantern. "Each time a person leaves this room, the traps reset themselves. More than that, they move around, shifting where they are and what they do."

"Wizardry?" Wick asked. In the romances in Hralbomm's Wing there had been any number of stories about moveable traps. All of them had been fueled by magic.

"I don't know. It has to be." Quarrel walked into the room slowly and began lighting other lanterns hanging on the wall. When he touched one of them, a section of the opposite wall popped open and a crossbow fell into position. It fired automatically and the bolt leaped across the space.

Quarrel dodged out of the way. The sharp blade, not

blemished at all by rust, smacked into the wall right where the young man had been standing.

"Forgot about that one," Quarrel admitted. He went through the room and turned off five other traps. "That's not all of them, but it will allow you to enter and look at the passageway down to the sea."

With the lanterns lit, the room stood revealed. Instead of a simple stone floor, this one held a patchwork of blue and black tiles measuring two feet square. It looked like a giant chessboard. When Wick counted the tiles, he found they were arranged eight by eight, exactly like a chessboard. A bloodred border ran around the room.

Friezes decorated the walls, depicting human heroes in battles on the land on snow-covered mountains as well as in rich woodlands, and on the sea. Ships under full sail were frozen in battle against others while sea monsters roared up from the depths.

Cautiously, and curiously, Wick peered into the room. "Maybe I could just stay out here," he suggested. "Like you said, if there was something here to find, you would have already found it."

"Then why did we come down here?" Quarrel sounded angry. "I've already been down here. I could be looking in other places."

"No," Alysta said, easing into the room. "What we seek is here. Somewhere."

"The sword?" Quarrel walked toward the cat.

Despite his trepidation, Wick's curiosity about the friezes drew him into the large room. He stayed to the outside walls as well, circling the chessboard floor. "Is the floor booby-trapped?"

"Yes," Quarrel answered. His attention remained on the cat. "What makes you certain the sword is still here?"

The cat padded silently to the wall with the image of the sea battles. "I can *feel* it."

"You can't do that." Quarrel approached the frieze as well.

Alysta stretched up and touched the frieze. "I can."

Wick studied the frieze. There was something familiar about it. In seconds, his fear was forgotten. The frieze wasn't merely carved into the stone wall. Shaped colored stones were set into the hollows, bringing more immediate color to the images.

Looking around the room, Wick saw that none of the other friezes were like that. He wondered why this one was different. He took one of the lanterns from the wall and walked closer, studying the images.

Then it came to him.

"This is the Battle of the Dancing Waves," Wick whispered.

"What?" Quarrel demanded.

"The Battle of the Dancing Waves." Wick touched the frieze. "Of course, it wasn't called that at the time. It was just a skirmish between Captain Dulaun's ship, *Tolamae*, and a pirate ship called *Death's Grin*." He pointed at the flag on the second vessel, almost lost in gray fog.

"I've never heard of the battle or those ships," Quarrel said.

"I have," Alysta said. "It's an old story. Handed down to me by my father, and his father before him. This was the battle where Dulaun harnessed the power of the waves with Seaspray for the first time."

"That's right." Wick scanned *Tolamae* and saw Dulaun standing on her foredeck with his sword pointing straight into the air. The ship's captain was spare and lean, a man long hardened by the sun and the sea. His brown hair had streaks in it. He wore rolled-top black boots, tight black breeches, and a blue and red striped shirt. "That's Captain Dulaun."

Quarrel peered at the man's image made up of specially selected stones. "He's not as tall as I'd thought he would be."

"No," Wick said, remembering the pictures he'd seen of the human. "Dulaun wasn't heroic in stature, but in his heart. He never once gave up."

"Dulaun was killed in the Battle of Fell's Keep," Quarrel said. "When the dwarven blacksmith Oskarr betrayed the Unity defenders who stayed to protect the evacuation of the southern Teldane's Bounty."

"Master Oskarr didn't betray them," Wick said.

"That's the way I've always heard it told," Quarrel said.

"So have I," Alysta said.

"I only recently learned that story was false," Wick said, remembering the time he'd spent in Master Oskarr's forge. Neither of his listeners appeared interested in his opinion.

"This could be the ship the map referred to," Alysta said.

"I'd already thought of that," Quarrel said. "But what would that have to do with the sword?"

"It was during this battle that Captain Dulaun harnessed the power of the sea for the first time," Wick repeated. "The Old Ones gave the power of the water to humans, and those powers were invested in a few weapons made by humans. Seaspray was one of those enchanted creations. While locked in this battle, coming to the aid of a stricken merchant, *Tolamae* and her crew were vastly outnumbered by pirates from the Cage Islands. For a time, it looked like the end."

"But Dulaun used the sword, right?" Quarrel asked.

"They say Dulaun had always been blessed by the Old Ones," Wick said. "That from the day of his birth he was destined to be a hero. He'd studied the ways of the sea, and when he forged the sword himself, he asked the Old Ones to infuse it with power. The way most scholars interpret it, Dulaun asked only that the sword not break during a battle. Instead, given the way he led his life and tried to champion those not able to stand up for themselves, he was given much more."

"He commanded the seas that day," Alysta said. "When he thought all was lost, he stood upon that deck and hoped that the sea would rise up and swallow his enemies. It did."

As he listened to the cat speaking, Wick felt a curious

warmth dawn in the frieze. The chamber itself was near freezing and only his traveling cloak managed to keep him warm. He ran his fingers over the stones.

There's a puzzle here, he realized.

"What?" Alysta asked.

"Steganography."

"What's that?" Interested, Quarrel stepped forward.

"It's a craft, very deceitful and very sly," Wick said, "of hiding a message within a picture."

"What message?" Quarrel demanded.

"That," Wick replied, "remains to be seen." Picking at one of the stones with a fingertip, he was surprised to find that it easily popped out. He quickly searched out others. When his hands filled, he laid the stones down on the floor.

"Why did you pick those?" Quarrel asked.

"They're of fish." Wick scanned the images of fish jumping in the water. Not all of the pieces were the same shape, which was what he had expected. The message wasn't in the fish; they were only the link.

"There are plenty more of fish," Quarrel said.

"Yes, but not all of the others are depicted cresting the ocean with their tails tilted to the left." Wick worked to fit the pieces together.

"The fish shouldn't be in the picture," Alysta said.

"Very good," Wick said, smiling at the cat. "Why not?"

"Because whenever a large predator is in the water, all the small fish leave the area."

"Right," Wick said. "A sea creature's first instinct is survival, as are many others'. In the sea, if you're small, you're prey. Food for someone else. By the same token, small fish often avoid dead things in open water because they attract larger predators."

"But the fish are in the frieze," Alysta said.

"Yes." Wick reached for another piece, testing it. As he'd quickly discovered, not all the frieze pieces were loose. Most were mortared into place. Gazing at the pieces, Wick saw that they created a pattern. He wasn't tall enough to get all the pieces he thought he needed. Quarrel had to get a few of the higher ones for him.

"They were put there to draw attention," Quarrel said.

"I believe so." Wick's fear of his situation had all but vanished, its bones taken away as his curiosity filled him.

"To what purpose?" Alysta asked.

" 'Throughout the course of his life, a man's hand often slips from the tiller,' " Wick said softly.

"What's that?" Quarrel asked.

"A quote," Alysta said. "That's one of Captain Dulaun's most prized sayings."

"Dulaun was referring to the fact that most men tend to wander through life without purpose or aim," Wick said. "They go wherever the sea dictates." He surveyed the fish tiles in front of him. There were seventeen of them. "I'm certain that these pieces were put in that picture to provide direction for those who came looking for the sword."

"You believe Thango left clues?" Alysta asked.

"This frieze," Wick said with grim certainty, "is far older than Thango's time." He continued moving the fish pieces around, fitting them together so they were almost seamless. The design was flawless.

The cat crept in closer, sitting nearby and curling her tail around her paws. "I've never heard of this frieze."

"Neither have I," Wick said absently. "But I've heard of the artist."

"What artist?"

Wick pointed at the signature in the lower right corner. It was an icon of a gleaming star. "Lazzarot Piknees," the little Librarian answered. "He was one of the finest artists the Silver Sea Trade Empire ever saw." He turned his attention back to the tiles. "He was a contemporary of Captain Dulaun."

"They knew each other?" Quarrel asked.

"I didn't say that. It's possible, of course. And Piknees did make this mural."

"A signature at the bottom doesn't necessarily mean that Piknees made this mural," Alysta challenged.

"I," Wick said forcefully, "am familiar with Piknees's work."

The cat blinked at him, obviously ready to fight further, but she chose not to.

"What are you doing?" Quarrel asked, kneeling beside Wick. He eased his bow from his shoulder and laid it close to hand.

"These pieces form a puzzle," Wick said. "I'm trying to figure out what their secret is." As he worked, another piece slid to a neat fit.

"This one," Quarrel said, "goes here." Using his forefinger, he pushed one of the pieces against two others. When the sides touched, all three fused with an audible *clank* and triggered a brief spark of blue light that rivaled the lanterns' glow.

Wick leaned back, thinking that the pieces were going to catch fire. When nothing happened, he asked, "What did you do?"

"I just fit the stones together. I didn't cause that." Quarrel had his sword in one hand and a long knife in the other.

Wick had never seen the young man draw either weapon. The little Librarian tried to slide the piece Quarrel had touched from the others.

It wouldn't move. Somehow, the pieces had fused.

Returning his attention to one of the pieces he'd placed, Wick found he could easily slide it away. He lifted his hand from it and pointed at it. "Do this one."

Hesitant, Quarrel laid his blades aside and nudged the new piece into contact with another. The *clank* sounded again just before the blue light flashed.

"You're causing this," Wick whispered.

"It's not me," Quarrel said.

Wick thought again of the leather-maker's symbol on the bag that Quarrel carried. He tested the two new pieces and found they were fused as well.

"This is magic," Quarrel said. "I don't know magic."

"Apparently," Wick said, "the magic knows you."

"But how?"

"This makes no sense," the cat spat.

"Perhaps you'd care to piece the puzzle together," Wick offered.

Haughtily, the cat stepped forward and pushed pieces together with her paw. The pieces fit but there was no other reaction.

"It doesn't mean anything," Alysta said. "Maybe it's just because he's been down in this room before. Whatever magic is here could have an affinity for him."

"Perhaps," Wick said noncommittally. At his direction, Quarrel continued fitting the pieces together. Each time the pieces touched, they fused with a *clank* and the bright explosion of blue light.

The cat sniffed at each one, but her efforts grew less certain.

In a short time, the seventeen pieces had become a rough oval with flukes on one end.

"A fish," Quarrel whispered.

In truth, the assembled piece did look very much like a fish. Wick lifted it from the floor, amazed at the way it held together, as if it had always been of a piece. He turned it over, switching the side of the tiles that showed fish cresting the waves with their tails turned for the blank one on the other side.

Only now the other side wasn't blank. Words were written there. The language was the high trader tongue from the Silver Sea. He translated, amazed that the words rhymed even in the common tongue.

Fair blows the wind,
Driving iron men and wooden ships.
A hero far from home,
Unafraid to die alone.
Say his name, friend,
And ride the fierce Silver Sea as she dips!

"What does it mean?" Quarrel asked.

"Captain Dulaun," Wick said.

Nothing happened.

The little Librarian looked at the young mercenary. "Say his name."

Quarrel hesitated.

"Say his name," Wick repeated.

"Captain Dulaun," Quarrel whispered.

Immediately, the inscription on back of the fish lit up in roping, bright blue veins. Wick felt the piece vibrate in his hands. "Again. Louder. Put your hand over the inscription."

Dropping his hand over the inscription, nervousness showing bright in his eyes, Quarrel licked his lips. And he spoke the name of the hero of the Silver Sea once more. "Captain Dulaun!"

Abruptly, the fish piece flew from Wick's hand, sliding out from under Quarrel's. In an eyeblink, the fish elongated into a boarding plank. One end of the plank dropped against the floor and the other fell against the frieze.

Wick tried desperately to catch the plank, certain that it was going to destroy the image wrought from hundreds of stone pieces. He missed. The end of the plank fell *into* the frieze, coming to a shuddering rest on the edge of the artwork like it was a window ledge.

Fog spewed from the image.

Suddenly, the noise of crashing waves filled the underground chamber, followed immediately by the salty smell of the sea. Heat swept some of the chill away, warming Wick as he gazed up at the fog-covered frieze. He could no longer see the images there.

"Come aboard!" a deep voice rang out.

15

Captain Dulaun

Quarrel slid his bow over one shoulder, then took up his blades. He started forward.

"Where are you going?" the cat asked.

Placing a foot on the boarding plank, not even looking back at Alysta, Quarrel said, "To see where this takes me." He walked forward, leaning into the incline. The fog reached for him, softening his image as it took him into its embrace.

Alysta hesitated only a moment, then followed, quietly padding up the board.

Unwilling to remain behind, though drawn more by curiosity than by a fear of being left behind on his own, Wick reached down and took up the nearest lantern. He stepped onto the board and followed it up.

The fog swirled into him until he couldn't see. The rhythmic sound of waves crashed against the prow of a ship. Seven steps later, he felt the familiar up and down sway of a vessel at sea.

Then he was through the fog and could see the blue sky open around him. He stood on the ship's deck and knew that he was nowhere near Wharf Rat's Warren.

Quarrel and Alysta stood in front of the ship's captain. There was no mistaking him.

Captain Dulaun was an unassuming man. Sun-streaked brown hair that blew in the gentle wind and a warm brown-eyed gaze looked average, not heroic. He wore a mustache that curled on the ends, and he smiled as if he'd never seen a sad day in his life. His clothing was plain, black boots and breeches, a red shirt with belled sleeves.

"Welcome, my friends," Dulaun said.

"This can't be," Quarrel whispered, dazed. "You're dead. You died a thousand years ago."

Dulaun smiled again. "Of course I'm dead. Otherwise you wouldn't be here now seeking Seaspray." He laid an affectionate hand on his sword hilt.

"How did you arrange this?" Alysta asked.

"Magic, of course. Borrowed from Seaspray and linked to me through my family." Dulaun clasped his hands behind him. "You are my family. At least one of you. Otherwise you would never have figured out the secret of the frieze and would not have been able to activate the spell that allows you to come here."

Family? Wick thought. Then he realized another of the truths that had been staring him in the face. He gazed around at Dulaun's crew. The captain's men all looked battle-hardened and ready.

Beyond them, the Silver Sea shimmered under the midday sun. An albatross glided through the cloudless blue sky. The white canvas sails trapped and held the wind, mastering it as the ship continued to crash through the waves.

Dulaun walked to the ship's prow. "Come. Come. I'll tell you how you came to be here. But first I would show you my world. Hopefully it's still your world."

As if hypnotized, Alysta and Quarrel trailed after Dulaun.

"Due to the construction of the spell and certain constraints that are part of the nature of time," Dulaun said as he gazed out to sea, "I can answer your questions here and now, but I won't remember them."

"Who made this spell?" Alysta asked.

"A wizard named Rivalak." Dulaun sounded pleased.

"Rivalak," Wick said, "was one of Dulaun's contemporaries."

"More than a contemporary," Dulaun insisted. "He was a friend." He gazed at Wick. "And who might you be? I know you're no relative because you're a dweller. Not unless something went truly and drastically wrong with my lineage."

"No, I'm not family," Wick answered. "I came here with these two. As an advisor."

"Splendid." Dulaun smiled again.

Wick had to wonder what the man had been doing before they arrived. Dulaun was too pat, too sure of himself. Even before the Battle of Fell's Keep, Dulaun's self-confidence had caused fights that had sorely tested him upon occasion.

"Why are you here?" Wick asked.

"Because of this." Dulaun whisked the sword from his hip, slashing the blade through the air. "You know my blade?"

"Seaspray," Wick answered. "It has the power to call on the magic of the waves."

Seaspray was a gleaming length of steel three and a half feet long. Double-edged and inscribed with runes that blazed blue even in the bright light, the sword commanded instant respect. The guard above the hilt was shaped like two dolphins swimming around the blade. They had sapphire eyes and lines of carved gold filigree. It was beautiful.

"Aye." With a flourish, Dulaun returned the blade to its sheath. "There are many who want this sword. But no one can have it but one of my descendants. That's why this place was made."

"Where are we?" Alysta asked.

Surprised, Dulaun knelt and reached for the cat. "A talking cat?"

Alysta drew back, flattening her ears and hissing a warning.

"She's not exactly a cat," Wick said. "Her name is Alysta. She's one of your descendants."

Surprised and dismayed, Dulaun stood. "That's impossible."

"It's the truth," Alysta said.

Dulaun shook his head. "But a cat can't wield my sword." He looked at Wick. "I have no issue to give my sword to?"

"You do," Quarrel said.

"You do," Wick said. "It was her touch that activated the spell in the frieze."

" 'Her'?" Alysta looked at the young "man."

"This," Wick said, "is your granddaughter. Rose." He knew it could be no other.

"You?" Alysta padded around to better survey Quarrel. "*You* are Rose? I left you and your mother when you were so young."

Quarrel looked at Wick then, and her eyes were soft. "You knew?"

"Not until you put the puzzle together," Wick said. "I talked to Karbor the leathermaker. He told me that he adopted the daughter of friends who were related to Captain Dulaun."

"My granddaughter," Alysta whispered. She padded up to Quarrel. "You are Rose?"

The young woman smiled, but there was sadness in her eyes. "I am. But that was the name Karbor gave me when he found me and kept me hidden. I am Quarrel now, and I will be Quarrel until the day my parents' murderers are brought to justice."

"I'm your grandmother."

Quarrel's eyes widened. "Alysta?"

"Yes."

"We thought you were dead."

"I very nearly was." The cat touched her chest in a very human gesture. "After this happened, I couldn't return. Then I heard your parents were dead. When I returned then, I found no trace of you. I believed you dead as well.

Until that night Karbor talked of rescuing you—only to lose you again."

"Captain Gujhar's men came for me," Quarrel said, "but I escaped."

"Your mother," Alysta said pridefully, "trained you well."

Quarrel smiled. "She always said she had a good teacher."

"*You* are my descendant?" Dulaun asked. "A girl?"

Quarrel looked at him and lifted her chin in reproach. "I'm a woman."

Dulaun laughed and shook his head. "You're a slip of a thing. If you're sixteen I'll eat my boots."

"I'm seventeen," Quarrel said, "and I won't be made sport of. Not even by you. My mother gave her life to save me so that our line would be complete to take up your sword once more."

The captain shook his head. "You won't get my sword, girl. You would only take it from this place and lose it."

"How dare you!" Alysta hissed angrily.

Quarrel moved before Wick knew she was in motion. In an instant, she doffed her cloak in the warm breeze that propelled *Tolamae* through the Silver Sea. Her long blond tresses were tied back and hung below her shoulders. She was all suppleness and grace—and her sword leaped into her hand like a live thing. Her body fell into perfect line behind the point, which hovered only inches from Dulaun's right eye.

The crew drew their weapons and started forward at once.

Captain Dulaun held up his hand and stopped the sailors in their tracks. His lips twitched into a smile. "All right, child. You've got fire in your belly. I'll admit that. But you're not good enough to challenge me."

Without a word, without warning of any kind, Quarrel followed her blade and nicked Dulaun's right ear. Bright crimson blood dripped from his lobe.

"Don't disrespect me," Quarrel said. "I'll kill you. My

mother gave her life to live out your legacy. You died at the Battle of Fell's Keep, and you lost your sword."

"I . . . *died*?" Dulaun pronounced his sentence in grave dismay.

"Yes. At the hands of Lord Kharrion's goblinkin."

"No!" Wick shouted. "Don't tell him anything of the future! If you change the past, none of us might be here! If Captain Dulaun isn't at the Battle of Fell's Keep, the evacuation of the south won't take place! Or more might be lost! You could change the course of the war! Lord Kharrion could win!"

Too late, Quarrel realized what she might have done.

Dulaun held up a hand. "There's no reason to worry about that. This place, this moment, it's all stolen. Riva-lak engineered this spell so that this crew and I will never remember these visits."

"'Visits'?" Wick repeated.

Touching his bleeding ear, Dulaun nodded. "When the sword is lost from my descendants, it can be returned here for safekeeping till one of them comes to claim it. The magic of this spell won't open until the riddle is solved, and only my descendants can trigger it." He wiped his crimson-stained fingers on his shirt. "Now, where were we?"

The captain's question was deceptive by design. Even if Quarrel wasn't going to reply, she at least thought about it. That was enough time for Dulaun to rip Sea-spray from its sheath and take a step back. His blade crashed against Quarrel's.

Without a word, the battle was joined. Steel met steel, and the ringing clangor filled the air, beating back the noise of the creaking canvas and rigging.

Then the cheering began. The sailors rallied around their commander, calling on him to give greater and greater effort.

Quarrel fought well past her years. Her reflexes were honed and certain, unflinching in spite of Dulaun's attack. The captain smiled, arrogant and filled with confidence.

He knew his skill in a thousand battles and more, and was in the prime of his life. The Battle of Fell's Keep lay months or years in his future.

Despite her youth and speed, Quarrel gave ground more often than Dulaun did. They fought in a tight circle, and Wick knew from his research and reading of sword-play that it was Dulaun's skill and expertise that drove the fight. Neither combatant seemed willing to be the first to call enough. Sweat streamed down both of them.

Then Dulaun flicked his blade, stepping up the pace and tempo. He slammed Quarrel's sword aside with more power and authority. In another blinding pass that was too fast to follow, the Silver Sea captain suddenly had his blade at Quarrel's throat.

Quarrel froze, looking up at Dulaun fearlessly. "If you're going to do it, get it over with," she stated.

Laughter burst from Dulaun's lips. He reversed his sword and handed it to her, hilt first. "You're blood of my blood," he acknowledged, "and fit enough to carry the sword of your ancestors."

Slowly, Quarrel took the proffered blade. Holding it in front of her, the blade pointing at the sky, she admired the sword.

"It's beautiful," she whispered.

"It is," Dulaun agreed. "And now—it's yours. Take it and use it in good health against your foes."

Lowering the sword to hold at her side, Quarrel looked at the sea captain. "What about you?"

Dulaun smiled at her. "I'll go on to whatever fate has in store for me. There's no other way."

"But you're going to die."

"Everyone dies, girl," the captain said softly, but this time there was no disrespect offered in his words. He smiled. "Even if this spell were not crafted in the way it was, and I could remember meeting you after you are gone, I can't change who I am. Wherever I die, however death comes for me, I trust that I chose to be there because of the man I am. I couldn't turn away from that."

"It's worse than death," Quarrel said. "At the Battle of Fell's Keep, you're betrayed. By one of those that you assume is your ally."

Some of the lightness vanished from Dulaun's smile. "Then I hope that my descendants stand truer for me than some of my friends."

"You shouldn't go there."

Dulaun shook his head. "There's no other way for me, Quarrel. I chart my life by the same stars I always have. If I were to remove those stars from the heaven, what would be the reason for living?" He took a breath. "I'd rather die than surrender. But tell me one thing."

Quarrel tried to speak and couldn't. Tears glimmered in her eyes and trailed down her cheeks.

Wick felt the heat of tears on his own face as well. Their presence surprised him. He looked at the young captain and his crew. He knew from his reading that Captain Dulaun and his men had always acquitted themselves bravely against pirates, enemy crews, goblinkin, and sea monsters. But they would soon be sailing to their deaths. Would it truly have been the same if they had known that? Looking at the man, Wick believed that it would have been.

"What?" Quarrel asked in a voice tight with pain. Wick knew the young woman wasn't just facing Dulaun's loss, but those of her parents as well.

"My death," Dulaun said. "Did I die well? Was it for something I would have been proud to die for? And did my death make a difference, or was it all a waste?"

"You helped save a great many people," Alysta said. "Lord Kharrion's goblinkin forces would have slain them all if they'd been able. Your sacrifice, and that of your companions, it made a difference."

"Good." Dulaun smiled again, nearly as cocky as he'd been when they'd arrived. "That's all I've ever asked." He looked at Quarrel. "Be true to the spirit of the sword and it will never let you down."

"I will," Quarrel said.

"Now go, and may the Old Ones watch over you." Dulaun placed his hand on the hilt of Seaspray sheathed at his side. Quarrel still held her own version of the sword. For the moment, with the power of the spell, the sword—past and present—existed in the same time and space.

The gray fog rose suddenly around Wick, Alysta, and Quarrel, obscuring the Silver Sea and the blue sky. The fog seeped into the little Librarian's lungs, bringing with it the biting cold of the buried keep.

He blinked, and they were once more standing in front of the frieze. Only Seaspray hanging at the end of Quarrel's arm testified that the incident had happened. The walkway had disappeared and the pieces containing images of the fish had returned to the frieze.

"We're back." Quarrel examined the sword, which gleamed like it was newly minted in the lantern light. Blue fire ran along the edges and the runes.

"But not any safer than we were," Alysta said.

Quarrel sheathed the sword and took up her bow. She looked at the cat. "It's true? You're my grandmother?"

Alysta padded over to Quarrel and placed a paw against the young woman's boot. "I am. But when I knew you, your name wasn't Quarrel."

"No," Quarrel agreed, kneeling down and touching the cat's head and scratching. "I was Nyssa."

"Yes."

"I chose my name after my parents were killed." Sadness touched her pale blue wolf's eyes. "My father nicknamed me 'Quarrel' because he thought I was argumentative. He always insisted that I came by my nature honestly, that I got it from my grandmother."

Alysta preened. "That's true. You did."

"He thought my querulousness was a bad thing."

"Well," the cat said warmly, her breath gray in the cold, still air of the chamber, "your father was a good man. You'll never hear me say anything else but that. However, he was a man after all, and not always capable of the best judgment when it came to the nature of young women."

Her eyes blinked at Quarrel. "Frankly, I like the way you are."

"Perhaps we could save the family reunion for later," Wick said. "We're still trapped on this mountain with Captain Gujhar, Ryman Bey, and the Razor's Kiss thieves."

Quickly, they gathered their things and prepared to leave.

"We could use the passage to the sea." Quarrel pointed to the opening beside the frieze.

"You've been that way?" Alysta asked.

"Yes."

"Is there a boat?"

"No."

"Dawdal's still back at camp," Wick reminded them.

The cat sighed. "He could probably make his way back to Wharf Rat's Warren on his own. Then again, Dawdal doesn't have a true sense of direction. He could get lost out here. Or goblinkin or a bear could eat him." She shook her head. "We'll have to go back for him."

Quarrel took the lead once more.

16

Pursued

Long minutes later, after all the surviving traps had once more been navigated, Wick and his two companions stood at the entrance to the excavation site. The snowfall had increased, filling the air with thick flakes that obscured vision.

The snowfall helped, Wick knew, but they would still stand out against it if someone saw them. Staying there till the dawn was out of the question and would be tantamount to suicide. They had to press on.

The thieves' camp was still in turmoil. Gujhar and Ryman Bey were convinced that the interlopers hadn't escaped over the wall. The thieves were searching the campsite and the inner courtyard, brandishing torches to drive back the darkness and cursing their luck.

"Quietly," Quarrel whispered, "and stay close to me." She went, hunkering low to the ground. She carried her sheathed sword in her left hand, her right hand resting on Seaspray's hilt to draw it quickly.

Fear hammered inside Wick. Even though he'd been through several horrific struggles over the last few years, he didn't believe he would ever get over the fear of dying suddenly in some violent manner.

They slipped through the night without incident and

crouched in the shadows at the base of the wall. After a moment, when it seemed none of the torches carried by the thieves was near, they scaled the narrow steps leading up the wall.

At the top, the clouds parted and silver moonslight streamed down, raking the wall with incandescence, blunted somewhat by the swirling snow. Wick was reaching for the crenellation on the other side when Alysta hissed, *"Look out!"*

Ducking instinctively, Wick put both hands over his head and hoped nothing bad would happen to him. Something with leathery wings skated just above him and raked claws through his hair. An eerie, ululating, screaming whistle ripped through the still of the night.

"Up on the wall!" someone shouted down in the inner courtyard. "There they are!"

"Get up, Wick," Quarrel called. "We've been spotted."

Wick lifted his head, holding his arms up to protect himself. He got warily to his feet and looked up into the night. The ululating whistle continued, circling low overhead. Scrabbling for the crenellation, he spotted the winged zarnk diving at him again.

The creature was a flying scavenger with a five-foot wingspread. Three horns, two over its fierce eyes and one at the end of its cruelly curved beak, made the zarnk's face look like a knotted fist. Copper-colored scales covered the elongated body, leading down to a darker shade along the whiplike tail with the barbed end. Opening its razor beaked jaws, it screamed again.

Three others joined it.

Terror raced through Wick. Although he'd never seen the creatures outside of an ecology book, he knew what they were. According to the information he'd read, a dozen zarnks could strip a cow down to a mass of bones in minutes. He didn't want to find out if that was true.

Alysta moved, bunching then unbunching, hurling herself at the attacking zarnk and landing on its back. Knocked aside by the cat's weight and fury, the zarnk screech-whistled again as it tumbled to the top of the wall in a flurry of wings. The feline struck with clean, white teeth. Even though the zarnk was bigger than Alysta was, she weighed easily three times as much. The zarnk flailed helplessly as it tried to get up.

Another zarnk veered toward the cat, reaching for her with razor claws. Wick reacted almost immediately, unable to face the thought of Alysta ripped to shreds in front of him. He threw himself at the predator, and that was what saved him from the third's attack as it glided in at him.

Wick grabbed the zarnk's wing and neck, riding it to the ground. *Don't let it bite me! Please don't let it bite one of my fingers off or permanently damage one of them!* Nightmare images of the creature doing exactly that plagued him as he held on. He was surprised at how light the zarnk was, but it also possessed a wiry strength.

"Break its neck," Quarrel said.

Wick tried to find leverage but couldn't. In truth, he didn't know if he could actually kill the zarnk. He didn't like killing. He wasn't a warrior; he just didn't want to watch Alysta get hurt. The zarnk flailed and dug its claws into the wall, crawling up despite Wick's efforts. Lying on his back, suddenly trying to keep the zarnk from his throat, Wick saw Quarrel smoothly nock an arrow and track one of the other two flying zarnks.

The bowstring thrummed. The arrow pierced the heart of its target. Like a broken kite, the zarnk tumbled from the night sky and disappeared over the edge of the wall. Then Quarrel nocked another arrow, drew, and fired. The shot didn't hit the second flying creature's body, but it shattered a wing and dropped it into the inner courtyard.

Wick fought to keep the zarnk's curved beak from his eyes, yanking his fingers back each time he turned his attacker's efforts. Without hesitation, Quarrel flicked out her foot and slammed the zarnk's head up against the wall. Bone crumpled. The zarnk suddenly became dead weight in Wick's arms. He shoved the dead thing from him and scrambled to his feet.

Only a short distance away, Alysta jumped away from the dead zarnk she'd fought. Her muzzle was bloody. The winged predator lay curled up in a ball, its throat torn out.

"Is that all of them?" the cat asked more calmly than Wick felt she had any right to.

"For the moment," Quarrel answered just as calmly.

Then the first arrow from the thieves splintered against the wall. Sparks leaped from the razor-sharp iron blade.

Below, the thieves raced toward the wall. Two of them stopped long enough to nock arrows and draw back. They released too early, though, and both deadly missiles went wide of the mark. By an uncomfortable few feet.

"Go!" Quarrel ordered, drawing back another arrow. She centered herself, calmly and dispassionately despite the crossbow bolt that skidded from the stone only inches below her boots.

For a moment, Wick watched her, drawn by the sight of the elegance of intent that the young woman evidenced. She reminded him of an elven archer, every line of her centered exactly so behind the bow. Her fingers opened like the petals of a flower, releasing the shaft. The missile sped true, catching a man just above the breastbone where a chain mail shirt would have ended, then pierced him and knocked him back.

By then Wick was scrambling over the crenellation, realizing too late that the side they'd gone over on faced the sea. He was also more than twenty feet above the ground.

"Hurry!" Alysta growled as she leaped to the top of the crenellation.

"It's too far," Wick protested. "I could break my leg. Or my neck."

"You say that like staying here is an option."

Wick turned to face the cat, figuring to appeal to Alysta's good sense. *If we're not killed outright, and we shouldn't be—maybe—Craugh and Cap'n Farok will be after us soon enough.* Only before he could say anything, the cat launched herself at him, striking him heavily in the chest.

Off balance, Wick went over the wall backward. Alysta hooked her claws into his traveling cloak. He yelled in surprise and fear as he fell. The cat yowled. For a moment, her furry face was nose to nose with his. He flung his arms around her and held on.

When he hit the ground, the snow cushioned his fall. The impact still drove the breath from his lungs, but nothing felt broken. He plunged down into a drift that was taller than he was, disappearing at once inside the snow.

"Get up!" Alysta commanded, detaching herself from Wick and squirming from his panicked grip. "They'll be on top of us in seconds."

Wick nodded, still struggling to suck air into his deflated lungs. Grabbing fistfuls of snow, he heaved himself from the drift till he stood on his feet. He caught half a breath, then another, and finally—*thank the Old Ones*!— he could breathe again.

Then Quarrel plummeted into the snowbank beside the little Librarian. She came up out of the snow like a dervish, throwing snow in all directions. It suddenly looked like it was snowing *up* as much as it was down.

"Run!" Quarrel ordered.

"Which way?" Wick asked frantically.

Neither the cat nor the young warrior answered him. Both of them ran straight for the tree line nearly forty yards away.

"Dawdal isn't that way," Wick cried after them. He had to struggle through the snow because it was up to his chest in most places.

Alysta scampered across the snow and Quarrel ran in quick strides that seemed to defy gravity.

Wick took another breath, ready to protest the direction again, then an arrow hissed into the snow ahead of him, probably only missing him by inches. He reconsidered the value of protesting the direction and decided that *any* escape would be a good thing at the moment. He spared a fleeting glimpse at the thieves and saw a half dozen men scrambling over the keep wall and dropping to the snow. When he turned back around, he stubbed his toe and pitched headlong into the snow.

Quarrel stopped and came back for Wick, grabbing him by an arm and jerking him to his feet. Together, with the cat urging them on, they ran for the trees while arrows rained down around them.

Later, Wick was never able to completely remember the struggle they had as they dodged through the forest. Several times they tripped over fallen trees or had to fight their way through drifts and brush. Pines and firs tore at their faces and eyes. Snow dropped down on them from the limbs by the bushel.

The land remained roughly level for a time, then quickly fell away toward the sea. In a short distance, they were falling down the treacherous landscape at nearly the same speed they were running.

Wick bounced and thudded against the mountainside. The wild cries of the thieves, excited now because their prey was almost at hand, filled the little Librarian's ears. Terror raked at him.

Before he knew it, they were all out of running room. They burst free of the forest unexpectedly and found themselves out on a pointed shard of rock covered in snow that hung above the sea a hundred feet below.

"No!" Wick gasped. It wasn't fair. They'd risked everything to claim Seaspray, solved the puzzle of the boat room when the Razor's Kiss thieves hadn't been able to do that. They couldn't end up without a place to run.

Quarrel turned, bow in her hand and an arrow already nocked. Her breath exploded out of her in ragged gasps that stranded gray clouds in the cold air. Even Alysta seemed winded.

Wick gazed around, spotting an incline that went down the side of the mountain that offered him a fleeting hope. With luck, it went all the way to the bottom of the mountain. And with greater luck they would never lose their footing on the narrow trail.

"This way," Wick said.

"Too late," Quarrel said in a low voice.

Turning, Wick spotted the predatory shadows gathering in the tree line. Moonslight glittered on swords and knives. Involuntarily, he took a step back and nearly stepped over the ledge. Quarrel reached for him without taking her eyes from their enemies and steadied him.

"Careful," she said.

Wick almost tittered at the idea of being careful. *We're one word away from being dead. Careful doesn't even figure into this.* Or maybe they were two words. If Gujhar decided to say, "Kill them," instead of, "Kill."

"Who are you?" a man's voice rang out.

"Someone who will kill you if you give me half a chance," Quarrel replied.

"Then I shouldn't give you a chance." The voice mocked her.

"Are you a coward then?" she demanded.

"Actually," Wick whispered, "now wouldn't exactly be the time to antagonize him. Orlag Sonder, in a very excellent work called *A Sharp-Tongued Diplomat Stays Only One Step Ahead of Impending Retribution*, suggests that when overpowered and outnumbered, remaining pacifistic is the best way—"

"I am Ryman Bey," the man declared as he stepped from the tree line. His eye patch caught the moonslight, marking him instantly. "I lead the men that will kill you if you don't surrender what you took from the keep."

Showing no apparent strain, Quarrel kept her bow bent. "I could kill you where you stand. And I will if you don't call off your dogs."

Ryman Bey laughed, confident in his ability. "Even if you succeeded, these men would cut you to doll rags."

Quarrel smiled, but Wick could see that the effort was forced. "You won't live to see that happen."

"Oh, but I might," Ryman Bey taunted. "I just might. You'd be surprised to know what I've lived through."

Wick talked from the corner of his mouth. "We don't have to do this. Not yet."

"They're going to kill us," Alysta said. "They don't want to try to take us alive."

"They do at the moment," Wick said quietly.

"That's because they're afraid Quarrel will fall into the sea with the sword after they've killed her." The cat's voice was quiet and didn't go far.

"C'mon, girl," Ryman Bey said. "Make it easy on yourself."

With no indication of what she was about to do, Quarrel released the arrow. Wick's senses were spinning so rapidly he heard the shaft passing on the polished wood, then the deep, basso *thwang* of the string. He started to demand why Quarrel had fired the arrow when they were at the mercy of their enemies, then realized that her arm must have been growing tired holding the powerful bow ready. Knowing she'd never have the chance to draw back again, she'd obviously chosen to loose.

The arrow flew straight and true for the center of Ryman Bey's face. Incredibly, the thief leader whirled to one side and took a step back. The arrow sliced through his hair and several strands were sheared.

"No!" Ryman Bey shouted, throwing his hand up to still his men. "I don't want to lose that sword!"

By that time, Quarrel had thrown the bow down and slid Seaspray free of the sheath. The blue-etched blade caught and reflected the slight moonlight. Snowflakes whirled around her.

"Before I allow you to take this sword," Quarrel promised, "I'll throw it into the sea."

"Throw it!" Ryman Bey showed his teeth in a wolf's grin. "If I can't stop you, I'll recover the sword from the sea. I'd rather not if we could come to an arrangement."

Wick stood frozen, not knowing what to do. It was plain to see that Quarrel felt the same way. The little Librarian looked out to sea, hoping against hope that *One-Eyed Peggie*'s sails were visible. Only a pale, ghostly fog drifted in atop the waves crashing against the jagged rocks below.

"The only arrangement we can come to," Quarrel said, "doesn't involve me giving up this sword."

"Perhaps I could take you with us," Ryman Bey said. "We only need the sword for a short time, so I'm told."

For what? Wick wondered, curious again at Gujhar's purpose and who had sent the man on his mission.

"No," Quarrel replied. "I don't trust you. I'll never trust you."

A voice from the ranks of the thieves spoke in a cant known only to them. Wick was familiar with the language from his studies, though he wasn't as fluent as he would have wished to be.

"I'm ready," the voice said.

Ryman Bey responded in the same tongue, never taking his eyes from Quarrel. "Do it."

Wick turned to Quarrel. "Look out. They're planning—"

Before he could finish speaking, an arrow sped from the darkness pooled at the tree line. A thin cord trailed after the missile.

Quarrel saw the speeding arrow, or perhaps guessed from the sound of the bowstring that she had been fired on, and tried to spin away. Wick believed that the hidden archer had aimed at Quarrel's chest, but the young woman managed to avoid the arrow for the most part. Instead, it transfixed her left shoulder with a *thunk*.

Staggered by the blow, Quarrel barely remained standing. She looked down at the arrow in disbelief. She thought fast, though, recognizing the cord attached to the arrow and what it represented. Bringing the sword up, she tried to cut the cord, but whoever had hold of the other end pulled on it and yanked her from her feet.

17

Escape

Screaming in pain as the arrow twisted in her flesh, Quarrel tried to fight, but she was dragged through the snow like a sled, plowing a furrow. Ryman Bey waited with his drawn sword.

Turning over on her back, Quarrel threw Seaspray toward the cliff.

"No!" Ryman Bey shouted as he watched the enchanted weapon spin through the air.

But Quarrel wasn't able to get enough strength behind her effort. Seaspray fell short of the ledge and lay on the snow, naked and vulnerable.

"Wick!" Quarrel yelled, drawing a knife from her boot and grabbing the cord in her free hand. "Throw the sword over!"

Alysta lunged across the snow and nuzzled the sword, trying to move it with her head. Unfortunately, she wasn't strong enough. She turned to Wick and yowled, *"Hurry!"*

Ryman Bey raced forward, grabbing Quarrel's knife hand in one of his and staying her blade. He plucked her easily from the snow and grinned at her. She tried to fight him, but he was too strong and too quick with his hands and feet, and she was wounded. He grabbed the arrow with his other hand and twisted it savagely.

Quarrel screamed and almost passed out, dropping down to her knees for a moment. When she rose again, she had the thief leader's knife at her throat.

"Don't vex me, girl," Ryman Bey said. "At the moment you yet live."

Wick sprinted toward the sword, but one of the Razor's Kiss thieves got there before he did. The man grabbed the hilt and lifted the blade, grinning in triumph.

"Keep coming, halfer," the thief taunted, waving Wick on with his free hand. "We'll see how you like the taste of cold steel. And maybe we'll see if this sword lives up to the legend that surrounds it."

Having no choice, Wick stopped.

Alysta threw herself at the man, but he was prepared and fast enough to slap her away. She hit the snow-covered ground and flopped miserably, mewling in pain.

"Take them to the edge," Ryman Bey ordered.

At sword point, the thief guided Wick to the ledge. He couldn't help looking down at the waves thundering against the rocks. The cliff wall was almost sheer, but there were ledges scattered along the way. None of them were close enough to safely drop down onto.

Ryman Bey brought Quarrel to the edge and stood her there in the wind. Several of the thieves kicked Alysta and drove her away, and the cat had no choice but to go.

Wick's mind worked desperately. *They're going to kill us. Ryman Bey just wants to gloat first.*

"Who are you?" Ryman Bey demanded of Quarrel.

"He's a mercenary," one of the thieves responded. "I've seen him around the Tavern of Schemes."

"This is no man." Ryman Bey pushed back Quarrel's hood and revealed her hair and soft features. "I will weary of asking you, girl. If you would live, you'll answer my questions."

Quarrel only returned the thief chieftain's gaze full measure.

Ryman Bey grinned. "You've meddled in something

that you've no business being part of." He held out his hand and the thief holding Seaspray handed the sword over.

"I have every right," Quarrel replied.

Gujhar stepped forward then. "Get me a torch."

One of the thieves pulled a torch from his equipment pack and lit it.

Taking the torch, the mercenary captain held the flame up and toward Quarrel. The wind whipped the flames, seeking to extinguish them. "I know you," he said. "I recognize your face." He reached inside his cloak and took out a book, flipping it open to a familiar section.

"A *book*!" one of the thieves gasped.

Most of them stepped back in consternation.

"If the goblinkin discover you have that," another thief said, "they'll be down on you in a second with naked steel and clubs. They hate books."

"I'm certainly not going to tell them," Gujhar replied. "And even a goblinkin would think twice about taking a wizard's book of spells."

A wizard? Wick didn't believe for a moment that Gujhar was a wizard. He was like none of the wizards Wick had ever seen. Wizards were proud and haughty men. (And sometimes women, though he'd only encountered one of those.)

But the book was magical in nature. Gujhar spoke a couple of words and the blank pages that Wick could see suddenly filled with images. One of them was of Captain Dulaun and his wife. Quarrel favored both of them.

"You are one of Captain Dulaun's descendants," Gujhar said excitedly. "That's how you were able to find Seaspray when we weren't. I knew it had been hidden, but I had no idea where."

Quarrel said nothing, but she couldn't hide the truth either. "You're not fit to carry that sword."

"Oh, I won't be carrying it," Ryman Bey said. "I'm ransoming it to Gujhar's employer." He eyed the blade appreciatively. "As pretty as this sword is, it's worth a lot of gold." He smiled. "Consider me crass if you will, but I'd rather have the gold. Besides, I could never unleash the power it wields."

"Neither can Gujhar's employer," Quarrel said.

"Gujhar's employer has other intentions for the sword than using it as it was created," Ryman Bey said.

"Careful," Gujhar cautioned irritably. "You're speaking out of turn."

Ryman Bey smiled. "A few minutes from now, it won't matter."

Wick swallowed hard. For the first time he noticed that the other end of the rope attached to the arrow in Quarrel's arm was looped around one of the bigger thieves' waist. A desperate—and risky!—plan formed in Wick's brain.

You've clearly been reading far too many romances from Hralbomm's Wing, he told himself. But it was doable. Neither he nor Quarrel weighed half of what the thief weighed.

All they needed was a moment. And a lot of luck. By the Old Ones, they would have to be *awfully* lucky to survive what he had in mind.

"That sword," Quarrel said, "is meant for our family."

"Not anymore." Ryman Bey held the sword level before him. "Gujhar's employer plans on stripping the magic from this blade and using it for something else." The thief chieftain looked at Gujhar, who stood in silent fury.

"That can't be done," Quarrel argued.

Ryman Bey smiled. "I'm told it can be. The betrayal at the Battle of Fell's Keep ran deep. Deals were struck and the people involved trusted each other far too much. Lord Kharrion placed his agent within the ranks of the defenders and planned well."

The news shocked Wick. It was the first confirmation of a traitor among the defenders that he'd ever heard of outside of rumor and the elemental in Master Blacksmith Oskarr's forge. The story was becoming more tangled, and more relevant to things that were going on in the world now.

Just as Craugh and Cap'n Farok had told him. It even lent to the belief that it was something of a legacy Lord Kharrion had left.

"When Gujhar's employer is done with this sword," Ryman Bey taunted, "it won't be anything but a trinket."

During the thief chieftain's exchange, Gujhar had been gazing with deep interest in Wick's direction. "You were in the Cinder Clouds Islands."

The accusation hung in the cold despite the harsh wind coming in from the sea.

"No I wasn't," Wick squeaked. He cleared his throat, hoping he sounded more firm. "I've never been to the Cinder Clouds Islands."

Then one of the thieves spoke up. "There was a halfer there."

"There were a lot of halfers there," another thief snarled. "The goblinkin had slaves working those mines."

The first thief shook his head. "You don't often see red hair on a halfer. This one has red hair. So did the one in the Cinder Clouds Islands."

"I think you're right," a third said. "I saw him, too."

Gujhar approached and stood in front of Wick. "You *were* there. Searching for Master Oskarr's axe."

"It was someone else," Wick insisted, but his voice cracked and he knew he sounded like he was lying. "Some other dweller. Not me." He hated the way his voice came out. Just as guilty sounding as it did when Grandmagister Frollo wanted to know who'd smeared jam on the pages of a book or who had (accidentally!) forgotten to return a much-used reference book to its proper place. He hated sounding guilty. Terrible things always followed.

"It was you," Gujhar said. "What were you doing there?"

"I escaped," Wick said. "I was one of the mining slaves."

"You," Gujhar stated clearly, "were with the dwarves searching for the axe. They found it when no one else could."

"Not me," Wick said weakly.

"And now," Gujhar mused, "you helped this girl find Dulaun's sword in a place we had searched repeatedly." His eyes narrowed. "What do you know about this, halfer? What do you know about Deathwhisper?"

Deathwhisper. So Gujhar was looking for the third weapon from the Battle of Fell's Keep. Just as the journal had indicated. But why? The question tumbled endlessly through Wick's mind. Why was Gujhar's master planning to strip the action from the weapons? How had they been bound together a thousand years ago? Had that been why they'd been lost all that time?

He didn't know. The fact that he didn't have a clue made him so curious he couldn't stand it.

"Do you know where Deathwhisper is?" Gujhar asked.

Wick didn't say anything. Dread filled him. He knew what was going to happen next, and knowing that gave him strength to think about the wild scheme that had occurred to him.

"You should tell me," Gujhar said casually, as if he were talking about the price of apples or whether the ale at the top of a tankard was more flavorful than the ale at the bottom. "It will save you a lot of painful torture."

Actually, Wick was for anything that saved him painful torture. If he'd known where Deathwhisper was, he'd have told. Immediately. However, he also knew that he'd probably be tortured anyway because Gujhar wouldn't choose to believe him till he'd been tortured for a while. Of course, if he told the truth immediately, there was also the possibility that Gujhar would torture a *lie* out of him. It would be a clever ploy.

But that meant putting up with the torture, and Wick

wasn't looking forward to that. Even when he ascribed to the fantasy that *One-Eyed Peggie* would arrive with Craugh, Cap'n Farok, Hallekk, and the crew, Wick didn't care for even a *little* torture.

Without taking his cruel eyes from Wick, Gujhar asked, "I trust you have someone who's good at torture?"

"I do." Ryman Bey cleaned his nails on his cloak. "I usually attend to it myself. I'm the best we have."

"Good." Gujhar smiled. "I wouldn't want anyone but the best available to handle the chores on this."

"We'll have to discuss the price, of course. Helping you recover these things is fine, but you didn't mention anything about torture when we made our bargain."

Frowning, Gujhar turned to glare at the thief leader. "Do you really want to spend more time looking for the elven bow? When you have someone right here who knows where it is?"

"*Might* know," Ryman Bey countered. "I find I believe the halfer. I don't think he's lying."

"He lied about being at the Cinder Clouds Islands."

Ryman Bey grinned coldly. "Yes, but we all knew he was lying about that, didn't we? He's not a very good liar. Doesn't come by it natural enough."

Idly, Wick wondered if he should feel insulted. Then he decided there really wasn't any room for considering an insult with all the fear running rampant in his mind. Maybe he was quiet on the outside, but he knew he was running around screaming inside his thoughts.

"We had a deal," Gujhar protested. "I can't have you just assigning new costs to every little thing."

Shrugging, the thief leader said, "You can always take care of the torturing yourself." He paused. "If you don't have any tools for it—spikes to drive up under his finger-nails, crimpers to shred his ears, knives to split his fingertips—"

Wick shuddered and sour nausea bubbled at the back of his throat.

"I don't have any of those things," Gujhar said.

With a smile, Ryman Bey said, "I'll be happy to rent you a set."

Wick knew that he'd never have a better chance of escape. He steeled himself for the course of action he'd chosen, then hoped that he didn't get Quarrel or himself (or *both* of them!) killed.

He sprinted forward, quicker than the thief watching him had expected. Wick felt the man's fingers brush against the back of one shoulder, but he was free, running straight for Quarrel.

"The rope!" Wick yelled. "Grab the rope!"

A startled look flashed across Quarrel's face as she realized Wick was coming too fast to stop short of the ledge. Instinctively, she braced against his charge. If she'd been a full-grown man or a dwarf, perhaps even an elf, Wick knew he would have never been able to knock her from her feet. But she was slight, and she was weak from her injury. He just hoped she wasn't too weak to help save herself. She thought quickly on her feet. He knew that and he was counting on that skill.

"Stop him!" Ryman Bey yelled.

"Stupid halfer!" one of the thieves said.

"No," Quarrel said, trying to move out of the way.

Then Wick was on her, hitting her at her waist, below the arm she threw out to stop him. He reached up and caught the rope with his right hand, flipping his arm to catch a loop behind his right elbow.

For an instant they hovered on the brink of the cliff, teetering as Quarrel fought back and tried to stop the impending fall. "Grabtherope!" Wick yelled. *"Grabtherope!"*

They fell, spinning over the empty space above the sea and the jagged rock. Wick slammed against the cliffside and felt the breath leave his lungs. He got his left hand around the arrow in Quarrel's shoulder and snapped it off so that it wouldn't be savagely jerked from her flesh. She screamed in pain, or it might have been she was already screaming in fright, he wasn't sure. But she grabbed the rope with both hands.

Wick hoped that his arm wasn't torn out of its socket when they ran out of slack. He was still screaming—*something*, he wasn't sure what—when that happened.

They hit the end of the rope still seventy feet from the sea, slamming into mountainside as the thief above (evidently figuring out what was going to happen and fearing the worst) tried to dig in. Whatever the thief did, Wick knew, was potentially doomed to failure. That was quickly proven true when he and Quarrel began falling again. Only this time they were close enough to the mountainside to slide down to one of the ledges.

Wick hit the ledge with bone-jarring force and skittered along, flailing helplessly as he shot over the edge. He managed to grab hold of the ledge and chinned himself, mewling with fear. Quarrel had landed on the ledge and was in no danger of falling off. She lay silent and still, and he feared she was dead. Blood covered her wounded shoulder.

Motion above Wick caught his attention. He looked up and saw the thief falling from the ledge, arms and legs flailing. His scream echoed, growing closer. Then Wick realized that the rope was still around his arm. He whipped his arm from the coils as the thief fell within inches of him, screaming, "Letgooftherope! *Letgooftherope!*" to Quarrel.

Weakly, she shifted and shook free of the rope as well. Wick got the rope off his arm last, noticing from the stiffness in his fingers and palms that he'd suffered burns and abrasions from struggling to hang onto the rope. The cold wind threatened to tear him from the ledge and he didn't think he had the strength to climb up.

The thief turned end over end and smashed against the rocks below. His body lay there for just a moment, then the waves crashed in and carried it away. Somewhere in the foggy darkness, the dead man disappeared without a trace.

Wick tried to pull himself up, digging his toes into the mountainside and heaving with all his strength. Above him, he heard the shouts of the thieves. Two arrows splintered against the stone as archers tried to pick him off. Quarrel lay sheltered under an overhang, but she leaned out with her good arm and caught hold of Wick's cloak. Leaning back, she helped him clamber up while another arrow whizzed by. He huddled under the overhang.

"That was idiocy," Quarrel accused.

Nodding, Wick said, "It was. But if we'd stayed up there, they would have killed us."

"That shouldn't have worked."

"You only think that because you haven't read Daslanik's *Practical Applications of Dual Penduluming Bodies*. It's a fascinating book. Daslanik did a lot studies regarding penduluming weights with no fixed points."

Quarrel shifted and got to a sitting position.

"You shouldn't be moving," Wick said. Blood smeared the stone surface where the young woman had lain.

"Staying here for them to climb down and slit our throats isn't a good idea. Neither is staying here to freeze to death."

Wick nodded, realizing that it was a lot colder on the mountainside. He helped her to her feet. They crouched under the overhang, then peered upward.

Gujhar looked down at them over the side. "You got lucky, halfer."

Wick didn't bother to argue or point out the mathematics of his actions.

"If you know what's good for you," Gujhar went on, "you'll make certain we never cross paths again."

"I'll have my sword back," Quarrel promised.

Gujhar smiled at her. The light from the torch he held exposed the cruel lines of his face. "You're welcome to try, girl. I don't like leaving loose ends."

The thieves had spread out along the cliff, but none of them had yet found a way down to the ledge where Wick and Quarrel were. But their efforts to find one were reason enough to go.

"Can you walk?" Wick asked.

"If I can fall down a mountain and live," Quarrel said, "I can walk."

Wick took the lead, marking their path with a trained eye. He hadn't navigated the steep and twisting staircases of the Vault of All Known Knowledge's subterranean recesses without learning a few things. They went slowly, but they went, switching back and forth as they needed to. Occasionally, till they reached the rocky shore seventy or so feet below, arrows still skittered down the mountainside or splashed into the sea.

At the water's edge, they walked east along the coast, thinking that the more distance they put between themselves and Thango's keep the better. Wick felt certain Gujhar would return to *Wraith* and set sail as soon as he could.

After all, the elven bow Deathwhisper yet remained to be found.

Quarrel stumbled and almost fell. Wick took her good arm across his shoulder and supported her as well as he could. He kept them moving through the snowstorm. A few minutes later, he heard footsteps behind them. His heart stopped inside his chest, then he turned around and saw the cat had joined them.

"Is she going to be all right?" Alysta asked.

"Yes," Wick answered, though he wasn't sure. The wound looked horrible, and the rough trip down the mountain (the climb as well as the fall) hadn't been good on her. "She just needs some rest. We need to find shelter." He turned and continued on.

The cat fell into step beside them, trudging through the snow with a definite limp.

"Ryman Bey and the Razor's Kiss thieves are leaving the keep," Alysta said. "They have what they came for."

"And they think we're as good as dead," Wick said grimly.

"If we live through the night and manage to return to Wharf Rat's Warren, they'll be waiting."

Wick went on, forcing himself to move through the physical pains and exhaustion that plagued him. The pain was dulled somewhat by the questions that revolved endlessly inside his head.

epilogue

Safe Harbor

"Over here!" someone cried. "They're over here!"

"Thank the Old Ones!" a familiar voice growled. "Are they still alive?"

Wick struggled against the lethargy that filled him. He tried to move but wasn't able to. Even fear seemed walled off by the cold that filled him. He sat hunkered in the folds of his cloak where he, Quarrel, and Alysta had decided to take shelter beneath a stand of spruce trees when they could go no farther.

They'd walked for an hour or more and found no sign of habitation. That part of the coast appeared completely desolate. The bright spot was that they hadn't crossed paths with the Razor's Kiss thieves, either.

Unless they've come calling now, Wick thought grimly. He kept still, trusting the snow that had fallen to keep them covered. The snow now felt several inches thick. He wondered how they'd been found. With the snow around them and falling fast, he'd believed they'd safely dug in and disappeared.

Then hands dug at the snow and uncovered them. Torchlight burned bright and hot against his eyes.

Hallekk peered at Wick. "Are ye truly alive, then?"

Snow clung to his beard, and his breath had formed ice crystals in his mustache.

"I am," Wick whispered. Heartened by the sight of his friend, the little Librarian tried to stand. Past Hallekk, *One-Eyed Peggie* sat at anchor well away from the rocky shoals. A longboat sat beached on the shore. Craugh stood nearby, his staff blistering the frigid air with a trail of green sparks. "It's good to see you. I hoped you would come soon—soon enough." He tried to take a step and almost fell.

"Go easy there with ye," Hallekk cautioned, throwing his big arms around Wick and lifting him as he would a child. "I got ye. Don't ye fret none. I got ye."

"What about Quarrel and the cat?" Wick whispered.

Hallekk peered into the cloak nest. "They're alive. We'll take care of 'em."

"Please," Wick asked. Then the fatigue that filled him claimed him and took him into the yawning blackness.

When Wick woke again, he was on *One-Eyed Peggie*, sleeping in a bed this time instead of a hammock. For a while he simply lay there, luxuriating in the warmth he'd thought he'd never again feel while he'd huddled in the thin protection of his cloak. The ship was in motion, riding the ocean waves, rising and falling regular enough to let him know they were making good time—wherever they were headed.

Thoughts of Quarrel and how the young woman was faring drove Wick reluctantly from the bed. He still wore the clothes he'd gone roving in while at Wharf Rat's Warren. A bath, he knew, was in order at his earliest convenience.

He found his cloak on a chair beside the door. He pulled the garment on, then went out into the waist. In the hallway, two dwarven pirates carried supplies up from the cargo hold to the galley, replenishing Cook's supplies. After a brief conversation, Wick found out that Quarrel was resting and that Craugh and Cap'n Farok were topside making plans to pursue *Wraith*. While the idea of the two making further plans didn't make Wick's heart leap for joy, he was still glad that Gujhar and Ryman Bey hadn't escaped undetected. Although he was afraid of crossing paths with the two again—and the mysterious master Gujhar worked for—the little Librarian didn't like leaving any mystery unsolved.

And this one looked like the biggest he'd ever seen.

On the main deck, Wick found the wizard and the ship's captain on the stern castle, heads together as they consulted a map. Wick hailed them.

"So," Craugh said, "you've risen." He didn't look particularly relieved or glad to see Wick. Doubtless, he was thinking that Wick had managed to let yet another of the weapons escape their grasp.

Wick gazed at the sun and judged it was only a couple of hours past sunrise. "I have. And you're lucky that I did after all that I've been through. You found us early this morning. I've only gotten a few hours of sleep. I'm surprised I'm even up."

"You've gotten more than a few hours' sleep," Craugh said. "You slept through one whole day."

The news shocked Wick. He never slept that long. His ability to sleep so little had helped him keep up with the work Frollo assigned him at the Vault of All Known Knowledge.

"A day?" Wick repeated.

"Aye," Cap'n Farok said. He ran a withered hand through his gray beard and smiled a little. "Me, I never seen a halfer go so long without a meal. Unless he was chained up somewheres an' food couldn't be had, of course."

"Of course," Wick said, dazed. *A day? I slept a whole day away?* He looked at Craugh. "We've lost time."

"We have," Craugh agreed. "But we've learned more."

"What?"

"We've learned that the three owners of those mystic weapons had hidden them," Alysta said. "They didn't just disappear over the years."

Wick turned toward her voice only to see her leap gracefully to the table where the map was. The cat sat on her haunches and wrapped her tail around her feet. "So?" he asked.

"That means someone was looking for them a thousand years ago," Alysta said. "Otherwise there would have been no reason to hide them."

"Who's looking for them?"

"That's just one of the questions we need answers for," Cap'n Farok said. "There's somethin' more than meets the eye to this."

"The monster's eye?" Wick asked, thinking of the great eye kept in the jug under the captain's bed.

Cap'n Farok frowned and waved a hand. "No. This doesn't have anythin' to do with that there eye. I meant the eye." He pointed to one of his eyes. "Me eye. Yer eye. Just . . . just . . . the *eye*. It were a figure of speech."

"Oh," Wick said, realizing he was thinking too literally. Then he thought of something else. "How is Quarrel?"

"Mendin'," Cap'n Farok said. "Hallekk took the arrow out of her shoulder. He says it missed everythin' important. Gonna be painful comin' back from it, but she'll get it done all right. She's young yet. Got a lot of healin' left to her."

"She's a very strong young woman," Alysta added. "I look forward to getting to know her."

"I'm glad," Wick said.

"Although I'm not too happy with you." The cat focused her unblinking gaze on the little Librarian. "When you threw both of you over the cliff, I thought you'd committed suicide and taken her with you."

" 'Threw yerself over the cliff'?" Cap'n Farok looked totally shocked.

"It had to be done," Wick insisted. "It was the only way."

In a disapproving tone, Alysta quickly related the events.

"Ye hadn't mentioned that when we talked," Cap'n Farok said when the cat finished her tale.

"We had other things to discuss," Alysta said.

Cap'n Farok dropped a trembling hand on Wick's shoulder and grinned, pleased and proud. "Jumpin' offa cliffs, is it? Wait'll I tell Hallekk. Or Cobner! By the Old Ones, that crusty warrior'll have hisself a laugh now, won't he? An' claim all the credit fer yer courage an' skill. 'Course, he'll probably leave ye yer trickery an' such fer thinkin' of such a thing."

In spite of the situation, Wick grinned. Cobner, who still claimed that Wick had saved his life that night in Hanged Elf's Point, would rejoice in the telling of the story. No doubt Cobner would further embellish it when he told it in taverns. By the time Cobner was finished with it, Wick was likely to be nine feet tall and to have taken at least fifty Razor's Kiss thieves with him. It would be something to hear, that was certain. He looked forward to it and felt a pang of wistfulness to see his friend again.

"I swear," Cap'n Farok said, still grinning, "since ye started a-hangin' out with proper pirates, Librarian Lamplighter, ye sure have picked up some almighty un-Librarian ways."

"I suppose," Wick replied, but he felt proud of his accomplishments. He felt proudest of the fact that he'd lived through everything. Looking at Craugh took some of the celebration out of the moment, though.

Craugh gazed out to sea, his brows knit in consternation.

Wick hadn't often seen the wizard worried. "Do you know where *Wraith* is bound for?"

"Perhaps," Craugh said.

"Where?"

Craugh glanced at Wick in a way that let the little Librarian know he'd rather not answer that question. But

Cap'n Farok and Alysta were waiting on a reply as well.

"There can be only one place," Craugh said. "The Forest of Fangs and Shadows."

A chill passed through Wick. He'd spent a little time in the area, but never enough to get completely comfortable with it. The Forest of Fangs and Shadows was a dangerous place, filled with monstrous spiders, elves that had chosen solitary lives apart from the rest of the world and didn't welcome intrusion, and frightful beasts left over from the Cataclysm.

"Why there?" Wick asked.

"Because Sokadir lives there," the wizard answered. "Somewhere."

"Sokadir is still alive?" Wick asked. Sokadir was the elven warder hero who had taken up arms with Death-whisper, the enchanted bow, at the Battle of Fell's Keep more than a thousand years ago.

Craugh nodded and took out his pipe. He tamped it full, then muttered an incantation to light it. "He is an elf, you know. They live for a long, long time. Unless they're killed, of course."

"You never mentioned Sokadir was still alive," Wick said.

"No."

Wick couldn't believe it. "That's something worth knowing."

"Now you know it."

"I could have known it days ago, before we left Greydawn Moors."

"Knowing Sokadir was alive wouldn't have helped us find Boneslicer or Seaspray," Craugh replied testily.

"If we truly want to know what happened at the Battle of Fell's Keep," Wick pointed out, "all we have to do is ask Sokadir."

"Except that Sokadir doesn't want to be found," Craugh said. "I went looking for him before I went looking for you."

Wick thought about that. It was the first admission

Craugh had made that his arrival in Greydawn Moors
hadn't been exactly fortuitous happenstance.

"I couldn't find Sokadir," Craugh said. "But I encountered others who were looking for him as well." He
paused. "These were very dangerous beings."

Beings. The description slammed into Wick. *Beings.
Not people. Not creatures. Beings.*

"It was their interest," Craugh said, "that made me
most curious about why they would be looking for him
after all these years."

Wick cleared his throat. "What . . . *kind* of beings?"

A small, mirthless smile pulled at Craugh's mouth.
"The very dangerous, murderous sort, of course."

Of course. Wick sighed. "Gujhar believes that with
Boneslicer and Seaspray in his possession he'll be able to
track down Deathwhisper because of the magic spell that
bound them at the Battle of Fell's Keep."

"That's probably true. Magic ties all things together,
after a fashion. Those three weapons shared a binding."

"Then we need to catch *Wraith*." Wick looked at the
ocean, but there was no ship in sight.

"I'm keeping watch over *Wraith*," Craugh said. "I can
do that for a time. I've managed to place a compatriot on
board that ship while it was at Wharf Rat's Warren." He
puffed on his pipe. "More than that, though, I can also
track Sokadir and Deathwhisper. When the time is
right."

"How?"

"Through Master Oskarr and Captain Dulaun's descendants."

"Why couldn't you have done that before?" Wick
asked. "Bulokk is with us, and you sent Alysta to me.
You had their descendants before I ever entered Wharf
Rat's Warren."

Craugh regarded the cat. "Alysta is not . . . quite who
she used to be. When she lost her old body, she lost that
tie to Captain Dulaun."

Wick looked at the cat, feeling a little sad for her and

all that she had given up. After all, how could a person live as a cat after years of having hands?

"Now we have my granddaughter," Alysta said, "and we have the scent of our enemies. I will have my ancestor's sword back where it belongs."

"We'll have them all back," Cap'n Farok promised. "Afore this affair gets any more outta hand." Then he shifted his gaze to Wick. "There's breakfast a-waitin' belowdecks, Librarian. Best get at it while it's hot."

At the thought of breakfast, Wick's stomach rumbled. He was too hungry after a day's sleep to feel nervous over where *One-Eyed Peggie* was headed. He took his leave and headed belowdecks. Whatever trouble was brewing, it would come soon enough. He chose to be fortified for it.

In the galley, Bulokk and the Cinder Clouds Islands dwarves were regaling each other with tales while stuffing themselves with breakfast. *One-Eyed Peggie* never stinted on feeding her hands and passengers.

As soon as Wick arrived, some of the pirate crew greeted him and called him to their table, which sparked an immediate good-natured battle between them and the Cinder Clouds Islands clan as they entreated Wick to sit with them. In the end, they made way for Wick in the middle of both groups and he gave in to their demands for his stories in Wharf Rat's Warren.

With a full plate ahead of him and plenty more to hand, Wick sat among the pirates and warriors and spun his tales. He couldn't help thinking how out of place Grandmagister Frollo would have thought him among them. But surely there was no finer place for a storyteller than in front of a willing audience.

A Note from Grandmagister
Edgewick Lamplighter

*a*fter my recovery, which was thankfully short in returning, I spent time at my journals. I have written this one and placed it with a friend of mine in Deldal's Mills. Since you have that book, my apprentice, doubtless you know that my friend was none other than Evarch. Hopefully the Ordal that helped you solve the riddle to find this journal was known to me. He was a good friend.

Better yet, you should never be given this book, for it will mean that an Old Evil has once more risen. And, quite possibly, that an end has come to me. If that is true, try to find time to come to my grave and read to me every now and again.

I'm reminded of Alysta, the cat, in this instance. At least she had paws to turn the pages of a book with if she had a mind. I shudder to think of an eternity spent without books. I have hopes that every book that was ever lost is somewhere waiting for me when my life here finally ends.

There is yet a third book, of course. One that will complete this trilogy you've come seeking. You'll find it deep within the Forest of Shadows and Fangs. Look for that journal in the Crocodile's Throat at Jaramak's Aerie just off Never-Know Road.

Due to circumstances beyond my control, I couldn't take that book from that place. Even that book is somewhat unfinished, though. I fear you're going to have to write the end to that one.

Just don't let it be the end of you. You're facing horrible foes who don't know the meaning of mercy. If the Old Ones are willing, Craugh will be with you. He was the one who helped us escape from the madness of the Darkling Swamp when the time came. But even he couldn't destroy Lord Kharrion's foul legacy.

That's all I can say for now. To say any more would reveal too much at the wrong time. A story has to unfold at a natural pace, and—sometimes—so does life.

If you've come this far, and you're the one I taught my secrets to, then I must have cared for you. Hopefully you cared about me. Even more so, I hope that my life mattered and that I did good works. But mostly I hope that I got to read every good book there was.

Go forth then, my apprentice. Step lightly and with care. Everywhere you go now, there will be only danger. I wish that I could save you from this undertaking, but obviously I can't. So I wish you good luck from afar.

> *Sincerely,*
> *Edgewick Lamplighter*
> *Grandmagister*
> *Vault of All Known Knowledge*
> *Greydawn Moors*

afterword

Tears wet Juhg's cheeks as he finished reading the last words in his mentor's second journal. The fire still blazed brightly in Evarch's fireplace, so someone must have kept it fed while he was reading, though he'd been swept away by Grandmagister Lamplighter's words and hadn't noticed.

He wiped his face with a hand and looked to his companions.

"Are you all right?" Yurial asked. Concern showed on her youthful face.

After a moment, when he found his voice, Juhg nodded. "I am."

"It must be hard," she said.

"What? The translation?" Juhg shook his head. "Grandmagister Lamplighter taught me his codes. Most of them are almost second nature now."

"I meant it must be hard reading his last words."

"These aren't his last words." The declaration came out more defensively than Juhg had intended.

"Wick isn't here," Yurial said quietly. "If this is as important as you say it is, as important as Craugh has led you to believe, I know that Wick would be here." She smiled a little. "Despite his protestations contrariwise, he was never one to miss out on an adventure." Her eyes searched his. "You don't know if you're ever going to see him again."

Juhg returned her gaze and found he couldn't lie to her. Or to himself. "Wick is gone," he whispered, "off on an adventure like none have ever before taken." He shook his head. "I don't know if he will ever return. Or if he will even be permitted."

"That's why this journey is hard," Yurial said. "You're being offered one last chance to walk in your mentor's footsteps. I felt the same way when I found songs in my father's things that I'd never heard him sing." She smiled a little. "Wick taught my father the secret of writing."

"Grandmagister Lamplighter did that?" Juhg was surprised. Grandmagister Lamplighter had always taken pains to keep his abilities secret, and had believed that none on the mainland knew how to read except wizards.

"He did," Yurial said. "Learning to write didn't come easily to my father. If it hadn't been for Evarch's wines and spirits, I don't think either of them would have made it through that education."

"Do you know how to read?"

She nodded. "I do. It was hard not to learn with them railing at each other. My father made me practice the lute every day for hours. While I played the lute, he worked with ink and paper till he finally grasped what Wick was teaching him." She smiled at the memory. "I think I learned more than my father did, but he learned enough to capture songs on paper. While he was busy at that, I taught Wick to play the lute. He'd played the lute before, of course, and I never found anything he couldn't play, but he didn't quite have the fingering down. I helped him with that."

Juhg felt the weight of the book on his leg. Fatigue leached the strength from him and he could barely keep his eyes open.

"When I first started playing my father's songs," Yurial said, "I felt only sadness and despair. Gradually, I came to love my father's songs. Someday you'll be able to feel better about these journals you're after."

"There's only one more," Juhg said. "After that—" He couldn't go on.

"There are others," Raisho said, leaning forward with his hands on his knees. He looked tired as well. "Just in readin' that book, ye've learned that there are other books the Grandmagister wrote what ye 'aven't read yet."

"I know," Juhg said. *But do they still survive?* There were days, sometimes, when he didn't think of the trap he'd unwittingly brought to the Vault of All Known Knowledge that had destroyed so many books. Even with the addition of the second Library he'd discovered while looking for *The Book of Time*, several of those books hadn't been replaced.

They were gone. Forever.

"It's only the end when ye give up on it," Raisho said. "Ye used to tell me that when I'd get to feelin' dispirited. I'd 'ate to think ye were just a-tellin' me that."

"It's just that I don't know if I'm up to this task," Juhg said. "We were nearly killed last night—" He stopped himself, then corrected his statement. Gray dawn was already touching the windows of Evarch's distillery. "—*two* nights ago. Someone is looking for us." Tired as he was, he dreaded sleep, knowing the scarecrow thing would be waiting for him in his dreams.

"You can do this," Evarch said. "Elsewise Wick wouldn't have put you on the track like he did."

"He didn't put me on the track," Juhg said. "Craugh did. And now he's missing." He could still see BEWARE written in blood in the wizard's cabin aboard *Moonsdreamer*. What had happened to Craugh, and who had taken the wizard unawares on board a ship full of Raisho's best pirates?

"That's where you're wrong," Evarch stated evenly. "Wick put you onto this trail." He pointed his pipe at the journal Juhg held. "He's even talking to you through those pages, asking you to finish what he started."

"It wasn't just what he started," Juhg said. "It was what he *couldn't* finish."

"Have you ever read Krumwirth?" Evarch asked.

"Yes." Juhg frowned. "Don't tell me that you read as well?"

"No, no. I knew Wick did, but I never had an interest."

"There's a lot you could learn about wine and spirits," Juhg said. "At the Vault of All Known Knowledge, there are thousands of books about fermenting and distilling."

Evarch waved the idea of the books away. "You can keep them. I know all I need to. I can't keep up with the orders I get now." He puffed on his pipe. "Anyway, what I was getting to was a quote Wick gave me at one time that stuck with me. Of course, he was talking about wines and such at the time, but I've found the quote fits a great deal of occasions. It fits this one now." He cleared his throat. " 'For every vine there is a season, for every rhyme there is a reason, to do less than all you can is treason.' "

"I remember the quote," Juhg said.

"Good. Then you'll know Wick put a lot of store by that thought." Evarch grew more serious. "All those years ago when Wick passed through here, I knew what he was dealing with was dangerous. I saw him go up the Steadfast River, and I saw him come back down it. He looked better going up it. When he came back, he didn't talk about all that he'd lost, or all the warriors that he'd gone with who didn't come back. I didn't ask. I've seen men who've gone through war before, and I knew that was what Wick had been through."

For a moment, silence filled the room except for the crackle of the wood burning on the fire.

"Juhg," Yurial said.

Juhg looked at her.

"Could you really turn around now? After you've come so far?"

Taking a deep breath, Juhg shook his head. But he couldn't help wondering if all the schools he was trying to get started would still be built and organized if something happened to him. Could he better protect the future he was trying to build by continuing to build, or by tracking down whatever villainy lay in the past?

Then he knew there was no choice. Old villainy had a habit of popping up when least expected. Just as it had now.

"No," he said. Then he looked at his three companions. "But if we're going up the Steadfast River to combat whatever Grandmagister Lamplighter was unable to defeat, we're going to need help."

from the annals of
the vault
of all
known
knowledge

A Tale of the Silver Sea Sailors

1

Swim, you bilge rat. Swim or you're going to die out here. And what's left of the rest of the ship's crew will die with you.

Dulaun stared up at the moons as Jhurjan the Swift and Bold and Gesa the Fair, the lesser moon, grew dark. Cold water surrounded him and soaked into his bones, leaching the warmth from his body. He knew the moons only looked like they had dimmed. Actually, he had slid down into the Silver Sea and the increasing depth had washed away the moonslight. His lungs pounded for air.

For a moment his limbs refused to move. His head ached fiercely, though he had no clue why. Then, reluctantly, his arms and legs responded to the panic he barely controlled. His vision cleared as he swam toward the ocean's surface. He thought briefly of shedding his boots, but they were fancy roll-tops he'd paid good coin for down in Dream, and he didn't intend to let them go so easily. Since the city had fallen to Lord Kharrion and the goblinkin, the chances of getting another pair so fine seemed unlikely.

He'd let go of the boots before he jettisoned his sword, though. Seaspray hung at his side in its customary place.

His muscles warmed as he swam. The moonslight nearer the surface revealed the debris in the water.

Wavecutter lay in pieces above and below. Sundered and broken, the ship released its cargo to the sea's cruel embrace. Dulaun's heart ached at that. The old ship took a lot of memories down to the bottom with her, as well as profits the captain and crew had invested in.

A tangle of sails and timbers suddenly unfurled in an ocean current and blocked out the moons. Dulaun angled his body to the side and managed to escape it. A body floated from inside the folds.

Old Ones help me, Dulaun thought. Although his lungs threatened to inhale the sea, he swam for the body and grabbed a fistful of the man's blouse. A dark cloud clung to the man's head. In the dim light, Dulaun didn't recognize the man. He hoped he was crew, not one of the Cage Island pirates that had attacked them and caught them unawares.

A moment later, just when he thought it impossible to hold his breath any longer, Dulaun surfaced. He sucked in a draught of air and immediately turned his attention to the man in his grasp. He turned the man around, locked an arm under the man's chin, and treaded water to keep them both afloat. An eerie fog drifted over the sea. A lantern, one of those used as running lights on the ship, bobbed on the surface thirty feet away. It rode a curler and illuminated the face of the man in Dulaun's arms.

"Alarat, can you hear me?" Dulaun asked. The crashing ocean waves drowned his voice. He put his mouth next to the man's ear and repeated the question.

The man he held gave no response. Blood leaked down from a terrible head wound. It didn't spurt, however, and experience told Dulaun that meant bad things. Head wounds bled fiercely—unless there was something wrong with the heart.

"Can you hear me?" Dulaun repeated. He shook the man.

No response came.

"Leave him go, Dulaun," a husky voice said. "It's too late for him. I think they killed him before he hit the water."

Dulaun glanced over his shoulder. Krahzir, one of the ship's warriors, clung to a timber that floated nearby. The older man looked like a bear as he held on. Fear widened the man's eyes. He didn't know how to swim. Most of the sailors didn't.

"Help me." Dulaun swam toward the timber and hauled the man after him.

Krahzir shook his big, shaggy heard. "Ain't no use. That's a dead man you're holdin' onto. He's just ballast you don't need weighin' you down."

Angrily, Dulaun threw an arm over the timber and took it farther underwater. Krahzir yelped in consternation. For a moment he looked like he might fight over the floating timber.

"Help me," Dulaun ordered in a commanding tone he was still learning. He was young, easily half the older sailor's age.

Cursing, Krahzir caught the sailor's shoulder and tugged him over to the floating timber. Dulaun fought to keep the man afloat. Then, when Alarat flipped around, Dulaun saw the massive head injury. No one could have lived through that.

"I told you," Krahzir said. "He was gone before you fished him up out of the drink."

For a moment, despite his harsh life at sea, sickness twisted through Dulaun's stomach. Ten years and more at sea, he'd seen a lot of bad things. He kept his gorge down with effort. Then he cursed and released the man.

"Go," he whispered as the corpse sank into the depths. "With the blessing of the Old Ones. May your next way be smoother."

Dulaun wrapped his arms around the timber and scouted the nearby water for other survivors that needed help. Here and there, other heads bobbed as they held onto remnants of the ship. Little chance remained of finding those beneath the waves.

Wavecutter was gone. Except for the floating debris—timbers and a few barrels—the ship had vanished. She carried forty men, enough for two lean crews. She'd been ready to claim another pirate ship and split up the sailors so the confiscated vessel could be sailed back to a friendly port and sold.

The next seaworthy prize ship taken in battle had been intended for Dulaun. Captain Neldar had pronounced Dulaun fit enough to captain a ship of his own. Dulaun had looked forward to the prospect.

That's not going to happen now.

Dulaun surveyed the wreckage. If twenty of the forty men had survived, he'd be surprised. Now it remained to see if they continued to live.

2

"Where's the captain?" Dulaun asked.

Krahzir shook his head. His long hair and thick beard threw off water droplets off. "Don't know."

"Who attacked us?" Dulaun scanned the heaving sea for sails. The eight- and ten-foot swells made that venture hard to do.

"Pirates, most likely. This part of the Silver Sea is full of 'em. They got hidey-holes all through the Horns. Nobody even knows how many islands are out here."

"You didn't see any of the pirates?"

Krahzir shook his shaggy head.

"Nor a flag?"

"No. They came outta the fog. They carried no running lights. They pounced on us like a cat on a mouse. I don't think they was hunting us. Just took advantage of finding us." Krahzir glanced around fearfully. "Old Ones help us if they decide to come around and kill any survivors."

"They had the wind with them when they attacked," Dulaun. "Probably seized the moment and rammed us. Their captain evidently decided tacking around into the wind to come back at us wouldn't be worth it."

"Most of our cargo went down into the brine. All them profits we had put back. Wouldn't be much for them to pick over was they to return." Krahzir looked at Dulaun. "I got to admit, I'm scared. There's a lotta water betwixt us and land, and we ain't gonna be safe as long as we're in the Horns." His rough voice lowered to a whisper. "The sea around here is known to harbor monsters as well as pirates."

"Let's not go borrowing trouble," Dulaun responded. "We've enough as it is." But now that the older sailor had mentioned it, the thoughts of monsters had firmly wedged into Dulaun's mind.

Marshaling his courage, Dulaun swam for the floating lantern. Within only a few strokes, he lost Krahzir in the darkness.

"Dulaun." A weak voice came from the left.

Treading water, Dulaun stared through the darkness and found a pale face bobbing beside a thick timber that barely held him up. Young and fearful, the youth clung to the timber with a death grip.

"Jasta," Dulaun called.

"Help. Please help me." Jasta claimed to be twelve years old, old enough to become a ship's boy. Dulaun doubted the age was true. Jasta was at least younger by a year or two. Before Captain Neldar had taken him on, Jasta's life had been hard, leaving him scarred and thin. He'd put on a little weight since coming on board. Things hadn't been easy, but they'd been better than wherever he'd come from.

"I will," Dulaun said as he looked around for the nearest floating timber.

"Hurry. My arms are getting tired. And I'm afraid."

"It's all right to be afraid, lad. We're all afraid. At a time like this, there ain't no shame in that. But you have to keep your head. Can you do that?"

"Aye. Just don't leave me out here."

"I won't. Hang on just a little longer." Dulaun swam to

a timber floating in the water and got behind it. Slowly, he propelled the timber toward Jasta. Trying to grab hold of the boy in his present state of panic would probably have gotten both of them drowned.

With Jasta's help, Dulaun pushed the two timbers together. He shed his shirt and used it to tie them together in the middle. He swam to the lantern and held it over his head.

Light reflected from a handful of faces scattered around him. All of the men called out to him.

"Has anyone seen Captain Neldar?" Dulaun asked.

A chorus of *no*s followed the question.

"Who was the helmsman?"

"Ardne," Frampos replied. He was the ship's cook. He'd gotten old and fat and gray with the job. "Took him up a bowl of stew afore we was hit."

Dulaun felt a little better at that. Ardne had been the last scheduled in rotation as helmsman through the night. Dawn wasn't far off. Things would look better in the light.

"Where's Ardne?" Dulaun asked.

"Captain Neldar was with Ardne at the helm," someone said.

"Where were we struck?" Dulaun had been asleep at the time.

Neldar was a fair ship's captain and split the watches with Dulaun more equitably than most would have. Neldar also liked the night because the ship and sea had been quieter. It was, as he often pointed out, a contemplative time for a sailor.

"Aft of the stern," someone said. "I saw that big black ship appear out of the fog. It weren't there, then it were. And then it were upon us. I tried to shout a warnin', but there weren't no time. That ship was in the middle of us afore I could turn around."

"We need rope." A wave smashed across Dulaun's face. He sputtered, then spat out the salt water. Swallowing it would only make him sick. It dripped from his mustache and coated his lips.

Three of the sailors found rope attached to the timbers they clung to. Under Dulaun's guidance, they propelled them into one spot and started lashing them together. After a bit, the mass of timbers became a floating bundle of sticks that rolled loosely on the sea. They added some of the barrels, tying them underneath to create more buoyancy.

"Not exactly seaworthy, is it?" Krahzir asked sourly.

"Any port in a storm," Dulaun rebuked the big man. "Ain't that what they say?" He clung to the mass of timbers for a moment to rest. His body ached from swimming so much, and his head still pounded.

"How far do you think we are from land?" Krahzir asked quietly.

"Ten, twelve miles."

Krahzir nodded. "That's what I'm guessin' too."

Dulaun had taken a reading from the stars in the early evening and plotted the helmsman's course. Pirates roamed the nearby coastal waters and made them dangerous to cargo ships that hugged the land. *Wavecutter* had been a peaceable ship, sometimes freighting cargo, but she'd preyed on pirates, too. Many people fled the North lands as the goblinkin under Lord Kharrion marched south.

"The sea's carrying us back out into open water," Krahzir said.

"I know," Dulaun agreed. "Most of the others don't realize that. They've got vexations enough now. Telling them that ain't gonna do them no good." He looked at Krahzir. "I'm thinking we should keep that to ourselves. The men don't need anything more to panic over."

"Aye. That trouble'll blow our way soon enough."

"Dulaun! Dulaun!" One of the two other sailors that knew how to swim called from the east. The coming dawn scratched pink and purple lines above him. He looked like a silhouette against the dark sea.

"Aye," Dulaun called back. "I hear you."

"I found the captain."

3

Captain Neldar held onto a small, buoyant cask. The old man and his prize barely managed to stay afloat. He lay on his back and clasped the cask to his chest. Only his face, not even his ears, remained above the waterline.

For a moment after he saw him, Dulaun believed the old man dead, that only a death rictus kept his grip on the cask. Then he saw the captain's eyes move.

"Captain Neldar." Joy and fear warred within Dulaun as his saw the dire straits of his old mentor. Dulaun swam toward Neldar.

"Dulaun? Is that you, lad?" Neldar's head shifted slightly in Dulaun's direction. He spat out water, then hacked and coughed.

"Aye," Dulaun responded as he drew closer. He pushed a timber ahead of him. Pulling the captain from the sea wasn't going to be possible or safe. However, the timber would help.

"I thought—" Water sluiced across Neldar's face. "I thought I lost you."

"No."

"Blasted ship came out of nowhere. Didn't see it till she was upon us. Weren't no time to do anything."

Dulaun's body protested as he strived to reach the old

man. Neldar was in his twilight years, gone gray and slack
with age, but his mind remained sharp as a sword's edge.
Calluses covered his big hands, hardened by pulling ropes
and fighting goblinkin and sailors that sailed under a black
flag. He wasn't a big man, but he'd always lived big.

And he'd taught Dulaun everything he knew about
sailing and being a commander of men aboard a ship.

"They sunk my ship," Neldar went on. "Built her with
me own two hands, and those Horns pirates took her
from me. May they burn in the Pits."

Dulaun kept pushing the timber ahead of him. He
struggled against the waves.

"I recognized her," Neldar said. "That ship that struck
us. She's *Blackheart*. Had her a metal prow, she did.
Busted us clean in two with it."

Blackheart possessed a legacy. Sailing men all throughout the Silver Sea knew of her. Humans and the elves that
sailed told stories about the ships she'd won in battle, and
the crews the pirates had killed in bloodlust. No one
knew where *Blackheart* dropped anchor, though, but everyone assumed it was in the Cage Islands.

Dulaun reached Neldar with the timber. The old man
didn't move. Dulaun started to make his way down to
him.

"Avast there," Neldar ordered. "If you come down here
and try to pull me outta the sea, I'll have you on barnacle
duty for a month."

Dulaun stayed back with effort. "Grab hold, captain,"
he invited. He held the timber as close to Neldar as possible. "Just grab hold and we'll get you back to the raft
we've made."

Weakly, Neldar caught hold of the timber. Frustrated,
Dulaun watched as the waves almost tore the old captain
from the timber every time they lifted him and dropped
him into the trough. Dulaun experienced difficulty in staying above the sea as well.

Finally, Neldar had a decent hold and clung to the
timber.

Dulaun threw Neldar a piece of rope. "Lash yourself to the timber. I'll take you back to the raft."

With trembling hands, Neldar formed a sling around the timber and slid his left arm through it. "All right."

Dulaun forced the timber around and aimed it back toward the raft. The sailor that had located the captain swam nearby.

"You're gonna have to be careful with the men," Neldar said. "These waters ain't safe for none of us."

"I know," Dulaun replied.

"The Horns pirates are—"

The sailor swimming only a short distance away suddenly disappeared beneath the surface. At almost the same time, Dulaun felt a current against his legs.

Neldar cursed. "Something's in the water, Dulaun. Something took Pyarak."

Suddenly, the survivors aboard the raft yelled warnings and pointed toward the sea. Dulaun spun in the water and tried to spot what they saw, but the gleaming fresh dawn reflected from the sea and he saw nothing.

A blood trail surfaced along the water.

"Save yourself, lad," Neldar growled.

Panic spiraled through Dulaun. He reached for the long knife at his belt. He'd left Seaspray aboard the raft. He fisted the knife so the point angled down.

"Swim for it!" Neldar ordered.

"I'm not leaving you." Dulaun scoured the water for the predator that took Pyarak.

"There's no saving me."

"We can both—"

"No!" Neldar roared.

From the corner of his eye, Dulaun saw the old captain slip his arm free from the rope sling. Neldar flailed weakly for just a moment, then slowly sank beneath the surface.

Dulaun took a deep breath and plunged below the water. His vision was immediately limited. Straining his eyes, he spotted the captain sinking into the brine and went after him. He wasn't prepared to let the old man go.

Incredibly, Neldar pointed back at Dulaun. The old captain's face twisted into a mask of fear. Air bubbled from his mouth as he tried to yell a warning.

Dulaun twisted in the water. He experienced a brief impression of a wide mouth filled with jagged teeth, four black eyes, long whiskers, and a sinewy mottled gray body that moved with explosive power. The creature struck him almost hard enough to cause him to lose consciousness.

Instinctively, Dulaun managed to bury his knife in the monster's back, then it ripped the knife from his hand so hard it nearly pulled his arm from its socket. He spun in the water, then put out a hand and kicked to recover. As he whirled around, he searched for Captain Neldar.

However, he found no sign of the old man. Or of the predator or Pyarak.

Lungs burning, Dulaun kicked for the surface and swam as fast as he could back toward the raft. The crew yelled encouragement and panic at him. He powered his legs and arms as fast as he could. While in the water, he was just a target for an undersea predator.

The crew pointed with renewed alarm and Dulaun knew the monster relentlessly tracked him.

Keeping the panic surging through him under control, Dulaun concentrated on survival. He summoned Seaspray, calling the sword to his hand. In a heartbeat, his fist closed around the blade and he stopped swimming. With the sword in his hand, the sea suddenly offered no resistance to him. He stood in the sea as if he were on dry land. Those were two of the gifts beaten into the mystic metal that had made the weapon. He was loath to call on the power because it was new to him. He still didn't understand all the sword could do.

The maloch arrowed toward him. Twenty feet long and as thick as a man, the creature offered nothing but sudden death. Four eyes, a pair on either side, framed the gaping maw filled with razor-sharp teeth as long as a man's hand. Whiskers, most of them as long as an arrow, jutted out from its wedge-shaped face.

Before Lord Kharrion had risen to power among the goblinkin, no seafaring man had ever witnessed such a beast. Some said that the Goblin Lord had created the maloch as he had the Boneblights and other things that battled at his command.

Dulaun didn't know if that was true. Until today, he'd never seen a maloch. They tended not to hunt alone. He held Seaspray ready and hoped that whatever magic the dwarven Master Blacksmith Oskarr was said to have beaten into the weapon worked.

The maloch swam straight for Dulaun. Holding the sword in both hands, Dulaun waited. The maloch wrenched up from the sea, twisting violently so that half its body stood up from the water. A torrent gushed from the maw, and it squalled in inarticulate rage.

Dulaun steeled himself and trusted in the sword's magic as well as his own experience in battle. At the last moment, he threw himself to one side, rolled back to his feet, and slashed the blade into the underside of the maloch's jaw.

The creature missed Dulaun by inches and disappeared into the sea. The water below Dulaun's feet rolled and almost knocked him down. But the sword's magic held and kept him on top of the water. He peered into the sea and tried to track the huge predator.

You wounded it. Dulaun tried to take hope in that. *You can hurt it.*

"Dulaun! Come on! While you've got the chance!"

Dulaun didn't move from the spot he stood on. His breathing came in ragged gasps. The wind whipped over him and he rose and fell with the waves.

A chorus of frightened cries drew his attention back to the makeshift raft. Then he spotted the dark shadow gliding under the sea toward the desperate men.

Dulaun ran back for them. The uncertain waves made his way difficult because the sea surface rolled and heaved and dropped. As fast as he was, and as big as the maloch was, he knew he wasn't going to reach the raft before the monster did.

The monster reared up again only a short distance from the raft. The sailors cowered back, trying to find some place to hide even though that was impossible. With a lithe strike, the maloch grabbed one of the men from the raft.

Just as Dulaun reached the creature, a wave shoved him up almost to the same height as the sea predator.

Reversing his sword in his hands, Dulaun hurled himself forward and landed astride the great beast. He locked his legs around the maloch's body just behind its wedge-shaped head. In the next moment, the creature dove beneath the water.

Dulaun held on grimly as the maloch arrowed for the sea bottom far below. Although Seaspray possessed a number of mystical qualities, all given by the Old Ones according to Forgemaster Oskarr, giving Dulaun the power to breathe underwater wasn't one of them.

The sailor in the maloch's jaws continued to struggle for a moment. Then he shivered and stopped. One of his legs floated free as the maloch crunched down harder.

Knowing there was no way to save the man and that he would have to endure the loss of yet another friend, Dulaun struck fiercely. Seaspray penetrated the thick muscle that sheathed the maloch's neck at the base of the skull. With a twist and a wrench, the keen blade severed the creature's spine.

A cloud of blood spread through the water and covered Dulaun but washed instantly away. He felt the muscles of the predator go slack beneath him but it still slid deeper and deeper.

Dulaun kicked free of the monster and swam for the surface as he held Seaspray in one hand. He peered through the murky water and hoped that the maloch had been alone.

When he surfaced, Dulaun drew a deep breath and shook the water from his eyes. With the sword in his hand, he stepped once more on top of the water and studied the rolling waves for the raft. For a moment he feared the creature's attack had shattered the fragile craft. Then he saw it bobbing to the north and realized the maloch had carried him away.

Several of the sailors waved encouragingly.

Dulaun ran across the waves to join them.

"Where's the beastie?" Krahzir asked cautiously. He held a jagged length of wood.

"Dead." Dulaun stood beside the raft. Water squeezed between the cracks of the timbers as they thudded against each other.

"An' Laryan?" one of the men asked.

Sadness touched Dulaun. "Was that who was taken?"

"Aye."

Laryan was a year or two younger than Dulaun. During the last two years he'd been with *Wavecutter*, Laryan had always been a good hand, quick to help and twice as quick with a joke.

Dulaun shook his head and saw the desperate despair in the eyes of his companions. *Your men*, he corrected himself. *They don't need a friend out here. That's what Neldar would tell you. They need a captain.*

"We're gonna die out here, ain't we?" Boccoda rumbled in his thick voice. "If the maloch an' sharks don't get us, thirst will."

The sun warmed Dulaun's back. By noon the heat would almost be blistering hot on the water. Without shelter the men would be parched and burned despite their heavy tans.

"You'll die out here," Dulaun said. "Only if you've a wish to. For myself, I'm going to the Horns."

The sailors remained silent for a moment, then talked among themselves. Finally Krahzir said, "With that sword you've got, you can walk into the Horns, but what about the rest of us?"

Dulaun made himself grin despite the devastation that had filled their sails the last hour. "For that, I'm going to need your pants."

5

dulaun tested the line he'd made from the sailors' pants. When he was satisfied every knot seemed tight enough, he settled the loop over his shoulders and pulled it down to his waist. Once it was in place, he leaned into it like a dray into its traces. His muscles strained against the weight of the raft. Slowly, grudgingly, the raft started forward over the waves.

Concentrate. Just put one foot in front of the other. Dulaun tried to forget about the oppressive heat and the loss of Captain Neldar and all their shipmates. He also tried to forget that his sense of direction might be off and he might not be walking into the Horns, but into another stretch of open water. Forgetting that another maloch might wander by at any time, or that a shark might, proved even harder.

He carried Seaspray naked in his fist and hoped he'd be fast enough to save them all if it came to that.

Walking against the outgoing tide started hard and got harder. At first he struggled because most of the time he was walking uphill. Then he decided to tack into the curlers and head straight down on the other side. Once he had the raft moving, the task became easier. But his muscles still ached and burned.

The sailors stayed quiet behind him. He knew most of them studied the water, ready to cry out an alarm if they saw anything threatening, so he concentrated on the effort.

It's only ten or twelve miles, he told himself. *A man can walk more than twice that in a day easily.*

Hours later, Dulaun knelt on the ocean's surface and tried to catch his breath. His knees and feet got wet, but he didn't sink as he rode the waves. The line tying him to the raft yanked at him rhythmically. He resented the weight.

Judging from the sun, it was early afternoon. He didn't know how much distance he'd covered so far. From the way the blue-green horizon looked, uninterrupted, he'd made no headway. That couldn't be true, though. He wouldn't let that be true. But he knew he wasn't getting all the distance he needed with each step. The Silver Sea pushed back at him just as surely as he pressed forward.

Even now, resting merely to catch his breath, represented a loss of what he'd gained. The tide continued to carry them out to sea.

"Dulaun."

He turned back to the raft.

"Mayhap you need to come back in," Krahzir suggested.

All of the men had been burned by the sun. Their pale legs looked like liquid coals. Trying to cool off in the water only made the burn worse.

"I'm just resting," Dulaun said. "I'll be ready to go again shortly."

"Won't do none of us any good if you kill yourself out there today."

"I'm not going to kill myself."

"Dulaun—"

Turning his back on the man, Dulaun got to his feet, adjusted the loop of pants around his waist, and leaned into the weight of the raft. Sluggishly, the raft broke free of the water and started following him again.

It would have been easier if someone else could have held Seaspray and pulled the raft for a while. But that wasn't possible. Each of the three weapons that Master Oskarr had forged was magically linked with their bearers. No one outside their bloodline could touch the weapons.

Hours later, Dulaun paused for some of the bread and water they'd managed to salvage from the floating cargo. There hadn't been much. The full water barrels had sunk, leaving them with only dregs they'd found in nearly-empty containers. The sea had ruined most of the foodstuffs, but there had been a few loaves of bread, eggs, and jerked meat that had been salvaged.

The sun sat low in the western sky. But the tide had changed. Dulaun had noticed it almost at once. He no longer had to fight the pull out to sea as much. He took heart in that, even though he knew that it might not mean they were any closer to land.

At twilight Krahzir called for Dulaun's attention.

Dulaun didn't break stride. He was afraid if he stopped he wouldn't be able to get going again. "What?"

"I see a light to the east, nor'east."

Dulaun brought his head up and stared into the darkness. In the west, the sky was an ugly purple and black bruise as the dregs of the day drained into the ocean and some of the light gleamed across the water. Patches even flickered to the east where the foaming curlers caught the light as well.

For the most part, though, darkness claimed the east. The inky blackness, marred only by the stars, made the light dancing in the distance stand out even more.

"What do you make of it?" Dulaun asked.

"It's fire. Definitely fire. But it's not made for camp. Looks more like a warning fire."

Dulaun silently agreed. He took heart in the fire's presence. "We'll make for the fire, then."

"Could be dangerous," Frampos said. "A fire like that, here in the Horns, can't be meant for anything but pirates."

"A fire like that," Dulaun replied, "means dry land. As for danger, I don't think I've ever seen anything more dangerous than the sea."

Several of the surviving sailors agreed.

Dulaun shifted the harness around his waist and adjusted his course. He kept his eyes locked on the fire and told himself it wasn't too far away. Behind him, Frampos cursed their luck.

Full dark descended upon the Silver Sea. Dulaun walked for another two hours. With the sunburn fresh from the long day, the night chilled him to the bone. Although he walked on the sea's surface, curlers still splashed against him. He stayed soaked. The water and the wind cut into him and made him shiver.

The sailors clumped together on the raft and shared body heat. But their meager food and water stores were gone. They'd saved the last of it for Dulaun and not told him till he'd noticed they neither ate nor drank. He'd felt guilty because he should have been paying better attention, and he wouldn't have taken the last of it. But he'd been tired and not as observant as he might have otherwise been.

That guilt pushed him now, drawing reserves from him that he hadn't known existed within him.

The island took shape in the darkness as they neared. The bonfire raged at least ten or twelve feet high, but it sat on a cliff that shot straight up from the sea. When Dulaun had seen the climb it presented, his heart had sunk. Even on their best days, with years of climbing the 'yards behind them, the ascent would have proven grueling.

He'd walked to the north and hoped to find a proper beach. Atop the hill, figures occasionally stepped into view as they fed the fire.

It was a warning signal, a marker for ship's captains that sailed at night. Here in the Horns, though, those ship's captains would only be pirates.

6

$\mathcal{T}$he tide swapped around and started pushing the raft toward the land. The way got easier. Dulaun guided more than pulled there at the end, but he was all but undone. Fatigue wore at him. He felt numb and his eyes refused to sort out much from the darkness.

"Dulaun, there's a beach. Do you see it?" Krahzir asked.

Shaking his head to clear it, Dulaun focused on the coastal area before him.

White sand covered the small beach and caused it to stand out in the darkness. Not enough room existed in the lagoon for a proper ship's harbor. A fierce timberline closed the beach off and promised rough passage for anyone that ventured there.

When Dulaun pulled the raft at last into shallow water, the men who were able jumped from the miserable craft and helped him pull the wounded to shore. They cheered their good fortune.

"Quiet," Dulaun ordered as he stood on the white sand and finally sheathed Seaspray. The sword felt like a blacksmith's anvil dangling from his arm. "Don't forget where you are. These islands are the Horns. They belong to pirates. If they find us here, they'll kill us outright or take us for ship's slaves."

The men quieted at once.

Dulaun glanced at the curlers crashing against the white sand. Fatigue sapped his strength to the point that he could scarce stand.

Several of the men lay on the ground despite the pervasive cold. Exhaustion showed on all of them.

"Now isn't the time to rest." Dulaun swayed unsteadily despite his best efforts to stand tall. "We've got things to do before we take our beds."

Most of the men groaned.

"We're tired an' sick an' burned, Dulaun," Bytternos protested.

Krahzir walked over to the man and cuffed him about his ears. Bytternos covered his head with his arms and yelped in pain.

"Get up, you lazy dog," Krahzir snarled. "Ain't no man more tired than Dulaun, and if he's gonna walk, I'm gonna follow." He glared at the rest of the crew. "Any of you that don't take his advice is likely to end up with your gullets sliced come morning. If the pirates don't do it, I'll likely do it myself."

Reluctantly, with some grousing, the men roused and came to attention.

"We need to hide the timbers," Dulaun said. "Pull them into the trees. Then we need to find fresh water." He looked at the mighty oaks in the forest at the other end of the beach. "If those trees have found water in this inhospitable clime, then it's somewhere here to be had."

Krahzir picked four men for the task.

"Stay together," Dulaun ordered. "And go slow. With that signal fire out there, the pirates are probably close. Everything we do tonight must be done before morning. I don't want any of us moving around after it gets light until we get the lay of the land."

The four sailors drew their cutlasses and vanished into the darkness.

"We need food. Frampos."

"Aye," the big man said.

"You'll know more about what we're likely to eat in the forest. Take three men and see what you can find."

The ship's cook hesitated, caught Krazhir's fierce gaze, and quickly nodded. "Aye. I'll get it done." He picked his men and walked into the darkness.

"Jasta," Dulaun said.

"Aye."

"You claim to have been a fisherman."

"Aye." The boy smiled proudly.

"Ever done any night fishing?"

"Aye."

"See what you can fetch us from the lagoon."

"If there's any fish in those waters, I'll catch us a few."

Dulaun smiled at the young boy's sense of adventure. "I trust that you will. Voldt, take two others and go with him. See if he can teach you a trick or two. And there's likely clams out there along the beach. See if you can find any."

The men headed back toward the water.

Surveying the rest of the crew, Dulaun saw three of them were too wounded to help much. One had a broken arm. Another had both legs broken. And Solfak had a head wound and hadn't regained consciousness since getting pulled from the sea.

"Krahzir, let's get those timbers pulled up and stowed." Dulaun turned his weary steps toward the sea.

High up on the cliff nearly a quarter-mile away, the signal fire continued to burn. Dulaun took hope from that. The distance alone, as well as the thick forest, proved that the island was big enough to support life.

And it offered a chance for them to hide from their enemies. The morning might change that, though.

Light and soft voices woke Dulaun. He closed his hand over Seaspray but made no other move. During the night, he'd dreamed of his days aboard *Wavecutter*. For a time he thought he might be waking up in his hammock back aboard ship.

The hard ground beneath him convinced him otherwise. Even the layer of giant leaves from dragon's tongue plants hadn't softened the earth enough to make sleeping comfortable.

He cracked open his eyes and saw the fiery red color of the dragon's tongue leaves that gave the plant its name. Birds called to each other in the treetops. Out in the distance, the waves crashed against the beach. The scent of herbs and wood smoke tickled his nose.

As he sat up, he felt the twinge of overtired muscles and strains ache deep within him. Judging from the angle of the sun, it was midday at least.

The sailors sprawled along the tree line and stayed away from the beach. They all appeared tense.

"He's awake," someone said.

Krahzir rose from the twisted bulk of two oaks sharing gnarled roots and walked over to Dulaun.

"Keep your voice low," Krahzir said. "We ain't alone on this isle. Like as not, we won't be getting out of this place alive."

7

"What's going on?" Dulaun's dry mouth made his voice sound like a croak.

"It appears we've had the bad luck of landing on one of the pirate harbors instead of a deserted isle." Krahzir gestured to one of the men and took the water flask that got passed along. "The good luck is there's a spring back in the woods away. Water's sweet and good. Have a drink."

Dulaun took the flask and drank slowly, knowing if he drank too quickly his stomach would turn sour. He paused, then tilted the flask again and let his mouth fill with water. He felt refreshed almost immediately.

"Found enough edibles in the woods to make up a fine stew," Krahzir went on, "what with the clams we dug up and the fish Jaska caught. Frampos found enough herbs to season it up. We ain't gonna starve."

"How long have you been up?"

"A while. We been sleeping in shifts. Keeping a lookout."

"Why didn't you wake me?" Dulaun asked. He felt guilty that he hadn't been awake to take his share of the labors.

Krahzir shrugged. "Weren't no need to. And you did all the work yesterday. Thought it best if we let you sleep as long as you'd like." He nodded out toward the water. "Being up and about right now ain't the best thing we could do. We'd be better off doing any exploring after night falls. Horns pirates are still coming in to port."

"Have you found the port?"

"No. We stayed where we knew we was safe." Krahzir nodded toward the Silver Sea. "But they's pirates out there, sure as you're born. We've seen two ships come by. One this morning and one this afternoon."

Dulaun squinted up at the sun and realized it was afternoon. He slid Seaspray into its sheath and sat up with crossed legs.

"What ships?" he asked.

"Didn't recognize the one this morning," Krahzir answered. "But the one this afternoon was *Hound's Tooth.*"

Dulaun recognized the name at once. *Hound's Tooth* was almost as feared as *Blackheart.* "What kind of shape was she in?"

"Banged up some, but her sails was full and she cut through the water like a gull through air. Why?"

"Because there aren't too many reasons for a ship to put into port. To take on ship's stores and to handle repairs."

"Aye." Krahzir scratched his thick beard.

"So I have to wonder, why are the ships coming here?"

"There's one other reason I can think of." Krahzir grimaced at the thought. "They's a pirate town somewhere on this island."

Dulaun nodded.

"Well," Krahzir grumped unhappily, "we've stuck our head in a bee's nest right proper, ain't we?"

"Maybe. But you'll find more than bees in a hive. There's also honey."

Krahzir studied Dulaun. "What are you thinking?"

"We need a ship if we're going to get off this island. That pirate harbor should have a few of them. And if they're here because a pirate town is here, they might not be expecting to have one of them stolen."

"You're crazy, you know that, right?"

Dulaun sipped more water. "You know any better ways to get off this island?"

With a final rattle and a cough, Solfak died. His body quivered and he lay still in the long shadows of the evening. Dulaun had sat beside the man and applied poultices Frampos had put together from things he'd found in the forest. In the end, the old sailor never regained his senses, and Dulaun hoped it was better that way. After he died, Solfak's fever-ridden flesh finally started to cool.

"He's gone," Krahzir said quietly, a short time later.

"I know."

"You ain't gonna do him any good sitting there."

"I was just remembering him," Dulaun said. "Him and the captain."

Krahzir was silent for a time. "Ain't likely any of us is going to forget them. But we gotta get off of this isle if we're going to remember them and tell their families what become of 'em."

"I know." Dulaun pushed himself up. "Let's find a place to lie Solfak to rest properly, then see if we can scout out that pirate town."

Digging in the root-infested forest ground proved hard without axes, shovels, and picks. The crew made do with their knives and backs. Dulaun aided them, taking turns with them as the moons rose into the star-studded sky. Cries of night birds and cats turned the forest eerie. Several of the crew believed in superstitions and didn't care for life outside the ship or the towns where they'd grown up.

Finally, they put Solfak's body into the shallow hole and covered it over. They added a layer of rock to keep the scavengers at bay.

When they'd finished, they all stood around the un-marked grave.

"Ain't right just leavin' him here thisaway," Marnix stated. He shook his head. "Somebody should say some-thin'."

Gradually, all heads turned to Dulaun.

"I'm not a speaker for the Old Ones," Dulaun pro-tested.

"Cap'n Neldar always spoke over them what died aboardship," Frampos said. "You'll do."

A captain doesn't just lead the men on the ship, Neldar had told Dulaun. *He trains them, guides them, punishes them, and rewards them. And Old Ones forbid that the time comes, but the captain also buries them. If you want to be master of your own ship one day, Dulaun, that's what you've got to be ready to do.*

Dulaun took a deep breath and talked with favor of the old sailor, remembering things that he'd been known for. Then he asked the blessing of the Old Ones and declared the burial complete.

Krahzir dropped a heavy hand on Dulaun's shoulder. "That was a fine burying. The cap'n couldn'ta done no better."

Dulaun nodded and didn't trust his voice to speak. When he'd thought of becoming captain, he'd never seen himself performing duties like this.

But raiding parties? That was something he was used to. He looked forward to the next few hours.

8

The pirate town sat nestled at the bottom of a horseshoe-shaped canyon. Trees along the sides of the canyon guaranteed that few saw the hidden harbor. Although the moonslight offered bright illumination, Dulaun barely spotted the false walls that jutted out from the open end of the canyon. The walls reduced the expanse to one barely navigable by a single large ship.

"Got themselves a proper hidey-hole, they do," Krahzir whispered.

"They do. Hidden *and* defensible. Even if someone finds them, they can destroy them." Dulaun lay on his belly with a spyglass in hand. He trailed the glass across the false walls.

Guards stood atop the walls and watched out to sea. Upon careful inspection, trusting that the pirates wouldn't simply depend on archers for defense, Dulaun spotted nets filled with rock that hung suspended over the opening.

"Do you see the nets?" Dulaun asked.

"Aye." Krahzir shifted uncomfortably. "I figure they drop them down on attackers."

"Maybe."

"What other reason would they be there?"

"That's a lot of rock," Dulaun observed.

"Aye. And what of it?"

"The draft in that part of the port may be shallow. I have to wonder if there's enough rock there to dam up the opening."

"Oh." Krahzir scratched at his beard. "That could be a problem."

Despite Krahzir's protests, Dulaun crept down the side of the canyon and trusted the shadows to keep him hidden. A few warehouses lined the harbor area, but most of the buildings housed taverns. Festive lanterns hung on the walls by the doors, under eaves, and in windows. The stained glass created red, blue, green, and amber lights that reflected on the still water between the ships.

Seven ships lay at anchorage. Small boats ferried goods to the docks. The town depended on the goods for food and clothing, but plenty of other goods had been captured to sell or trade in other ports.

Captain Neldar had done the same thing with the confiscated goods of pirates they'd preyed on. With the vicious cycle of political alliances along the Silver Sea and the coast in the South on the mainland, a pirate—or a privateer—always stood a good chance to capitalize on the misfortunes of others.

Dulaun tried to guess how many men were in town. Assuming the ships crewed an average of thirty men apiece, that was two hundred and ten swords they'd have to face. He swung the spyglass over the dwellings behind the warehouses. Most of them looked like more than one family lived within the clapboard walls.

Call it five hundred men, Dulaun decided. He and his men were outnumbered twenty-five to one.

He turned his attention to the ships. The boats ferried goods, but there weren't many of them.

"They're active," Krahzir whispered beside him. "But I'm betting as the crews get deeper into their cups, they're lax about watching over them ships."

"I think so, too." Dulaun studied the defensive positions atop the wall. "If we hurry, if we're careful and fast, I think we can grab one of those ships and be out of this place before anyone's the wiser. Or, at least, before they can stop us from escaping."

"Those men atop them walls are going to be the problem."

"Well," Dulaun said, "we're just going to have to find a way around that."

Back within the forest, Dulaun laid out his plan for the men. He drew out the town with a dagger on a patch of earth he'd smoothed with his palm.

"We wait until tonight," he told them. He ignored the fear on their faces. He felt it, too. There was no way to do this without being afraid. "In the early morning hours, the pirates pass out or return to their homes. They don't post much of a watch. As hidden as they are, they don't think they need it."

"Inside the canyon like they are, them ships ain't likely to catch wind very fast," Voldt declared. He was a ship's helmsman and had considerable experience.

"I've been down inside the canyon," Dulaun said. "There's enough wind." He glanced at the reddened sky. "Judging from the sky and the heaviness of the air, we're in for a bit of a blow. If it comes tonight, that'll favor us."

"Aye, but you got them men at the walls to worry about."

"Not long we don't," Krahzir said. "I'm gonna take a crew up there and take out one side of them pirates. When the ship comes by, we'll make our way to you."

Dulaun looked at the somber faces of the men before

him and knew they didn't like the chances. "It's what we're left with," he told them. "As risky as it is, we can pull this off."

"If we don't," Frampos said, "there's no place to run. We'll be eyeball deep in pirates."

"Then we have no choice but to succeed," Dulaun told them.

"I'm for it," Voldt said. "I got a wife and babes to get back to. I don't intend to sit on this isle in fear for my life and wait for them pirates to find us. And they will, mark my words on that. Hiding out here ain't gonna work forever."

Dulaun let them think about that for a moment. "Tonight, I'm going down there to get a ship. I'm going to strike a blow for Captain Neldar, because I intend to take *Blackheart*."

Several of the sailors cursed.

"If our luck wasn't foul enough," Bytternos said, "then this will turn it plumb rank."

Krahzir slapped him on the head before he dodged. He yelped and fell over.

"If you speak out of turn against Dulaun again," Krahzir said, "I'm gonna turn you into chum."

"You didn't have no cause to hit me," Bytternos wailed.

"You show Dulaun the same respect you showed Captain Neldar," Krahzir ordered. "No. In fact, you show Dulaun more respect because he ain't told nobody to gut you and leave your worthless carcass in the woods."

"We need every man to handle the ship," Dulaun said, thinking for a moment that Krahzir might make good on his threat.

"I know that," the big man said. "That there's the only thing keeping this toad alive."

"You need me," Bytternos reminded.

"To steal a ship, aye. But once we're at sea, that's a different matter." Krahzir eyed the man fiercely. "Have we come to an understanding then?"

"Aye." Bytternos rubbed his aching head. "Aye. That we have."

"Let's get some sleep," Dulaun said. "We're going to need it for tonight." *And luck. We're going to need that, too.*

9

By nightfall, a storm descended over the isle. Thunder cracked and lightning burned zigzags across the black sky. Rain fell in heavy drops and turned the ground to mud.

Dulaun sat overlooking the harbor and watched as the cargo boats stopped work earlier than usual. The temptation to attempt the theft of the ship rattled within him, but he watched how the taverns filled up.

"We could go now," Frampos said.

"No," Dulaun said.

"I'm freezing out here in this rain. Ain't going to do any of us any good to be froze up while we're after that ship."

"Those pirates are sitting in the taverns," Krahzir said. "They ain't gone to bed, and they ain't gonna be abed for a time yet. We wait."

"Our chances of—"

"You're giving me a headache with all your yapping," Krahzir warned. "You'd best stop while you ain't got knots on your head."

Scowling, Frampos sat back.

Dulaun continued to watch. His stomach grew tighter in apprehension.

"A ship's coming in," Krahzir said a short while later. He pointed toward the harbor opening.

Dulaun turned his spyglass from the taverns to the ship. She was a three-master and rode low in the water. Her hull appeared to drag while sailing through the opening.

"Water's shallow there all right," Krahzir said.

Dulaun nodded. The ship's passage confirmed his fears. "We can't let them dump both loads of rock, Krahzir." He shot the big man a meaningful look.

Krahzir nodded. His long hair lay plastered to his head and on his broad shoulders. "I know. They won't. You got my word on that."

The ship sailed into the harbor. Several men inside the taverns came out and stood in the rain. Most of them huddled within their coats and slickers.

"Must be somebody special for them to get wet like that," Jasta said.

Dulaun noted the way the windows filled with archers. They stayed inside to keep their bowstrings dry, but they had a clear view of the harbor.

"Not special. Someone they don't trust overmuch," he said. After the ship docked, he found out who the crew was. It also explained the trust problem.

"Are those goblinkin?" Krahzir asked.

Through the spyglass, Dulaun studied the goblinkin. They were oddly shaped, with misshapen bodies and mismatched limbs. Many of them had arms longer than their legs. Their heads were triangular shaped and covered with thick black hair that sported finger and toe bones. They wore necklaces of bones as well. Their clothing was meager and uncared for. Goblinkin took what they wanted or needed from victims. They didn't produce much outside of fear and violence.

"Those are goblinkin," Jasta whispered. "What are they doing with the pirates?"

Dulaun couldn't answer the question. He continued watching as a figure in purple robes came up from the ship's hold and went forward.

"Who's that?" Frampos asked.

The purple-robed figure carried on a brief discussion with one of the pirates that seemed to be in charge. The discussion ended briefly when the purple-robed man gestured at a nearby crate. A blazing fireball arced from his fingertips and smashed against the crate, turning it into a pile of flaming boards despite the rain.

"Wizard," the crew whispered in fearful unison.

Dulaun's stomach almost curdled at the thought. Although his sword possessed magic, he didn't much care for wizards. They tended to be selfish and unpredictable.

And deadly, he reminded himself.

The fireball ended whatever disagreement went on between the pirates and the wizard. The wizard climbed from the ship and joined the pirates. Several of the goblinkin followed them into a nearby tavern.

Krahzir cursed the pirates. "They're probably selling out to Lord Kharrion. Gonna help him win the war against the nations in Teldane's Bounty."

Those areas were the linchpin of the resistance to the Goblin Lord's armies, Dulaun knew. Attacks across the land had proven costly to the goblins and they'd started balking. But if the pirates of the Horns could be swayed, the war's advantage could be changed again.

"We've got to escape tonight," Dulaun said. "If the pirates in these isles are going to work with Lord Kharrion, the Alliance needs to know."

"With the goblinkin in port," Krahzir said, "the pirates might be more watchful."

"I know." Dulaun thought furiously as a plan came together in his mind. "But that vigilance might work against them. Whatever agreement exists between the pirates and the goblinkin, they're still dealing with goblinkin. They won't forget that."

"And they won't overlook the fact that they're dealing

with a wizard neither. I'd be more afraid of a wizard. At
least you know what goblinkin will do."

Dulaun silently agreed.

Much later, the pirate town went to bed as drink flowed
to their heads and the small hours before dawn came
crawling. The storm continued unabated.

Soaked to the skin, Dulaun offered his hand to Krahzir.
"It's time. I wish you well."

"And you." Krahzir grinned crookedly. "Old Ones favor us all. And they should because I'm told they favor
the bold and the foolish. We've got a foot in each camp
tonight."

Dulaun smiled. "I'll see you soon. Keep your head
down."

"You do the same." Krahzir turned and headed along
the rim of the horseshoe canyon.

After Krahzir and the four sailors he'd chosen vanished from view, Dulaun hunkered back down to wait.
He stared at the goblinkin ship and noted that no guards
walked the deck. That was a fact he intended to use to his
advantage.

Lightning blazed the sky and flashed from the small mirror Krahzir had taken with him to signal that he was in
place. Dulaun waited tensely for it to repeat, in case the
flash had been from something else. But when the lightning burned again, the flash showed once more. If everything went according to plan, Krahzir was now in control
of the left side of the harbor opening.

"All right then," Dulaun said in a voice that suddenly
sounded far too dry, "it's up to us. Let's be about it."

He led the way down into the pirate town.

10

With the night and the rain and the distraction of their treacherous guests masking their approach, none of the pirates noticed Dulaun and the men he led. His stomach still knotted, though, and his head raced with all that could go wrong.

Being caught out in the open would be the worst thing. Trying to flee back up the muddy slope would prove nearly impossible, and even those that succeeded wouldn't have anywhere to run on the isle.

No. Dulaun calmed himself. *The ship is the only answer.*

"Like as not," Bytternos groused unhappily, "we're gonna end up in some goblinkin's stew tonight."

Before Dulaun could decide whether to address the comment, he heard the sound of walloped flesh followed by Bytternos's yelped curse.

"Be more hopeful about this," Frampos warned, "or I'll offer to cook you up myself."

Dulaun waved the sailors into hiding in the alley between two taverns filled with pirates singing dirty drinking shanties. Tension made the men stiff and nervous.

"We approach *Blackheart* in twos and threes," Dulaun said in a soft voice. "Even if the watch sees you, they may not think much of it. You'll just be pirates, deep in your cups, returning to your berth to sleep it off. Keep your weapons sheathed but close to hand."

They nodded.

"I'll lead the way." Dulaun named two of the sailors to accompany him. Both men were accomplished fighters, not trained as he was in the blade, but resourceful street scrappers.

Woldberg was a short, thin man who had been a cage fighter for a time. His specialty was knives. Halversom had grown up in his da's blacksmith shop until the sea called out to him. He wielded the short-hafted hammer he carried with deadly strength.

"Once we're aboard, the next group should follow." Dulaun turned to go.

"Luck be with you," Jasta whispered.

"And you," Dulaun said, then he stepped out of the shadows.

Despite the conviction he held for his plan, Dulaun's heart hammered as he strode across the rippled boardwalk in front of the taverns and shops. His hand itched for Seaspray, but he kept it away from the weapon.

The pirate watch glanced at him, then looked away. None of them appeared happy with their duty, and most of them drank from bottles they kept in their cloaks.

"Hey, you three," one of them spoke up as Dulaun neared *Blackheart*.

Dulaun turned toward the man. Woldberg and Halversom flanked him automatically as they had in ports around the Silver Sea and the mainland.

"Aye," Dulaun responded.

"I'm willin' to pay any man that'll stand my watch so I can get out of the rain," the guard said drunkenly.

"Not me," Dulaun said. "I'm for bed."

Woldberg and Halversom echoed similar sentiments.

"Weaklings," the guard protested. "The night's still young." He cursed them good-naturedly and foully as they went on.

Blackheart sat tall and imposing at anchorage. Dulaun ran his gaze over her iron-reinforced prow and thought how easily the ship had shattered *Wavecutter.* And the action had been out of bad luck and spite. The pirate ship hadn't even hunted them.

Dulaun squared his shoulders and walked down the pier to the gangplank leading up to the pirate ship. He drew Seaspray and felt himself go calm as he always did before a fight. His boots thumped against the wooden planks.

Four men stood on the deck around a pot of coals. The one nearest turned to Dulaun. The orange glow of the coals painted his features, and Dulaun saw the look of surprise dawn there. The pirate clawed at his cutlass.

"Woldberg," Dulaun called.

"Aye," Woldberg replied.

Orange light flickered against the two thrown knives that spun toward two of the pirates. A knife took one pirate in the eye and the other in the throat. One tumbled to the deck, dead instantly, and the other clawed at his throat as he sank to his knees.

Dulaun had no mercy in his heart. The Horns pirates were the most bloodthirsty of the lot. They killed innocents aboardship out of hand.

The pirate facing Dulaun tried to swing his cutlass. Dulaun grabbed the man's wrist to block the blow, then ran Seaspray through the man's heart. As Dulaun slid the corpse from his blade, Halversom brought his hammer down on the last pirate's head, shutting off the man's warning cry before it could be uttered.

Along the boardwalk, Jasta and two other sailors walked toward *Blackheart*.

Dulaun watched them for a moment, then turned back to Woldberg and Halversom. "Let's secure the ship. I want to be sure we're the only ones aboard."

Minutes later, all the sailors were aboard *Blackheart* and gathered on the deck. They gathered by the hooded brazier. Rain fell in among the coals and hissed.

"We've come this far without being noticed," Dulaun said, "but once we start dropping canvas aboard this ship, that'll end."

Nervous anticipation filled the faces of the men lit by the orange coals.

"Then let's be about it," Dulaun said. "Step lively and keep your weapons to hand."

The crew ran to their stations without a word. Excitement thrilled through Dulaun. He thought of Captain Neldar and knew the old rogue would have loved what they were about to attempt.

To do, Dulaun corrected himself. *We haven't come this far to fail.* He positioned himself at the prow near one of the thick hawser ropes that bound *Blackheart* to the dock. Then he raised his sword, held it for a moment, and swung. The enchanted blade sliced through the hawser with ease. The rope fell away and tumbled into the black water.

In the next instant, the men aboard the 'yards slid the sailcloth free and ran down the lines and the falling canvas. They tied it in place. *Blackheart* bucked at her traces, like a horse ready to break into a full gallop.

"Turn her into the wind," Dulaun cried.

The men pulled at the sails and caught the breeze

that blew in over the cliff. Fortune favored them because the wind boiled down into the canyon and blew toward the harbor mouth. The gale winds made the passage faster and more dangerous.

Warning cries spread along the docks. As Dulaun watched, the boardwalk filled with drunken pirates snarling curses. Then several of them drew weapons and ran toward the ship.

11

dulaun ran to the gangplank with Seaspray in his hand. "Bring her about! Bring her about!"

"She's slow, Dulaun!" Colvyr yelled back as he turned the great wheel. "Once we get her head into the wind, we'll be all right!"

But it was taking too long. Pirates swarmed up the gangplank.

"Dulaun!" Woldberg called, then flung one of the shields from the ship's railing.

Dulaun caught the shield and pulled it onto his arm. He stepped into the breach created by the gangplank and met the pirates' charge. Seaspray clanged and sparked as he hacked at the pirates. He beat a cutlass aside and split the skull of the man wielding it. He used the shield to catch another man's blade, then stepped in and shoved his sword through the man's neck, killing him and stabbing the pirate behind him.

The drunken pirates weren't at their best, but they had numbers. Others threw themselves from the docks and clung to the ship's sides, then kicked their feet and tried to scramble aboard.

"Get down!" Halversom roared.

Dulaun ducked and Halversom threw the contents of

the brazier over the pirates lining the gangplank. The hot coals and burning ash covered the pirates. Many of them howled in pain and beat at their hair and clothing as the coals got trapped in their clothing and cooked their flesh.

Then *Blackheart* finally gave up her berth and pulled away from the dock. The gangplank fell away and dropped a dozen pirates into the sea.

"Repel boarders!" Dulaun ordered. He ran to the nearest pirate and kicked the man in the face, tearing him loose from the railing and knocking him back into the sea. Another pirate rose to his feet, cutlass in one hand and knife in the other, and attacked.

Dulaun parried the blades with his shield and sword, then pierced the man's heart. The wet deck ran slick with blood.

Halversom laid waste to the pirates with his hammer. Gore covered him, but he roared with savage fury, gripped in a berserker rage.

"Coming about!" Colvyr shouted. "Grab aholt!"

Dulaun took hold of the nearest railing and held on.

Blackheart creaked and popped as she came about. The canvas snapped and the lines rang against the masts as the wind took her with grim passion. Almost in the blink of an eye, her sails bellied full with the wind.

The goblinkin ship swung into view.

Dulaun knew they didn't have much speed, but the goblinkin ship was vulnerable amidships, and she was heavy with cargo.

"Hold steady!" Dulaun yelled.

"Holding steady!" Colvyr replied.

"Ram that goblinkin vessel!"

"Hold fast!"

Dulaun watched as *Blackheart*'s iron prow smashed against the goblinkin ship. Timbers cracked as her hull gave way, but they didn't have much speed. For a moment he thought his plan might have proved the undoing of them. *Blackheart* stopped dead in her tracks and ground against the other ship.

Goblinkin heaved themselves over the side and came at Dulaun and his crew.

"Repel boarders!" Dulaun cried. "Grab the wind!" He launched himself at the goblinkin, slashing and hacking without finesse. Goblinkin dropped dead at his feet. Lightning blazed across the sky and turned the spilled blood black in the sudden white glare. Torrents of rain made the deck treacherous as well.

The crew dedicated to the sails brought them around again to seize the wind. Dulaun and the others battled. The goblinkin were fierce fighters and had more manpower, but they were unused to fighting aboard a heaving ship's deck. The sailors' sea legs proved the goblinkin's undoing.

Wood splintered as *Blackheart* tore free of the sinking goblinkin ship. The stricken vessel took on water fast.

Dulaun squared off against two goblinkin and engaged both their blades with Seaspray. Metal clanged in his ears and the impacts vibrated along his arm. Then he stepped forward and passed between them before they expected it.

He turned quickly to the left and smashed the goblinkin there with the shield's edge, caving in the creature's skull. Following through on the momentum, he lifted the shield to block the second goblinkin's overhand strike and sank to the hilt in his opponent's chest.

The goblinkin's black eyes opened in shock. He looked down, saw himself impaled, and died.

Dulaun kicked the corpse off his blade and turned to survey the deck. In the blaze of lightning, he saw that the crew owned *Blackheart*'s deck. The goblinkin were dead and dying.

"Clear my deck," Dulaun roared as the fever of the moment gripped him. He'd first heard Captain Neldar order that after a hard-won battle that had crawled onto their decks. "I don't want to trip over garbage while we're making off with our prize."

The crew quickly complied and yelled and cheered. One of the sailors was dead. Mortaine had a slashed throat that gaped obscenely.

Don't grieve for him now, Dulaun told himself. *There'll be time enough later. For now you've got to get these men to safety.*

Confusion reigned on the pirate town docks as goblinkin attacked the pirates and the pirates did likewise. Whatever bound them evidently wasn't strong enough to overcome the natural enmity the humans and goblinkin felt for each other.

Dulaun stood in the prow and watched as *Blackheart* gained speed and raced for the harbor mouth. He glanced at the walls and tried to spot Krahzir. The shadows made that impossible.

However, on the other side of the harbor, pirates hurried into positions. Torches marked them as they readied the nets to free the jumble of rocks.

"Hold her steady, Colvyr," Dulaun ordered.

"Aye," the man roared back.

Dulaun watched the pirates and wondered if they'd loose the rocks before they arrived or while they passed through. Either could prove devastating.

"Prepare to take shelter!" Dulaun shouted.

The sailors aboard *Blackheart* stood close to the railings. Dulaun hoped it would be enough to keep them safe.

Only a hundred yards or more separated them from the harbor's mouth.

"Dulaun!" Woldberg shouted. "They've set a ship upon us!"

Dulaun glanced back. A ship pursued them, catching the wind and cutting sleekly through the choppy water. He squinted against the rain to see the figures lining the prow. If they were archers, the rain would—

A lightning bolt sizzled from the hand of one of the figures. It cut across the distance and hammered the stern sail. The top third of the mast cracked and fell over. Fire claimed even the wet sailcloth. Flaming canvas and lines tumbled to the deck.

12

"*Wizard!*" someone yelled.

"Had that figured out, you melonhead," Halversom yelled back.

"Get that fire out!" Dulaun commanded.

The sailors grabbed buckets of wet sand and threw it over the flames to extinguish them. Luckily the rain kept the fire from spreading too rapidly, but the magical blaze remained stubborn.

"Hold to port, Colvyr!" Dulaun ordered. "And keep an eye peeled for Krahzir and the others!"

"Aye!"

Dulaun scoured the wall and finally made out Krahzir and the three sailors that had scaled the wall. "There!" he shouted, pointing at the four men gathered on the bank. "Stand ready with the net on the portside!"

A group of sailors raced to port and readied a cargo net that had been lying on deck. They set up in the stern.

"Colvyr, keep us close! I don't want to have to depend on those nets!"

"Aye."

"Look out!" someone yelled. "They've set fire to the rock!"

At the top of the wall to starboard, the pirate sentries applied torches to the rocks. Evidently they'd been made of flammable substances or had been coated in them. They caught fire and the flames quickly spread throughout the net. In the next moment, the nets were loosed. Burning, flaming rocks tumbled down the hillside like a rush of comets.

Dulaun concentrated on Krahzir and the other sailors. As *Blackheart* ground against the wall to port and the scraping sound filled the air, Krahzir and his mates leaped for the ship. Krahzir and two others landed on the deck and tumbled across the prow. The fourth man fell short, hit *Blackheart* amidships, and fell back into the sea.

"Throw the net!" Dulaun ordered.

The sailors heaved the cargo net and it unfurled to slap against the water. The strands landed atop the sailor. He caught hold for dear life and was dragged in the ship's wake while flaming rock thudded against the ship's deck.

Dulaun used the shield to scoot the burning rocks over the side. He shouted orders to clear the decks. Then *Blackheart* shivered as her bottom scraped against the rocks that partially closed the harbor mouth. She hung for just a moment, then the wind caught her sails again and shoved her through.

While the crew in the prow continued throwing the burning rock overboard, Dulaun raced to stern. His knees and back protested against exertion as he climbed the stern castle stairs. Nothing but the open sea lay before them, but the pirate ship with the wizard aboard continued to pursue them.

A fireball spun from the wizard's hand as that ship, too, crested the pile of rock. The flaming mass sped toward *Blackheart*.

"Hard to starboard!" Dulaun yelled.

"Hard to starboard!" Colvyr repeated. The wheel spun in his practiced hands.

Blackheart heaved to the side. The fireball missed by

only a few feet. Dulaun was certain he could have reached out and touched it with his sword. The heat tightened his skin and set his sunburn on fire again.

Seaspray glowed with an incandescent light. Dulaun stared at the weapon. When Oskarr had crafted it, he'd said that the magic within it would awaken in stages, and that the sword would grow more powerful as the years passed. None of them had known for certain, though, because no one had ever worked the vidrenium metal or those spells before. The three weapons—Boneslicer, Seaspray, and Deathwhisper—had been forged for use against Lord Kharrion and the goblinkin hordes.

Power built up inside Dulaun. He felt it trembling, almost ready to explode his body. Instinctively, he unleashed it at the ship that followed them. A wave of force blurred across the intervening distance and touched the sea in front of the pirate ship.

Immediately, a towering wave rolled up from the sea. The wave only stood for a moment, but it reached eighty feet or more in height. Then it crashed down across the pirate ship's deck and took the vessel from sight.

When the wave settled and the sea was smooth again, only pieces of the pirate ship remained. No survivors appeared.

Dulaun looked at the wreckage in stunned fascination. For a moment he'd felt locked into the sea, had felt the strength of the water and had guided its savage fury. It was unlike anything he'd ever before felt.

He tried to do it again, to prove to himself that it had actually happened, but a fatigue like no other he'd ever known descended upon him.

"By the beards of the Old Ones," Krahzir said in awe. "Did you do that?"

Wearily, Dulaun let Seaspray hang at his side. "I think so."

Krahzir clapped him roughly on the shoulder. "Then good for you. But if you could do that, why didn't you do it earlier?"

"Because I didn't know I could." Dulaun stared at the harbor mouth. Another ship had sailed through, but it showed no interest in pursuing them.

Still, the crew stood tensely waiting for a time. *Blackheart* chased her sails out into the open sea.

Morning arrived too early. Dulaun roused from the hammock he'd thrown between two masts after they'd finally sailed past the storm. He felt stiff and exhausted, and he wondered how much of that was due to whatever magic the sword had unleashed.

"Ah, you're finally awake, you slug-a-bed," Krahzir greeted. He stood on deck, doing mate's duty and commanding the crew.

"You should have woken me," Dulaun protested.

Krahzir grinned. "Your watch ain't for a bit yet."

Dulaun glanced at the morning sun lying in the eastern mists above the Silver Sea and saw that it was true. He wasn't yet late.

"Me and the crew talked while you were asleep," Krahzir said.

Dulaun waited warily.

"Somebody has to fill Cap'n Neldar's boots, Old Ones rest him," Krahzir said.

Dulaun prepared himself for the worst. There had been plans for him to take over a second ship when they captured one, but Krahzir was due to take over *Wavecutter*. Dulaun tried to figure out how he'd feel taking orders from the man. He didn't like his honest answers.

"We all agreed that back on the isle, you already pretty much done that," Krahzir said. "You got us out of a lot of trouble."

Dulaun looked at the sailcloth-wrapped body on the deck. "Most of you."

"I wouldn't have wagered on any of us getting out alive."

The crew gathered around Dulaun as he stood on deck. They were ruffians, without breeding or station, but they were men he'd learned to trust over these past years.

"We decided that since Cap'n Neldar wasn't here to do the job properlike, we'd make you captain ourselves," Krahzir said. "If you're interested in having us."

Dulaun smiled. His da had planned for him to be an officer in the Silver Sea Navy, one of those that patrolled the Trade Empires in the Silver Sea. He'd never wished for such a thing. That was why he'd abandoned his studies at the Academy and thrown in his lot with Captain Neldar when the old man would have him.

"Aye," Dulaun said. "I'll have you. By the Old Ones, I'll make proper sailors of you all before I'm through."

As one, the crew groaned and protested.

"Now," Dulaun said, "has anyone been down in the hold of this ship to see if there's any ale aboard?"

"Aye, Captain." Frampos walked up with his arms around a keg. "Appears to be of the finest stock, too."

"Then bust it open and let's judge for ourselves."

The crew cheered and cavorted on the deck.

Dulaun watched them, feeling the weight of the burden he'd taken on. He'd have to tell the families of Captain Neldar and the others what had become of them when they returned to their home port. And he'd have to recruit a few more hands to manage the ship. All of that would be hard, as hard as surviving the coming years as privateers.

But with the wind in his hair and his boots solidly on a heaving deck, Dulaun knew he was where he was supposed to be.

"As fine as this ship is, Captain," Krahzir said as he handed Dulaun a cup of ale, "I shouldn't be surprised if her last captain comes looking for her one day."

"Let him come," Dulaun said. "I've still got a bone to pick with him myself. It'll save me from tracking him down. I promised vengeance for Captain Neldar, and I mean to keep that promise."

TOR

Award-winning authors
Compelling stories

Please join us at the website
below for more information
about this author and other great
Tor selections, and to sign up for
our monthly newsletter!

TOR

Voted
#1 Science Fiction Publisher
20 Years in a Row

by the *Locus* Readers' Poll

———•———

Please join us at the website below
for more information about this
author and other science fiction,
fantasy, and horror selections, and to
sign up for our monthly newsletter!